A FLOCK OF SHIPS

My hands gripped the rail in front of me as I stared, frozen to the spot while the eviscerated corpse of the corvette tried to push into us. She bumped and grated blindly aft, shedding bits and pieces of ship and fittings into the hungry sea between us.

I remember seeing her White Ensign still streaming proudly from her box-like counter, and watching men jumping from under it with an unspeakable, goddamned unbelievingly disciplined silence, into the oil-fouled water.

We could save a lot of those silent, jumping, fresh-faced seamen if we stayed. But under our keel were thousands of pounds of high explosive, liable to detonate at any second . . .

BRIAN CALLISON

A Flock of Ships

 FONTANA / Collins

First published by Wm. Collins 1970
First issued in Fontana Books 1971
Ninth Impression April 1974

© Brian Callison 1970

Printed in Great Britain
Collins Clear-Type Press London and Glasgow

TO HUGH C. KEITH
LATE CHIEF ENGINEER
BLUE FUNNEL LINE

PROLOGUE

The ship had lain there for many years—Ten? Fifteen? Maybe even twenty? One of the old, pre-war cargo liners with her high, straight stack and the strangely anti-quated vertical lines of her midships accommodation. From nearly two miles away at the entrance to the island's inner lake it was hard to see detail but it looked as though she was slightly down by the head and there was an odd, untidy geometry in the ragged shape of her wheelhouse and bridge structure.

Which was very odd indeed, because this island hadn't been visited for nearly half a century—or so the Navigator's *South Atlantic Pilot* said.

From his post in the bows of the slowly moving survey-ship the First Lieutenant took one disbelieving glance and said, 'Jesus!' Farther aft the Commander—concentrating only on conning his ship through the narrow gap between the towering, nerve tensioning black cliffs that pressed in on either side—didn't notice anything strange until, one hundred and ten seconds later, the bridge also broke out into the blinding South Atlantic sunlight that swamped down over the hitherto uncharted inland sea. He, too, stared for an incredulous moment at the ship that couldn't be there and grabbed for the 8×50 Ministry of Defence (Navy Department) binoculars slung round his neck.

By the time the stern had crept infinitely slowly past the huge, weed-skirted rock marking the inner periphery of the apparently natural anchorage the only man aboard who hadn't expressed surprise was the phlegmatic Chief Petty Officer leadsman in the chains who, unconcernedly, continued to barrage all within earshot with the mystical information that the depth was now 'By the deep . . . Six!', or 'And a quarter . . . Seven!' as he leant pre-cariously out over the silent green water yet again to heave the bunting and flannel-decorated line. Despite the half-million pounds' worth of sophisticated electronic sounding and measuring gear condensed in the sleek hull below him the Commander still clung to the comfort of a good, old-fashioned leadsman when he was feeling his way into places strange and uncertain.

An urgently hailed warning from the First Lieutenant, hanging insecurely out over the ship's stem, a few staccato commands to the Coxswain at the wheel, and she was turning on her screws, swinging fast to starboard with an almost complete absence of forward way while the anchor party on the foc'slehead watched as the thing they had nearly hit vanished again in the concealing anonymity of the waters.

The Commander flashed a look of relief at his Navigating Officer and leaned over the voice pipe. 'Stop engines . . . Dead slow ahead both!' Then, as the ship's head steadied on a course to take her towards that non-existent freighter which still sat, nevertheless, as stolidly and patiently at the end of her rusty cable as she had done for the past two decades, the Commander swivelled slowly with the binoculars pressed hard under his bushy brows and surveyed the black, forbidding land formation that pressed in on them from all points.

A glint of yellow almost directly astern, down past the far side of the entrance they had just squeezed through. Sunlight reflecting on billions of tiny, incandescent grains. A beach? Warm and beckoning after the bleak inhospitability of the surrounding rock. 'Damn good,' he thought. 'Give the men a run ashore while we're . . .'

Then he stopped thinking and fumbled for the knurled focusing wheel. 'My dear God!' he said this time, not so much compounding the blasphemy as requesting reassurance, and the stubby finger moved the wheel another eighth of an inch until the thing on the beach jumped into brilliant, clear-cut detail.

And the Commander had now found *two* ships where there couldn't have been any.

Or, perhaps not two ships so much as one and a part, because the monstrous deformity on the beach couldn't really be called a ship any more. It was still possible to make out the line of her hull form, with the greater proportion of her floors still sheathed in rusty red tank top plating. There was even a vaguely nautical suggestion in the few frames and pillars that rose from her bier of sand like the bones of some skeletal, stranded whale. But, otherwise, the thousands of tons of corroded, heat-twisted steel that lay carelessly scattered by some incredible internal force were almost unrecognisable for what they had once been—the complex deck housings and engine parts and entrails of a mighty vessel.

The Commander had barely time to note the twin tracks that still marked the sand where the huge phosphor-bronze propellors had gouged deep into the surface as they drove the ship farther and farther up on to the beach; then the Navigator was pointing to yet another obscenely deformed mass that rose from the shallow water directly astern of the gutted steel corpse.

And, while the Commander swung his binoculars incredulously between what were now the *three* shells of the impossible fleet, the Navigating Officer whispered in a hushed voice: 'She must've been doing bloody near twenty knots to drive herself up on the beach like that, for Chrissake!'

The Commander stood silently gazing around while the rest of the boarding party shinned sweatily up the grapnel line caught in the aftermast stays and gathered wonderingly about him abaft the ghost ship's centrecastle. They could have come aboard by the bleached accommodation ladder which still hung dejectedly down her starboard side, but one glance at the rusty bridle and mildewed topping lift which suspended it had convinced the Commander of the folly of such a venture.

The First Lieutenant heaved himself over the bulwarks and uneasily took in the rotting hatch covers, the streaming, leprous steel of bulkheads and decks and the patches of creeping yellow fungus that sent out diseased fingers to explore every inch of wooden doors and awning spars. He shivered involuntarily despite the shimmering heat of the high sun and self-consciously eased the Webley and Scott .38 sitting so unaccustomedly in the sagging web belt around his white-shorted waist. The Commander saw him and smiled a little tightly: 'There hasn't been anyone to shoot at aboard this ship since you were getting your picture taken on a bearskin rug, Number One.'

The First Lieutenant coloured in embarrassment and

tried, doubtfully, to laugh it off. 'No, Sir. Though I saw a horror picture once . . .'

But the Commander wasn't really listening. Instead he was gazing aft at the incinerated mess of sprawling rails and shattered ventilators which scarred the high poop, and at the object which rose arrogantly and still lethally traversed almost on his own ship. 'Good God!' he gestured. 'That was the sort of museum piece the D.E.M.S. crown used to install aboard merchantmen back in '39 . . . An old 4.7 by the look of it.'

His Number One followed the oustretched arm and bit his lip involuntarily. Apart from the gun itself the rest of the deck aft had been practically swept clear of fittings, presumably by what must have been a virtual hurricane of gunfire. 'Poor bastards . . . Whoever made up that gun's crew, I mean.'

'Which seems to prove one thing,' the Commander said, almost to himself.

'Sir?'

'This ship, Number One. She's been lying here ever since the war, just rotting and rusting and dying of old age.'

'Yessir . . . Er, which war would that be, Sir?' said the First Lieutenant, for he was young and his first memory of angry guns was as fleet midshipman off the coast of Korea.

The Commander looked at him sadly. 'If you were a little older, Number One, you'd realise there only ever *was* one real war.' He turned. 'Petty Officer Torrance.'

'Sah?' The thump of rubber-soled boots.

'Take your party and, starting from aft, search the ship as thoroughly as you can. Don't attempt to enter any ill-lit spaces or go below to the engine room at the moment. I'll have the E.R.A.s fit up emergency lighting to-morrow. Just settle for a quick shufti through the main decks and accommodation for now. The First Lieutenant and I will visit the master's quarters; you can report to me there as soon as you're finished.'

He turned back to his Number One. 'I always was frustrated every time I read that damned *Marie Celeste* story, Number One. You know? That sailing ship found drifting with no one on board?' He started off up the shrapnel-pitted ladder from the well-deck, then hesitated momentarily. 'And I'm buggered if I could stand not knowing what happened here twenty-five years ago.'

They found the radio room as they climbed the last ladder up to the high boat-deck and, when they glanced apprehensively inside and saw the shambles of splintered dials and valves and wires hanging from the still grey enamelled cabinet, the First Lieutenant said 'Jesus!' again. There seemed no way it could have happened—unless someone had done it deliberately.

But what sane person could ever want to maroon himself without any means of communication on a ring of black rocks a thousand miles from anywhere?

They walked along the sun-bleached decking towards the curiously canted bridge and noted the empty, swung-out davits with the rotting, drooping rope falls terminating just above the glassy water in rustbound blocks, and the Commander muttered in angry frustration: 'From the looks of her, this bloody ship isn't all that badly damaged. Why, in God's name, did her crew leave her in the boats? Why didn't they just sail her straight out?'

They stood for a few moments surveying the partially collapsed wheelhouse and then walked cautiously across the vast plain of the bridge-wing—vast in comparison to the tight compactness of the survey ship's tiny navigating space—and entered the wheelhouse itself. Shards of shattered glass from the starboard windows scrunched under their feet as they moved silently into the dank shade. A faded black course-board hung from the deck-head forward of the lifeless telemotor and wheel, the faint lines of chalk still showing the last course some long-gone quartermaster had steered to. The Commander allowed his hand to rest briefly on the green verdigris of the binnacle while the First Lieutenant nudged his toe against a ragged, discoloured signal flag thrown carelessly on the coir-matted deck. It was still decipherable to a seaman, though.

'Letter "U",' murmured the Commander looking down, ' "YOU ARE STANDING INTO DANGER". I wonder: did they get it out, perhaps, to signal to that gutted wreck on the beach across there?'

The First Lieutenant squatted and fingered it with distaste. The discoloration wasn't all caused by the ravages of time. 'I don't really know what twenty-five-year-old blood should look like, Sir . . . but somehow I don't think this was meant to be used in any signal hoist.'

They only hesitated for a few seconds beside the section of teak planking that had, at one time, presumably formed part of the monkey island—that open area above the wheelhouse used primarily for taking azimuth bearings while navigating in narrow waters. The little white-painted silhouette they could see on it had weathered well through the years, protected as it was from the winds and rains by the break of the chartroom.

'Damn thing looks like a submarine, Number One,' the Commander commented, looking more closely.

And that was yet another odd factor to consider because, as the First Lieutenant pointed out, it was not uncommon for submarine captains to celebrate a kill by painting a little white merchantman on the side of their conning towers . . . But a submarine painted on a merchantman?

They stared, baffled, at the curling, mildewed chart which still lay spread out beside the long-stopped brass ship's chronometer in its rosewood box. They could see quite plainly the little misshapen ring indicating the island. They could also see the soft pencil line that had indicated the ship's course and the dead-reckoning positions marked as it had approached the island, but what they were so mystified by were the other tracks entered by the various officers of the watch during the earlier part of her voyage. Northings contradicted Southings, Eastings countered Westings—there was no rhyme or reason in the darting scribbles.

'They must've been either bloody drunk or bloody mad . . . or bein' chased by the very Devil himself,' muttered the Commander.

Yet even that explanation didn't bear close examination for, in a ship of this size, there must have been a lot of deck officers and they couldn't *all* have been drunk or mad.

And the Devil doesn't really exist—not in the South Atlantic anyway!

They entered the master's day-room under the bridge very cautiously indeed, the Commander slightly in the lead stepping over the low coaming while the First Lieutenant followed, this time with his hand unashamedly firm on the plastic butt of the pistol in its webbing holster.

The Commander smiled to himself in anticipation as he saw the pile of closely-written papers lying on the desk between the silver, company-crested coffee pot, now filled to overflowing with a leprous mould, and the yellowed pages of an open book. He stepped across the expensive and still curiously pristine Egyptian carpet, frowning slightly at the brown stain that marred it under the low coffee table, and leafed through the sheets of what appeared, at first sight, to be some form of manuscript.

They met the rather grimy and sweating Petty Officer Torrance as they stepped out into the sunlight which flooded the silent boat-deck. The Commander returned the salute, at the same time being careful not to drop the papers he held covetously under his arm.

'Proper rum do, Sir,' the P.O. said, in a voice of such low pitch that one might almost have felt he was afraid the dead ship would hear and resent the imputation of abnormality. 'The only sign we could find that she ever had a crew aboard was . . . this, Sir.'

And the Commander and the First Lieutenant stared uncomfortably at the yellowed officer's pattern deck shoe held unconcernedly in the Petty Officer's outstretched hand.

'Good God . . . There's still something in it,' the First Lieutenant muttered, taking an uncertain step backwards.

'Yessir,' the P.O. whispered conspiratorially. 'A bit of a foot, Sir. I thought, like, that you might want to . . inter it with proper respec', Sir?'

'Quite correct, Petty Officer Torrance,' boomed the Commander approvingly. 'Perhaps you would be good enough to . . . ah . . . take charge of the remains until we can conduct the appropriate ceremony.'

The First Lieutenant blinked doubtfully—did one perform a ceremony over what was, after all, only a very little part of a man? 'I now commit this deck shoe and contents to the deep . . .' 'Where did you find it, P.O.?'

'Sort of caught up in the traverse ring of the 4.7 on the poop, Sir. Proper bloody old cannon it is too.'

But the Commander wasn't really listening again, being more anxious to get back to his ship and begin his study of the manuscript clutched under his arm.

They left the Petty Officer and two rather unenthusiastic ratings aboard the mouldering ship and, on the way back to the survey vessel, took the gleaming black and white pinnace on a complete circuit of the rusty, once grey hull towering above them.

As they rounded the great, overhanging stern they could still see the ship's name and port of registration cut into the rounded steel plates of her counter: CYCLOPS . . . LIVERPOOL.

'It's a long time since she last saw the Formby Light,' said the Commander reflectively.

They cut sharply under the surprisingly modern flare of her bows and the First Lieutenant watched as the black shadowed line of the corroding starboard anchor cable ran quickly aft across the upturned faces of the Navymen. The once fine edge of the weed trailing cutwater was twisted and distorted, with some of the rusted plates gaping slightly at the seams.

'She seems to have been involved in some sort of collision,' he observed to the impatient Commander.

Which at least accounted for the slender hull being very slightly down by the head; though it was still strange, because one would have thought that her Chief Engineer would have had time to trim his tanks in the placidity of the island lake.

Dinner was served rather later than usual in the survey ship's wardroom that evening and, when her officers did eventually take their places round the table, the Commander's seat remained vacant.

Because the Commander was already sitting down in

his own quarters, and the plate of finely-cut ham sandwiches slowly curled at the edges while the pot of untouched coffee beside him grew colder. Outside, the sun
sank lower over the motionless, silent fleet of mutilated
ghosts that had sat there since before the survey ship had
been even a pensive twinkle in her builder's eye.

And the Commander sank lower in his solitary chair,
and read, and read.

THE PERSONAL LOG
OF JONATHAN KENT

Chief Officer
M.V. *Cyclops*
Voyage No. 13

CHAPTER ONE

I was eating a jam sandwich when the first ship of our
group went down.

At least I think it was jam, it was red and sticky like
blood anyway. I wasn't really enjoying it though—have
you ever tried eating jam sandwiches at five-thirty in the
morning in the South Atlantic? By the time the Third
Mate has picked out the best of them around ten p.m. the
evening before, then the Second has poked and prodded
them during his middle watch and forgotten to put the lid
back on the box when he's finished, they're more like
curled up little wafer biscuits when it's your turn. The
only consolation was that, being Chief Officer, at least I
had priority over Brannigan, the Fourth, and young
Conway, who shared the four to eight watch with me.

Stepping out through the chartroom door I stood
chewing gloomily and looking around for a few moments.
It was shaping up to be another hot, listless day, which
was what you'd expect with us well into the Benguela
Current and the coast of South West Africa nine hundred
miles away on our port beam. The stand-by quartermaster was already rolling down the canvas bridge

dodgers to allow what little breeze there was to fan the
bridge, and I mentally thanked God that at least we had
the advantage of a seventeen-knot passage to help create
a wind.

We were four ships altogether; all much faster than the
normal 1941 convoy establishment, but that was because
we were something special. I didn't really know why, not
then, but it was certainly an unusual set-up. Three
freighters and an escort corvette, all modern and all
capable of pushing at least nineteen knots—twenty even,
once the engineers heard the dull thud of underwater
charges rebounding off the hull. There's nothing like a
bit of explosive as an incentive for getting the best speed
out of a ship.

We were steaming in a sort of 'L' formation—my own
ship, *Cyclops*, at the head of the 'L', with the Frenchman,
Commandant Joffre, and our sister ship, *Athenian*, lying one
thousand yards astern and steaming abreast with about
six cables between them while, darting in and out of the
group like a frustrated moth round a candle, little *Mallard*
showed us with monotonous persistence just what an
eleven-hundred-ton corvette could do in the way of tight,
stern-skidding turns. I watched her morosely, thinking
that was about all she could do—she didn't have enough
fire power to fight *us*, never mind the bloody Germans,
with her single four-inch main armament! Even *Cyclops*
had an antiquated 4.7 mounted on the poop aft and I felt
some sympathy for *Mallard* since, while she had to be
facing the enemy to fire, we could at least make fearsome
if ineffective bangs while running away. Mind you, the
early escort corvettes were almost purely designed for
anti-submarine measures and, with the new Asdic gear
and the twin rows of depth-charges on their after-decks,
they were pretty well equipped for that.

The Junior Cadet, Conway, was hanging over the sand
and canvas scrubbed teak rail of the starboard bridge
wing. The backs of his knees looked very white under the
slightly too long tropical shorts, and I noticed how the sun,
reflecting up from the greenpainted starboard navigation
light screen, threw a sickly pallor over his pale features.
He was watching the skips of water as flying fish skimmed
across the oily swell with an expression of youthful

fascination. It was his first trip to sea, and four-winged fish that flew in the air for up to a quarter of a mile were still a source of constant wonderment to him.

So were torpedoes—to me!

I waved the drooping sandwich at him, 'Maybe you'd like me to send Mister Brannigan below for a deck-chair, Conway?'

He jerked as his mind came back to 1941. 'Thanky . . . er . . .No, Sir. Sorry, Sir.'

I looked grimly disapproving. 'Just remember where you are, lad. This is the bridge of a ship in a war zone—not the aquarium at Bognor.'

He nodded silently. I noticed the big eyes under the drooping lock of fair hair and tried to smile a little more reassuringly. He was shaping up to be a good lad one day, but good lads got killed just as often as bad ones in a war at sea. 'Flying fish will be there ten, twenty years from now for you to watch, Conway. If you miss one you'll see the next. But torpedoes? . . . They're different! You only get one chance to see them and, if you do, and God's in an expansive mood, then you might, just might, get enough time to put your helm hard over and . . .'

But maybe He wasn't feeling so tolerant that morning.

The column of dirty, yellow-stained water seemed to climb ever so slowly up the side of the *Commandant Joffre*, just abaft her tall, wire-stayed funnel. Nervous reflex made me bite another half moon out of the sandwich as I watched the spray reach its zenith and hang, suspended momentarily like a slow motion shot from some old film. It was a silent film, too, for a few eternal seconds. Nothing seemed to mar the noiseless passage of the four ships through the whispering sea, yet I knew that great mushroom of atomised water just shouldn't be there. Then the clap of the explosion rumbled across the thousand-yard gap and the Frenchman's funnel jetted a high spurt of white steam as she started to swing broadside, out of control, right across the bows of *Athenian*.

I didn't wait to see any more.

My deck shoes pounded across the coir matting of the wheelhouse as I threw myself at the telegraphs. The brass handles felt surprisingly cold as I grasped them and, throwing them fore and aft, gave two rings for 'Full ahead.' This was our emergency full speed warning and, while perhaps I should have waited for *Mallard*'s instructions, I wasn't going to leave room for regrets while I sat on a wet backside in a lifeboat—if I ever made it to one in the first place.

Before the answering jangle had come from below I was slamming my palm against the engine room phone buzzer. I heard the metallic clack as it was ripped off its hook sixty feet below me. 'Engine room! Second speaking!'

The shocked white face of the quartermaster at the wheel stared at me as I answered, 'The Mate here. I want full revolutions immediately, Bert. Open her right up. Check?'

The voice sounded tinny and distant. 'Aye, aye, John . . . was that a torpedo, f'r Christ's sake?'

I nodded at the phone, 'The Froggie.'

'We guessed as much, it seemed to come from the starboard quarter.'

I wasn't surprised they'd heard it, an explosion like that must have sounded to the white boiler-suited men below like being in a dustbin when someone was hitting it with cymbals. It wasn't the time for chat, though. 'I want you standing-by on the platform for manoeuvring down there, Second.'

'I'll adjust the governors . . .'

I slammed the hand set down with a crash and blew down the voice pipe to the Old Man's quarters while, under my feet, I could feel the vibration increase as the engines built up the revolutions. Somewhere behind me something started to rattle irritably. Impatiently holding the brass bell of the pipe to my ear, I took a swift glance at McRae, the helmsman. He looked scared and I didn't blame him.

'Just keep her steady as she goes, McRae,' I said, still waiting anxiously for the Captain to answer. 'Be on your toes for helm orders though, we might have to do a bit of dancing.'

He smiled weakly, 'Jus' like at the Palais.'

I didn't smile back; it wasn't that funny anyway. Then the Old Man charged up the port ladder, still shedding shaving soap from a half-finished toilet like an angry dandelion in a high wind. I shoved the voice pipe back in its brass clip and stepped aside.

Captain Evans was stark naked except for his gold-braided cap—and the shaving soap. Obviously the U-boat had picked an inconvenient time to introduce itself. I suppose I must have looked a bit startled as I stared at the Old Man, noting detachedly how the red beefy face and tanned bull neck faded away into a bleached expanse of snowy skin under matted black hair. Ship's masters never sun-bathe of course, but then, neither does God, I suppose, and they are more or less on a par.

Somehow I'd never imagined Evans would shave in the nude. It seemed a bit obscene and disloyal even to think about him like that and I was glad he'd had the time to put his cap on, what with Brannigan and young Conway and McCrae staring at him out of the corners of their eyes. Or maybe he shaved with his hat on every day?

'The Captain's trousers will be in his cabin, Conway,' I murmured discreetly as I turned and followed the Old Man's gaze aft.

The sunlight reflecting from the water sprinkled the grey hull of the *Commandant Joffre* with dancing patches of light as she lay tiredly over on her side. The two deck cargo railway engines, stopped down to rails welded on her foredeck, leaned right over at a crazy angle never allowed for by their designers. It was the only length of permanent way they were ever going to settle on, and not for much longer at that judging by the way the wire lashings must have been humming under the impossible strain of arresting over one hundred tons deadweight.

The boats on her port side were the only ones they could hope to use owing to the list, and we could see a cluster of gnome-like figures mobbing round her davits, looking like orange hunchbacks in their bulky kapok life-jackets. The steam from the funnel had died down to a trickle, but she was on fire round her number four hold, with the thick, oily smoke climbing almost vertically into the clear blue sky.

Suddenly I remembered *Athenian*, our Company sister ship, and swung quickly round, looking for her. Somehow they'd managed to shave past the careering Frenchman and there she was now, drawing up on our port quarter. The 4.7 on her poop was manned by her D.E.M.S. crowd, and the long barrel glared wickedly, if a bit pointlessly, out over the empty, burning sea. They were really pushing hard in her engine room judging by the way the white foam belched and tumbled under her rounded counter—she was going like a bomb, to use an unfortunate phrase under the circumstances. I grinned a bit to myself, despite the tension. It reminded me of the story I'd heard last time in about the plane that landed with a fused thousand-pounder still stuck in her bomb bay—the truck that hurried the crew away from the scene at top speed was overtaken by an L.A.C. on a bicycle.

Athenian was a beautiful ship though, almost as smart as my own, and, as she swept up abeam of us, a figure waved from her bridge. I waved back. It was Bill Henderson, her First Mate and my opposite number. We loved each other like brothers, Bill and I, apart from an occasional twinge of professional jealousy, and I hoped nothing was going to happen to the second-best ship in the Company. Not with Bill aboard her.

Conway arrived panting with the Old Man's shorts and, as Evans struggled into them, *Mallard* cut across and under our bows with heart-stopping elan, making the Old Man growl angrily under his breath: 'Bugger all week-end bloody sailors!'

She still looked damned good though as she creamed along our side, in between the two cargo liners which dwarfed her. The long sleek forefoot dipped into the slight swell and the white bone in her teeth rose nearly to a level with the foc'slehead as she raced past. We could still hear the clamour of her attack alarm system, while steel-helmeted ratings moved swiftly and automatically around the thin shield of the foredeck gun, their white anti-flash hoods giving them the sinister appearance of avenging monks. Aft, her White Ensign streamed out over the boiling wake and the sub-lieutenant in charge of the depth-charge crew raised a hand in salute. A solitary white cap cover defiantly caught the sun among the cluster of steel helmets on her postage-stamp bridge and I guessed it belonged to our escort commander, Lieutenant Commander P. Braid, R.N., otherwise laughingly known as Comescort. The Old Man and I had grinned when he heard them use that description first, it seemed a very grandiose title for a corvette captain sheep-dogging three freighters. In that case, Evans had said, with him being senior master, that sort of made him Comconvoy!

The Aldis spluttering from her bridge was obviously operated by a yeoman who held the signalling capabilities of the merchant navy in low esteem. It was so slow that it was insulting. Mind you, it did also mean that our junior mates could read it first time without having to request a repeat. Brannigan spelled it out as the Old Man finished making fast the cavernous pair of shorts.

'COMESCORT TO MASTER CYCLOPS: REPEAT TO MASTER ATHENIAN: MAINTAIN PRESENT COURSE AND FULL EMER-GENCY REVOLUTIONS U BOAT NOW PRESUMED ABAFT YOUR BEAM AND UNABLE TO MAKE FURTHER ATTACK NO ATTEMPT WILL BE MADE TO PICK UP SURVIVORS COMMANDANT JOFFRE REPEAT NO ATTEMPT WILL BE MADE TO PICK UP SURVIVORS SIGNED BRAID END.'

I stared at Brannigan in horror. 'Sure you got that right, Four Oh? They aren't going to pick up the French-ies?'

His face was very white. 'Yes, Sir. Positive.'

I swung round on the Old Man. 'The yellow bastards. We can't leave them out here, nine hundred miles from anywhere.'

Evans looked back at the *Commandant Joffre*. The way was right off her now and she was lying almost flat on her side, slightly down by the head. We could see a swirl of white foam against the sluggishness of the encroaching sea as the foc'sle windlass broke surface, otherwise the oily placidity of the water was uninterrupted until it curled sullenly round the near vertical steel hatch coamings.

Some poor bloody sailor was still left standing on the top side of the spindly funnel, masked occasionally by the swirls of steam that trickled from it, while two boats were sculling frantically in the shadow of the dead hull like grey water-beetles, overloaded with survivors. Suddenly I tensed. The boats were splashing fruitlessly and apparently aimlessly, instead of pulling straight away from the bulk of the dying freighter. Something was terribly wrong.

I groped for the Barr and Stroud 10×50's in the binocular box at my hand and lifted them, feeling a little sick. Those boats should have been well away by now, fighting for distance between them and the inevitable suction as thousands of tons of water poured into the cavity that would be left when the *Commandant Joffre* finally went. Instead they were piddling round in panic-stricken circles and getting nowhere fast. It was lunacy.

Then my nervous fingers found the knurled ranging wheel and the powerful lens fused into sharp focus. I found out why they were putting up such a pathetic attempt at self-survival—and it wasn't anything to do with Gallic excitement.

The French ship was lying with her great masts almost brushing the water. I could make out the heavy forward jumbo derrick gear as it dangled ridiculously in the slight swell like some gigantic black-varnished fishing rod. Between the mastheads, now only a few inches from the oil-scummed surface, stretched the heavy jumper stay and H.T. wireless aerial. Together, they combined to form an impenetrable fence—a sort of nautical corral—with the Frenchman's lifeboats trapped in the middle. They were trying to escape, though, with the desperation of the damned. One boat had nosed up to the stay and a gnome jerked frantically as he chopped at the heavy cables.

'Bastards!' I whispered bitterly, not really knowing if I meant the U-boat crew, the corvette's exec's or even the poor bloody Frogs and their pathetic attempts to save themselves.

Evans apparently thought I meant *Mallard*. 'Braid has his orders, Mister Kent—to get us through to Adelaide, no matter what. If he stopped to pick up the Frenchmen he'd be a sitting target for the bugger that hit her. They're still out there somewhere, still watching and waiting . . . and hoping we're heroic-minded enough to put humanity before common bloody sense.'

I watched as *Mallard* performed another of her tail wags round the far side of the stricken ship, then came racing back dangerously close to the lopsided masts, like an excited dog that's just recovered his master's walking-stick. Something splashed over her stern and, for one horrifying moment, I had the impression that she was depth-charging the area where the boats were, then I saw they were heaving over Carley Floats and yellow survival packs. Seemingly, Comescort Braid had it figured the same as me—that if any crewmen survived the inevitable massacre when the freighter sank, then they wouldn't have any boats left to swim to.

'Bastards,' I said again, thinking this time specifically of *Mallard*—but then, I wasn't feeling very logical, and I guess it's easy to be gallant and stupid when you yourself are steaming away from danger at twenty knots.

Then something blew deep down in the entrails of the *Commandant Joffre*—probably her boilers—and everything seemed to come to an end all at once.

The starboard railway engine went first, crashing almost vertically down on to its part-submerged twin and, between them, creating a tidal wave that itself threatened to engulf the little boats. The resultant loss of weight made the dying ship jerkily recover a few degrees and we saw the man on the funnel take off into the air like a wad of blotting paper from a kiddie's ruler before his tiny, spinning, star-shaped body crashed back somewhere round the after end of the promenade deck.

The funnel itself went next, keeling slowly forward and sideways, then crumpling into itself as it swept the bridge structure and monkey island into the hungry sea.

I had one brief, intimate glimpse right down the gaping hole where her stack had been, deep down into the pipe-webbed machinery space—then she monstrously turned turtle and everything was white foam and steel derricks rearing from the oilslicked sea like discarded matchsticks, and somewhere underneath it all were sixty-odd Frenchmen with bursting lungs and mangled limbs . . .

The rust-scarred double bottoms stared imploringly at the hot blue sky for one long, shocked appeal, then she went down by the head like an express train, while we listened to the lingering rumble of the internal explosions fading away as the boiling South Atlantic closed over the *Commandant Joffre*.

It was very quiet on the *Cyclops*'s bridge right then.

The Old Man moved first, slowly replacing his binoculars in the varnished box under the rail and turning away. He took the gold-braided cap off and looked sad, a slightly ridiculous fat man in a pair of baggy white shorts and a dried foam beard. Someone was sobbing behind me and, when I swivelled round, it was young Conway.

He'd never seen a ship die before, and the Frenchman had died hard. It had kind of dulled his interest in watching flying fish.

'You should be out on the other wing when the Master and I are here, Conway,' I snarled brutally, trying to cover my own sick horror.

He gazed wildly at me from tear-bright eyes for a moment, then rushed blindly through the dark wheel-house. Brannigan hesitated, then followed slowly. I could feel his anger burning the back of my neck, but I wasn't in the mood for apologies as I stared dully at little *Mallard* scurrying round the stained patch of oily wreckage like a bitch with worms chasing her tail. Then her siren whoop-whooped in a final lament and the white spray under her bows rose higher as she hurried anxiously after us and *Athenian*, still dipping to the slow swell broad on our beam.

Glancing over the six cables of tossing water compressed between our twin hulls, I noticed that Bill Henderson and a group of her officers were staring aft too. There wasn't much left to see by then though.

I didn't wave to him this time.

There were a few of the junior engineer officers at their places when I went below for breakfast, but the deck officers' table held only the solitary figure of Larabee, the Second Wireless Operator. He glanced up and nodded perfunctorily as I sat down, then the saturnine face bent again and he dug viciously at his cornflakes. Sam Ling, the Mate's Steward, appeared silently at my elbow and proffered a company-crested menu. I glanced at it, remembered the way in which the *Commandant Joffre* had taken her crowd down with her less than an hour before, and settled for toast and coffee. There wasn't even any butter when that came so I poured myself a black coffee and gave the toast a miss too. Larabee raised his head again.

'See the Frog go down, did you?' he asked, still chewing stolidly.

I swallowed a mouthful of the hot liquid gratefully, feeling the slightly acrid grounds stimulating the back of my throat. 'Yes,' I answered shortly. I didn't really like Larabee anyway, with his skull-like features and endless questions about how things were going in every department of the ship from engine room to bridge. He was only a bloody number-two sparks and these things were none of his damned business.

He scraped his plate noisily. 'She didn't get off a four-S call in time,' he said critically. 'She should have put out a proper distress call, you know.'

S S S S was the distress signal made by merchantmen under attack from a submarine, Q Q Q Q meant attacked by armed raider, all the A's for aircraft, and so on. I didn't feel much like talking, and certainly not to Larabee, but I glanced at him sourly. 'What did she need to put a call out for, Sparks? All the bloody Royal Navy in the South Atlantic's steaming right alongside of us anyway.'

It wasn't true of course—the Admiralty probably had at least another two ships somewhere between Africa and South America—but I wasn't an R.N. admirer at the best of times. Who was it said that the only thing more obscene than an R.N. rating's description of the merchant navy is a merchant sailor's opinion of the Royal Navy? Larabee wasn't put out either way.

The morose face inspected with suspicion the plate of Spam and dried egg that the silent Ling had placed before it. 'Bloody typical of the Frogs, mind . . . Gettin' snarled up in their own rigging.'

I slammed my empty cup down in the saucer loud enough to make Ferrier, the Third Engineer, glance over in surprise; then stood up and shoved my chair back, not wanting to get involved in an argument with anybody right then. 'Just hope, if your time ever comes, Larabee, you'll not be unlucky enough to get the chop from your own bloody wireless aerials.'

He raised an unperturbed forkful of Spam and solidified orange-yellow compo. 'Not me, Mister Mate. *And* I'll get a proper signal off first too, don't you worry!'

I gritted my teeth and stamped out of the wood-panelled saloon, conscious of curious stares from the engineers' table. The last thing I heard as I stepped out on deck was Larabee's high-pitched voice, 'Ling? Ling, you stupid bloody slant-eyed Chink. Where the hell's my coffee . . . ?'

Eight bells struck as I reached the top of the bridge ladder. I strolled into the wheelhouse, where Brannigan was just handing over the watch to Curtis, the Third Mate. McRae, the four-to-eight helmsman, had already been relieved and had disappeared aft, presumably in search of breakfast and to regale the rest of the crowd with a highly coloured version of how the Old Man had appeared on the bridge wearing nothing but his hat and shaving soap.

A still shaken-looking Conway was out on the starboard wing, talking in low undertones to his opposite number, Cadet Breedie. I felt a twinge of guilt about speaking so sharply to him while the *Commandant Joffre* was belching her guts out under the green Atlantic swell. Still, I'd had it pretty rough when I was a youngster too, back in the bad old days of the post-First World War shipping slump. We'd been damned glad even to get a ship—any ship— with or without an irritable first mate.

Brannigan finished passing on the watch information. 'Course 143. Emergency full speed until further notice from the escort . . . Right, Mate?'

Curtis nodded gloomily. 'Right, Mate. I have the watch . . . An' it's deep fried Spam an' yellow muck again for chow, while you're on it.'

The Fourth Mate pulled a face, 'Jesus! That bloody steward must have a nest of powdered chickens laying them under the galley.' He turned to me and raised an eyebrow, 'Permission to go below, Sir?'

I nodded, 'Off you go, Four Oh. Er, . . . where's the Captain?'

He grinned before he slid down the ladder, 'Gone down to put his clothes on, Sir. The rest of them anyway.'

Conway coughed diffidently behind me and I turned. 'Can I go below for breakfast, Sir?'

'Yes,' I said, then seeing the hurt still burning in his eyes I jerked my head. 'Conway!'

He swivelled back, tight-lipped, 'Sir?'

I had meant to say something light to him, make him feel a bit better but, somehow, after seeing the little-boy peevishness in his face, I just made things worse. 'Conway.

If you ever come that *prima donna* act with me again I'll have you on double watches from here right the way through to Aussie! Do you understand me?'

The kid swallowed nervously. 'Aye, aye, Sir. Can I go now, Sir?'

I nodded and watched him hurry down the ladder with the flat-topped cap still with the wire support in it and the Company badge gleaming with pristine newness. I hoped someone would tell him to leave it under the shower for a few hours so that it would get all floppy and more like an apprentice's headgear than a master's. The badge would go green in its own good time after the salt had got into it. Resolving to get Breedie, the Senior Cadet, to drop the hint, I wandered into the chartroom, feeling a proper bastard.

The Third Mate looked up from where he had been checking our dead-reckoning position on the chart. 'Morning, Mister Kent.'

I lit a Players from the fifty tin I kept on the shelf and stared moodily at the bearded old Jack Tar in the lifebuoy on the label, wondering if he'd ever suffered from sadistic officers who took their own fears out on helpless juniors. He probably had—the sea isn't the calling for anyone who believes in the rights of democracy. Now young Conway was well on the way to finding that out by courtesy of my good self.

Curtis took his cap off and riffled his hair vigorously. The pencil he had been using started to dance about in the rack with the vibration and I remembered we were still at emergency revs, which would have old McKenzie, the Chief, calculating out his increased fuel consumption like a miserly investor who'd just found the interest rate going down two points. The extroverted Lieutenant Commander Braid must have been on the same train of thought because Breedie stuck his head in through the starboard door. '*Mallard*'s signalling, Sir.'

Curtis crammed his cap back on and tumbled out on to the bridge, while I followed at a slightly more dignified Chief Officers' pace. The sun was really burning down by now and the steel helmets had vanished from the corvette's bridge, to be replaced by white cap covers.

Breedie handed me the signal. COMESCORT TO MASTER

CYCLOPS: REPEAT TO MASTER ATHENIAN: REDUCE SPEED
TO SEVENTEEN KNOTS ADMIRALTY ADVISE TWO REPEAT
TWO U-BOATS IN AREA IMMEDIATELY AHEAD COURSE ALTER-
ATION STARBOARD 5 DEGREES TO 148 DEG TRUE REPEAT 148
DEG ON MY EXECUTE SIGNED BRAID END.

I looked at Curtis. The *Commandant Joffre* had been hit
on her port side, now we were altering further to starboard, away from the African coast. It wasn't good news.
Anyone who went down now was going to have an even
longer row to safety and I wasn't the Bligh type of
adventure-sailor. On the other hand, if we had to deviate
at all, I would personally have felt safer leaving an even
bigger safety margin.

Curtis rested the Aldis on his forearm and flickered the
acknowledgement as I lifted the voice pipe out of its clip
in the wheelhouse. The Captain answered almost at once.
'Signal from escort, Sir,' I said. 'Course alteration to
starboard.'

There was a short silence. 'I'll be right up, John. Just
carry on as requested.'

I hooked the voice pipe back up and pressed the
engine room buzzer. When they lifted the receiver down
below the background noise of the machinery seemed
very loud. The voice at the other end rasped in my ear,
'Chief Engineer.'

'Kent, Chief. You can reduce to seventy-five revolutions again.'

'Aye? Thank Christ for that, Mate. The way yon fancy
Navy man acts ye'd think we were a bloody oil tanker.'

I grinned into the mouthpiece. 'Well, you can take your
kettle off the boil anyway, just as soon as you like.'

The Chief must have run to his precious throttle controls
because the vibration had died down almost before I'd
replaced the receiver. He was a real cost-conscious Company man was Henry McKenzie. Curtis appeared, framed
in the wheelhouse door. '*Mallard*'s taken down the "Execute", Mister Kent.'

I nodded at the helmsman. 'Starboard five degrees. Steady
on 148.'

'Steady on 148, Sir,' he echoed, putting the wheel three
spokes over, and I watched as the bow swung slowly
round. As the mast stopped steady on the shimmering

horizon again I walked over and glanced in the binnacle.

'Steady on 148, Sir,' the quartermaster affirmed as I looked at the floating card under the bright brass hood. I nodded. 'Watch her at that. You haven't a lot of seaway to play with between us and *Athenian*.'

I didn't like the idea of the two ships sweeping along directly abeam of each other. Not at that speed. It only needed a few moments of carelessness by either helmsman, and magnetism or interaction could take over, drawing the two enormous steel hulls together. The theory was that it made us a slightly less spread-out target for any predatory submarine though, at the speed we were travelling, he would even then have to take a snap shot at us from forward of the beam before we left him without a chance of catching up. It was a reassuring thought.

Then I remembered that the captain of the *Commandant Joffre* had probably felt as optimistic as I did, just before his ship lay over on top of him.

Breedie was chalking the new heading on the course board over the helmsman's head when Captain Evans arrived on the bridge. He glanced briefly at the figures, then jerked his head to me and stepped into the chartroom. I followed to find him stretched out over the table, tapping the chart thoughtfully with the dividers.

He looked up frowning, 'Did Commander Braid give any reason for the course change, John?'

I nodded. 'Admiralty intelligence seems to think there are U-boats directly ahead of us, Sir.'

He must have seen the doubtful look in my eyes because he raised his eyebrows queryingly. 'But . . .?'

I shrugged. 'The Navy must be one hell of a sure of their plotting to try and get us to skin past with less than half a point alteration. Maybe there is nothing to starboard apart from a few thousand miles of Atlantic Ocean, but I'd rather gamble on the possibility of a longer trip in a lifeboat to the West Africa coast than barely shave past an established danger area.'

Evans chewed his bottom lip and looked at the chart again. The thin pencil line marking our progress was creeping up to a point roughly abeam of Mocamedes, to the north of the Angolan border. 'Any substantial alteration now will mean a lot of ground to make up by the time we reach the Cape.'

I knew what he meant. If we swung well away to our starboard hand at this stage it meant we had to make good the distance of two sides of a triangle against a straight run into our refuelling point at Cape Town. As it was, we were already running well to the west of the normal shipping lanes in order to avoid presenting the German Navy with an almost guaranteed rendezvous. Still —apart from the Chief Engineer's penurious ulcers—I couldn't see why we had to save miles at the expense of a proportionate increase in risk.

'What's a couple of days extra steaming going to matter, Sir?' I queried.

The Captain dipped into my tin of Players and graciously offered me one too. I mentally resolved to carry them in my pocket from now on as we lit up and he blew a long, thoughtful streamer of smoke at the tiny blob on the chart marking St. Helena. I could see he had something on his mind so I stared out through the open door at *Athenian* taking long, graceful dips into the slow swell as she clung to the dubious protection of our flank. It was all a game of chance, even in the way we were hugging each other for solace. A split second decision by some waiting Kapitan Lieutnant on whether he could take us best from the port or starboard side would mean the difference between *Athenian* or *Cyclops* crewmen vomiting pink lung tissue in the wake of their luckier sister as the black diesel oil burnt its way down to their guts. I shuddered involuntarily. Sure, I loved Chief Officer Henderson over there like a brother, but . . . ?

'Have you ever wondered why we haven't been zig-zagging this trip?' said Evans, watching me.

I looked guiltily away from *Athenian*, hoping he hadn't been able to read my thoughts. 'Sir? Well . . . I assume that, at seventeen knots, we're presenting a pretty hard target anyway, without arsing about convoy-style.'

He smiled and knew what I meant. All our previous trips during wartime had been in convoy, where the slightest suspicion of submarine activity had been the signal for periodic alterations of course in an attempt to confuse any ambushing U-boat's attack plain. We'd seen a lot of ships erupting violently to prove that theory didn't always match

up with practice! It was a bloody nuisance for the officer
of the watch too, with twenty or thirty ships charging about
all over the shop like panic-stricken cattle. But then—so was
fighting a drowning man for a place on a Carley float.

Evans shook his head, 'Even vessels proceeding independently zig-zag almost continuously in submarine waters.
And maybe, after the practice they've had, the bastards are
getting better at hitting fast targets . . .'

I thought again about the climbing spray against the
hull of the stricken Frenchman a few hours before, and
the pathetic little matchstick man on her funnel, and suddenly the importance of taking every possible precaution
seemed very necessary and to hell with the inconvenience.
So, why were we being different?

The Old Man saw the query in my face before I had
time to frame the question. He wiped his red face slowly
with a large blue hankie and eased the sweat-soaked shirt
around his armpits. 'We're in a hurry, John. In one
hell of a hurry. Two days extra steaming just can't be
allowed on this voyage. You drew up the stowage plans—
you know what we're carrying in the forward strongroom?'

I nodded. We had two very hot consignments forward,
both brought aboard less than an hour before we sailed
from Gladstone Dock. The first shipment had arrived in
the traditional plain van, the secrecy having been somewhat dissipated, however, by the three Liverpool Con-
stabulary patrol cars that had accompanied it. Treasury
notes. Printed by the Royal Mint and shipped out to the
Bank of Australia. I didn't know how much there was but,
judging by the number of steel-bound cases, there was
more than enough to pay for *Cyclops* and a few more
freighters if anyone wanted to start up a shipping company
in style. I couldn't see that there needed to be any rush
to deliver them, though. Not if it meant risking valuable
ships and men in a headlong dash on a straight, easily
anticipated course through U-boat water.

The other strong-room cargo was veiled in considerably
greater mystery. Referred to on the manifest simply as
'Confidential Bags. Safe Hand. By British Master Only',
the three locked and lead-sealed bags had been brought
aboard just as the gangway was being shipped and hustled
up forward to be placed in the steel chamber under the

foc'sle. The two Naval officers delivering them had seemed extremely relieved at the handing-over proceedings under the wet glare of our shaded cargo lamps, but I hadn't thought much about it at the time. I was more interested in the excessive number of dockside longshoremen who were hanging about with apparently only casual glances at the ship but, at the same time, possessing an undefinable military bearing out of keeping with what they appeared to be.

Were these weighted bags the reason for our odd convoy set-up? For our having at least a token escort all to ourselves while many forty- and fifty-ship convoys had to make do with one warship per every eight or ten vessels?

'Those confidential bags?' I queried, looking suspiciously at the Old Man.

He nodded. 'I don't know what the security position is, John, but as you're my senior officer I feel I'm justified in explaining just what we have up forr'ad.'

Stepping with rather dramatic secrecy to the chartroom door he checked to make sure we were on our own. Over his shoulder I could see the flutter of a White Ensign as *Mallard* made another of her periodic, death-defying dashes under our looming, predatory bows, the ping of her Asdic definable even at this distance across the silent sea. 'She's going to do that once too bloody often,' I muttered to myself as Evans came back in and, removing his cap with the trimming of gold brain round the peak, used the hankie to wipe the leather sweat band inside.

He looked at me with a funny, sad expression in his eyes that I couldn't explain. 'You know that *Hesperia* passed us a few weeks ago, off Cape Finisterre, when we were homeward bound from our last trip?'

I remembered all right. It had been during my early morning watch when we'd seen her heading towards us out of the grey spindrift of the Bay. Biscay had been at her bloodiest that time, with great green and white-flecked waves rearing high over the foc'sle-head like greedily clutching fingers. *Hesperia* was another of the Company's fast cargo liners built, like us, just before this war had started. She'd scudded past us, going like a bat out of hell, outward bound to somewhere unknown, with the Red Ensign streaming out from her stern in tattered pennants and the long, flared bows crushing tons of water into flying gouts of spray which curled viciously aft over the plunging bridge and superstructure. Her Aldis had flickered through the ochre morning light. CAN OFFER YOU A TOW OR WOULD YOU PREFER US TO HEAVE TO AND WIND UP YOUR ELASTIC BANDS AGAIN SIGNED CLINT CHIEF OFFICER END.

I had grinned despite the rain which had found its way under my oilskins and the towel round my neck. Eric Clint, Bill Henderson and I had been cadets together in twenty-eight, on the China run, and no three human beings could have loved each other more than we did. I signalled back, SORRY BUT WE THOUGHT YOU WERE ALREADY HOVE TO SIGNED KENT CHIEF OFFICER END.

The last I'd seen of *Hesperia* was her high rounded stern being swallowed by the low overcast, and the signal lamp still flickering forlornly from her bridge. JUST PLAYING IT SAFE JOHN KNOWING YOU WERE DRIVING SIGNED ERIC A PROPER CHIEF OFFICER END. Two minutes later she was out of sight and the tumbling seas had erased all traces of her passing. He'd always been one for having the last word, had Eric.

'I remember. She was outward bound and going like the clappers,' I said.

Evans bit his lip nervously. 'She was reported lost with all hands three days later, John. I'm sorry. You were a friend of her Mate's, weren't you?'

I stared at him dazedly, feeling a sick knot compacting in my stomach. Eric gone? I couldn't accept it. Not Eric Clint? Oh, Jesus, the bloody, bloody War. The Old Man frowned in embarrassment at the chart and fiddled awkwardly with the parallel rules. 'I knew old Tom Everett, her master,' he murmured quietly. 'He was little Julie's Godfather.'

Julie was the Old Man's nine-year-old daughter and the apple of his rather fierce eye. I knew how he felt, too. We were all of one family in the Company, most of us had sailed with each other at some time in the past. We hadn't been at war long enough to harden ourselves to the realisation that we were going to lose a lot of friends before it was over. But big Eric Clint. I wondered whether Bill Henderson knew yet, over on *Athenian*.

'What . . . what had *Hesperia* got to do with us, Captain? Why should *her* being sunk affect *our* voyage?'

B

'Because we're carrying the replacement information that she should already have arrived with in Adelaide, John.' He took a deep breath. 'Those bags in the strongroom contain all the current Notices to Mariners, giving the very latest information on minefields and swept areas, the new Naval code conversion tables for masters, full details of convoy routes and procedures. Without them every ship leaving Aussie and what we have left of the Far East will have to play it strictly by ear, and you know that can be bloody dangerous. Until we get through there could be perhaps fifty, even a hundred ships a day leaving port without proper information . . .' He looked at me very hard and I shifted uncomfortably. 'Some of them will be sunk through the lack of it!

'*Hesperia* would have been there in plenty of time, but she's gone. Now it all depends on us. I'm not a religious man, John, but this is one time I'd even pray if I thought it would help any.'

Well, if he wanted to pray, it was all right by me—I was quite happy to accept any help I could get. There were a few things still bothering me, though. I lit another Players and nervously sucked the smoke down into the back of my lungs. 'What about *Athenian*, Sir? And the *Commandant Joffre*? Did they have the same cargo? And, if the Navy's in such a goddamned hurry, why don't they fly it out?'

He shook his head. 'The Admiralty can't afford to take any chances. Aircraft can be shot down, their contents are more liable to capture. I understand there are duplicate copies being shipped independently of us, just in case, but the other ships in this particular group aren't of vital importance.' He dropped his eyes, '*Athenian* and the Frenchman are—were—well, they're here to spread the selection slightly. To give us at least a one-in-four chance of not being picked as the primary target. Any U-boat sighting us would at least be stuck for choice.'

First, the news of Eric's death, and now—This! I felt my anger flushing into my face. '*Athenian*'s just a bloody decoy, then? And the Frenchie? She went down so we could save a few days by travelling in a straight bloody line instead of taking reasonable evasive action?'

Evans scratched his barrel chest uncomfortably. 'Not

so that we could save a few days—so that we could save a few *ships.* And the *Commandant Joffre* wasn't just thrown away, man. She was still loaded with cargo that had to be shipped one way or another. Any merchantman rounding the Cape is at risk. Good God, even a zig-zag can bring you right into a sub's range instead of taking you out of it.'

I stared out at the little corvette, now skipping playfully abeam of us. Aft, a torpedoman moved among the rows of depth-charges, seemingly unmoved by the knowledge that he was surrounded by tons of high explosive and that, in the event of *Mallard*'s being sunk, the water pressure acting on the charges would send the whole bloody lot up, back out of the Atlantic, as high as *Cyclops*'s mastheads.

I pointed accusingly at her with the butt of the Players. 'What about the Grey Funnel boat? Is she expendable too?'

Evans's face started to get red but he kept on trying to be nice. 'She's our escort, John.'

I savagely ground my stub in the Company ashtray on the chronometer case. 'Escort? That motorised skitter-bug? We'd be better off with a bloody yellow duck in a tin bath for an escort.'

Now the Old Man was really getting needled. I could see it would be 'Mister' any moment now. Maybe he didn't like the things that were happening either, but he had the sense to accept them and not keep knocking every idea the Navy had. 'All right, *Mister* Kent. If you must know . . . *Mallard*'s not so much with us as an escort— we both know she can't do much to protect us from submarines working on her own—she's with us more to ensure that the enemy don't get their hands on those confidential bags. If we are hit Commander Braid is charged with the duty of trying to take the bags aboard *Mallard*. If there isn't time, if the strong-room is inaccessible due to the ship being down by the head, say, or through any other reason . . . then he has orders to sink us himself!'

I stared at the Captain. This was getting better and better. Not only were we carrying enough secret information to make us the target of every Hun unit in the South Atlantic if they knew, but also, apparently, the Royal Navy were quite prepared to give them a hand with it, if convenient. I remembered Sparks's thin, self-

confident sneer at breakfast, and the contemptuous voice.
'. . . Not me, Mister Mate. *And* I'll get a proper signal off
first, too. Don't you worry!' Well, I was worried now—
bloody worried! And I had a sick premonition that Larabee
was going to have the opportunity to prove himself.

'What happens if the bags *are* captured, Sir?' I asked
without enthusiasm. 'If *Mallard*'s sunk, and we're boarded?'

He looked at me very hard, the warning cone was being
hoisted. 'In that case we must make every effort to jettison
them over the side, Mister. I repeat . . . every effort and
sacrifice.'

'But if they *are* captured?' I persisted, starting to get
bloody-minded. 'If there's no one left on board to dump
the goddamned things? What happens then? The whole
idea's crazy. The enemy will have enough information to
sink every ship in the Eastern Hemisphere by appoint-
ment . . .'

Evans slammed his fist down on the chart table savagely.
I had pushed my luck too hard with him and, as the
red, weatherbeaten face glared at me angrily, I remembered my own reaction to young Conway's display of little-
boy pique that morning. Now I was in his position. We all
had a superior to chew us out when we forgot ourselves.
A ridiculous, almost forgotten childhood rhyme started
running through my head. 'Big fleas have little fleas upon
their backs to bite them; And little fleas have littler fleas,
and so ad infinitum.' The particular flea on my back
crammed the gold-braided cap on his head and stuck his
jaw out ferociously.

'If you don't like it, Mister Kent, you can complain
to the bloody Board of Trade! Until then you will carry
out your duties as required by me, the master of this
vessel. My orders are *not* that you should dedicate yourself
to finding flaws in everything the Admiralty does, despite
your apparent capacity for so doing . . .'

He turned away and, reaching the chartroom door,
hesitated. The stern features softened slightly. 'I, myself,
confess to a little disenchantment with the circumstances
surrounding our present voyage, but I can, however,
pride myself on my ability to carry out my duty as master
of a British vessel. The Owners have dictated that I accept
my instructions from the Royal Navy without demur, and

this both I *and* my officers will continue to do.'

He smiled suddenly and it was like the sun coming
through a cloud. 'Duty, Mister Kent, does not necessarily
equate with common sense. But, if common sense pre-
vailed over every decision, then perhaps we wouldn't be
at war?'

I nodded silently, at the same time wondering how far
Eric Clint would go along with that profundity—washing
about face down in some anonymous patch of oily sea, his
long blond hair floating like dead tentacles and the wreckage of his beloved *Hesperia* as an obscene shroud—A
monument to 'Duty.'

The Old Man must have seen the doubt still in my
white face. 'Don't worry about the capture of the bags,
John. Common sense still retains a foothold, even in
Whitehall. In the event of our being unable to destroy
the documents we are to attempt to get a signal off advising
them . . .'

'Larabee fancies himself a bloody hero,' I murmured
sardonically.

He didn't catch the sarcasm. '. . . The Shipping Control
people will, of course, immediately alter all codes, sea
routes and so forth, rendering the majority of the captured
intelligence useless. If we are . . . er . . .'

'Sunk?' I suggested brutally.

'. . . sunk,' he affirmed smoothly, 'then they will pick
up a message either from us or either *Mallard* or *Athenian*,
wireless silence then being unnecessary. They will at least
know that the documents are still out of enemy hands and
they must hope to God the ships behind us get through.
The plans will remain unchanged.'

I didn't like to chance appearing bloody-minded again
—Evans in full battle rig was something to be avoided—
but there was one thing I just had to know. The most
obvious flaw in the whole proposition. 'I'm sorry, Sir . . .
but what happens if they don't receive *any* call from us?
If every ship in the group disappears without trace?'

To my relief he smiled tolerantly. 'It's hardly likely,
is it, John? I mean, for every ship here to just vanish into
thin air without leaving any indication of what's happened? But, to set your fertile mind at rest, if we don't
arrive on our E.T.A., and the Admiralty have no *certain*

proof that we have taken the bags down with us, then they are to assume that the documents have been captured and act accordingly. I trust, Mister Mate, that the Navy's proposals have your approval?'

He grinned fleetingly again to soften the sarcasm and stepped out into the glare of the sun washing over the bridge deck. I watched him go, then reached for the tin with the bearded Jack Tar on the label. Of course he was right. It was fantastic even to imagine for one moment that three ships like ours could vanish without trace, leaving no evidence, no indication of the way of their passing. Two ultra-modern cargo vessels and a warship, all with wireless equipment capable of blasting the ears off the operators at Simonstown Naval Base who would be listening specifically for us. I must have been bloody crazy even to consider it.

I lit up and felt a bit better.

At least, I tried to convince myself I did.

CHAPTER TWO

We were forced to alter course still further to the west just as I was starting my soup course at dinner that evening.

Charlie Shell, the Second Mate, was prodding doubtfully at his curried rice while bitterly bemoaning the trials and tribulations of being the only bloke on the ship who had to do a proper day's work on account of his standing the graveyard watch seven nights a week—which struck me as being a bit of an Irishism for a start—when I noticed the stand-by quartermaster hanging nervously around the saloon doorway trying to catch Ling's Oriental eye. The little steward finally consented to observe him and, after a bit of dramatic pidgin, came scuttling over to me. 'Number Four Mate, he say Mister Kent go up along blidge, chop-chop.'

I tried to console myself with the thought that the night was too hot and humid for soup anyway, and chop-chopped up to the bridge wondering what it was all about. As I hurried along the prom deck I didn't note any feverish activity over on *Mallard* or the looming *Athenian*, so I assumed we couldn't be under attack. As I swung up the ladder and into the wheelhouse I saw Brannigan deep in conversation with the elderly Mister Foley, our Chief Wireless Operator. He waved a signal form at me as I approached and I followed him out to the starboard wing.

'Just picked up an S S call, Mate,' Foley said, pushing his lined face forward to catch the stream of cool air flowing over the furled dodgers. It was a hot, airless little hole they had for a wireless room, perched as it was on the extreme after end of the boat deck.

I grabbed the flimsy. 'Position?'

Sparks shrugged, looking apologetic. 'He didn't have time to finish. I managed to get a D.F. fix though. It was bloody loud. Couldn't have been all that far away.'

I glanced at the neatly pencilled letters. SSSS: MV KENT STAR TO ALL SHIPS: TORPEDOED IN ENGINE SPACE WE ARE GOING POSIT . . .My mouth went tight as I imagined the poor bastard operator clinging grimly to his key as he felt the ship laying over with him still aboard. They could hardly have had time to realise what had hit them though, not with a garbled distress call like that as their only legacy.

'Is that all you got, Alf?'

He nodded and I caught a trace of whisky in his breath. 'That's all, Mate. The poor buggers must've gone down like a block of lead.'

I started to walk towards the chartroom. 'Nearly blew my earphones off,' Foley said behind me. 'Couldn't have been more than forty miles away, not at that strength. D.F. bearing 358.'

I stopped abruptly and stared at him, dead shattered. 'You did say 358, Alf?'

Then the Captain stumped up the ladder, fully dressed this time, and looked at the signal. I think the florid features went paler under the tan, but otherwise he didn't even blink. 'You didn't manage to get her position then, Mister Foley?'

'No, Sir!' Alf answered uncomfortably, and I felt sorry for him and the inadequate way he waved his hands.

'Mister Foley got a fix though, Sir,' I said quickly. 'Bearing 358, range approximately forty miles.'

Evans looked up sharply. 'My God!' he said.

Brannigan picked up the Aldis, 'Escort's signalling, Sir.'

The Old Man didn't glance at him. He just murmured, 'I don't want to know *when* she's signalling, Mister Brannigan. I'm only interested in what she has to say.'

'Aye, aye, Sir,' the Fourth Mate muttered, pulling a face at old Foley as he turned away towards the flickering blip on the corvette's bridge. Evans held the signal sheet up to me.

'You were right about our cutting it too fine, John,' he said slowly.

I nodded, but didn't feel very pleased with my vindication. Radio direction finder bearings are obtained relative to the ship's head only, which meant that Foley's bearing on the sinking *Kent Star* was only two degrees to the left of our present course. At seventeen knots we would be within spitting distance of the sub which sank her within two hours. Unless we altered course again . . .

'Cut in towards the coast, do you think, Sir?' I said.

The Old Man looked dubious. 'That would take us near to the regular shipping lane, John. We've already altered to avoid two U-boats suspected to the east and, with the *Kent Star* U-boat, which could even have been one of them, already fine on our port bow, I can only see Braid going farther west.'

Farther west! Which meant an even greater deviation from our refuelling berth at Cape Town. The Chief was going to have ulcers on his slide rule before this trip was over and I sympathised with him. The South Atlantic suddenly seemed a very large ocean. Behind me I heard the Aldis rattle a smart acknowledgement, then Brannigan appeared at the Old Man's elbow and handed him the scrawled message. Obviously the corvette's operators had caught the 'S' call too. Evans held out the signal for me to read. COMESCORT TO MASTER CYCLOPS: REPEAT TO MASTER ATHENIAN: DISTRESS CALL RECEIVED MV KENT STAR SUGGESTS FURTHER ENEMY ACTIVITY AHEAD COURSE ALTERATION STARBOARD FIVE DEG TO 153 DEG TRUE REPEAT 153 DEG ON MY EXECUTE SIGNED BRAID END.

'Execute from *Mallard*, Sir,' the Fourth Mate called. Obviously our Comescort wasn't wasting any time. I wondered if it had occurred to the dashing Commander Braid that there might be men coughing their lives out in the water less than two hours away, but it was maybe unfair of me. Compassion doesn't have any place in wartime, not when it conflicts with 'Duty.' It provided bloody good ammunition for unreasoning cynics like me, though.

I turned wearily into the wheelhouse. 'Starboard five degrees. Steady on 153.'

As our head swung even further into the wastes of the burning South Atlantic I looked at the distress signal still clutched in my hand. Something about it worried me. Something indefinable, but nevertheless there. I read it again more carefully: SSSS: MV KENT STAR TO ALL SHIPS: TORPEDOED IN ENGINE SPACE WE ARE GOING POSIT . . . Then the final break as her H.T. aerials shorted out into the rushy greedy sea. M.V. *Kent Star*. I chewed my lip nervously and tried to think. *Kent Star*? Maybe it was just word association. Chief Officer John Kent? Motor vessel *Kent*? I tried to shrug the suspicious feeling off. We had a small problem of our own to worry about—like just staying alive.

But Kent? The *Kent Star*? . . .

Poor bloody Alf Foley disappeared less than two hours later.

It was about ten p.m. and I was relaxing under a large gin in the Chief's cabin when it happened. Well, when I say relaxing I really mean I was getting on the outside of a welcome tot of Gilbey's best in between spells of watching an angry Scots ship's engineer pounding the hell out of the already battered, leather-bound Company Fuel Log lying cowering on his jumbled desk.

'Jesus Christ!' the Chief yelled, thumping the long-suffering book again with an oil-grimed fist. 'Does yon fancy Grey Funnel Line man Braid think I can run mah wee engines on sea watter? Does he?'

I grinned placatingly and reached for the bottle again. If it hadn't been the Royal Navy sabotaging his oil it would have been the perfidious Company Agents somewhere—and if it hadn't been them it would have been the fault of the Old Man, the Second Engineer or the ship's cat. For forty years the Chief had been fighting a running battle with the Phantom of the Fuel Bunkers, and the only time he'd ever won was when, as Second on the old China Steamship Company's *Fuktien*, they had brought her through the great typhoon of '21 by burning every stick of wood aboard, including the masts, saloon and cabin furniture, and the Old Man's rosewood sextant box, before the Mate had suddenly remembered they carried five hundred tons of coal as cargo in their number three hold.

'Henry,' I said, 'you know bloody well that if you'd been apprenticed in sail you'd have grudged the cook the oil he used to fry chow in the galley.'

He stood there in his red carpet slippers with the Chinese dragons embroidered on them and fumed impotently, 'And don't call me "Henry", Mister Mate! Ah'll remind you that ma name's McKenzie . . . *Chief Engineer* McKenzie to you.'

'Aye, aye, Henry!' I said as the knock sounded at the cabin door. The Chief flip-flopped across the cabin and opened it suspiciously. Young Conway stood outside in the alleyway.

'Whit?' growled the Chief ferociously.

Conway shuffled nervously at the confrontation and tried to see through the Chief's cellular-vested torso to me, 'Mister Kent, Sir. The Captain sends his compliments and asks if you would come to the bridge immediately . . . Sir!'

'The bloody man's no' going to change course further west again, is he?' yelled the bristling McKenzie. 'Over ma dead body, he's no'.'

I groaned inwardly. 'What's up, Conway?' I asked as I reached for my cap.

He looked very excited and flushed. 'It's Mister Foley, Sir—the Chief Sparks . . . He's missing!'

I looked sideways at the Chief, who stopped snorting abruptly and frowned at the cadet. 'He cannae be missing, lad. He's bound tae be somewhere. Mister Foley's no' a wee laddy on his first trip, tae get himsel' lost.'

'No, Sir. But . . . but he doesn't seem to be anywhere aboard. We've already had a pretty good scout round on deck and in the officers' cabins.'

I was already on my way through the door when McKenzie kicked the red slippers off and started struggling into his deck shoes. 'Ah'll have my gang search the engine spaces, Mate. Ye'll no' need to worry about them.'

On the way up to the bridge I asked Conway who had reported old Alf's disappearance. 'The Second Wireless Op, Larabee, Sir. He said Mister Foley should have been on watch but when he called into the radio shack to get a book the Chief Sparks had . . . well, he'd gone. There was no one manning the set at all. Mister Larabee's standing by just now.'

The velvety black air was still pleasantly warm on my face as I climbed to the darkened bridge. Only the dim green glow from the binnacle relieved the gloom, shining up on the underside of the helmsman's features like some Frankenstein colourwash. In peace time it would have been a lovely night to relax out on the wing, sixty feet above the rushing phosphorescent sea below, and think how nice it was to be a sailorman.

Tonight, though, I couldn't relax. I was too scared. The pleading message from the *Kent Star* had somehow unsettled me even more than the violent spectacle of the death of the *Commandant Joffre*. And Foley? Was poor, bumbling, white-haired old Alf choking dementedly only a few miles astern?

I couldn't get the thought out of my mind that, if it had to be anybody fighting for an already forfeited life back there in our shimmering wake, if it had to be anybody . . . then why couldn't it have been the Second Sparks instead? The thin-faced, coldly sardonic Larabee.

It took over an hour for us to rouse the crowd and go over the ship from truck to keel—crew accommodation, galleys, paint and lamp lockers, empty passenger cabins. We sent men up the masts too, watching them as they went higher and higher until their blue-jeaned backsides were lost in the blanketing darkness of the night. We even searched the strong room, with its steel-bound cases of banknotes and its three critically vital, lead-weighted mail bags.

But Alf Foley was gone. We never saw him again.

Larabee was still in the radio room when I went in, pulling the blackout curtain quickly to behind me. He was perched right back in his chair with his feet up on the transmitting table and the headphones slipped casually round the scrawny neck, reading a paper-backed wartime edition of some detective story or other. He heaved his legs to the floor and looked up.

'Find Alf, did you?' he queried, still with that half-mocking twist to the thin mouth.

I lit up gratefully without offering him one. I didn't like not being able to smoke on deck in the dark. 'No,' I said, briefly.

He shook his head critically, 'Stupid bastard!'

I felt the angry flush burning into my face as always when he spoke like that. 'Do you mean *me*, Larabee? Or your poor bloody oppo?'

The Second Operator still seemed to smile slightly. 'Oh, not you, Mate. Never you. No, I was thinkin' about Alf. Stupid bastard!'

My cigarette glowed fiercely as I dragged hard to keep control. 'Yeah? Well, he's a stupid *dead* bastard now, Larabee. Or don't you mind too much?'

He shrugged indifferently. 'He was an old man, Mate. Old men like Alf shouldn't be at sea if they can't keep off the bottle before they get to the stage of going over the wall.'

I knew what he meant. Foley was too fond of the hard stuff, especially when we were alongside and, unlike the rest of the ship's officers, the radio men didn't have a great deal to do when in port. Alf never went ashore more than once a voyage, when he would climb into a baggy, pin-striped blue suit, irrespective of the climate, and sweat around the local bazaars in search of a present for his wife, that elderly fly-blown woman who stared severely and almost reprimandingly from the cheap Woolworth's frame over the Chief Operator's bunk. The rest of the trip Alf —as soon as we were secured—would vanish into his cabin and drink steadily until 'Stand by' was rung for leaving harbour. I can't say, even then, that I ever saw him really three sheets in the wind, but on the other hand I never saw him really sober either. It still didn't fit together though.

'How do you know he went over the side, Larabee?' I asked suspiciously.

The almost hairless eyebrows went up in exaggerated

surprise. 'There's an alternative? A bloke disappears off a ship in mid-ocean—which *must* be true 'cause the Mate says so—and you think there's some other place he could be, other than over the wall?'

'No,' I muttered, trying to ignore the sarcasm and feeling a bit stupid. 'But how, in God's name, did he manage it? Alf wasn't the kind of bloke to put himself over.'

Larabee shrugged again. 'Like I said, Mate. He was stoned, stepped outside for a breath of air, and . . . splash, splash!'

'I've never seen him drunk as that when we were at sea. He could maybe absorb it pretty well off duty but I can't ever remember Foley drinking much on passage. And it's bloody hard to go over the rail on a dead calm night like this, too.'

The Second bent down and, picking an empty whisky bottle from a drawer, held it out. 'I found this sculling about under the desk. It wasn't there when I went off watch at eight bells, I'd swear it.' He waved it from side to side like a pendulum. 'And when a bloke's got outside this much stuff in a few hours, well . . . the boat doesn't need a wave to make it seem like it's rolling, Mate.'

And that was that. Epitaph for an operator. Cause of death—drowning, with ninety per cent proof complications! I took the bottle and turned away. 'I'll tell the Captain, he'll need to enter it in the Log. You may have to sign a statement, Larabee . . . about your finding this bottle, I mean.'

He picked up the paperback again. 'Anything you say, Mate. We . . . er . . . aren't going back to search then?'

'No,' I answered, feeling helpless and very sad. 'No, we won't be going back for Alf.' I put my hand out to the blackout curtain, then hesitated as a thought struck me. 'We'll signal the escort as soon as it gets light. Ask for a temporary replacement operator.'

Personally I didn't give a monkey's damn if Larabee had to sit there twenty-four hours a day 'til his hand mummified round the key, but I was Chief Officer of *Cyclops* and, as such, had a responsibility to give him every assistance. He didn't seem to appreciate my solicitude very much though, judging by the violent way in which he swung round, thin face working angrily. 'You tryin' to make out I can't do my job without a bloody gaffer to watch over me, Mate?'

I stared at him in surprise. I knew we were all a bit on edge—my own nerves were beginning to strum like wire stays in a gale—but Larabee's reaction seemed curiously out of keeping with his previous indifference to everything that went on around him.

'No, I'm not, Larabee!' I answered sharply. 'I'm saying that you can't do your job twenty-four hours a day without even a W.T. rating from *Mallard* to stand by the set while you get some kip.'

The veins stood out in the scrawny neck as he stabbed a bony finger at me. 'If you think I'm goin' to let some fuggin' poncy Bluejacket get within three cables of this set you can stuff it, Mate. Right up your hawse pipe!'

That did it! I'd had just about as much as I could take for one day. First, the sick horror of the *Commandant Joffre*'s agony, followed by the Old Man's revelations about our cargo, then the far too close death rattle of the *Kent Star*. And pathetic old Foley with his lonely passing. And now . . . Larabee! I threw the empty bottle on the bunk and leapt at the wireless operator, lifting him out of his chair and shaking him like a kiddy's teddy bear so that the earphones rattled against the back of his skull.

'You ever speak to me like that again, you little bugger, and I'll break your goddamned back!' I yelled, spraying flecks of spittle on to the staring white face close to mine. 'I'll break your bloody back, d'you understand? You talk to me like I'm the First Mate of this bucket and not some bloody Hong Kong steward in the galley. You're a rotten, stinking little man for my money, Larabee, but by God, you'll do as you're bloody well told while you're on this ship or so help me I'll put you over the rail to keep that poor bastard company . . . !'

Then, suddenly, I felt sick. Terribly sick and tired of it all. My anger evaporated, leaving me swaying with fatigue and the fear of what I somehow knew was going to happen. The little doll in my hands jerked convulsively and, almost absentmindedly, I let him flop back into the chair where he sat, tugging fretfully at the torn collar of the white tropical shirt. I noticed that the two thin, wavy gold bands on his epaulette had come adrift and he sobbed a bit as he picked ineffectively at the slender badges of rank. He reminded me a little of inadequate old Foley the way he slumped there so helplessly.

I couldn't bring myself to touch him again so I just waved my hand, vaguely apologetic. 'I . . . er . . . I shouldn't have done that, Larabee.'

He didn't seem to hear me. 'I jus' want to be left to get on with my job, that's all. Just to get on with my job.'

'Sorry,' I gritted, at the same time hating myself for having to say it.

The plaintive voice was almost tearful, 'I don't need no bloody sheepdog to help me out. Not with the amplifier on and me in the bunk next to the set.'

I understood what he was getting at. Not so many years ago very few ships had carried more than one operator, if they had any wireless at all. Internationally agreed radio watches allowed for normal message traffic during set periods and, while the Sparks slept, it was accepted practice to leave the receiver on and amplify all incoming calls. Operators were mentally tuned to react to the emergency and distress frequencies and, even while asleep, the twitter of an S O S or M A Y D A Y call would bring them to instant wakefulness. The same thing applied to their own ship's signal letters.

I looked at him with a little more respect—at least he appeared to have some professional pride. 'You think you could manage it yourself?'

He nodded morosely and sniffed. 'It's all incoming traffic with us bein' under radio silence. The only outgoing stuff I'm likely to transmit is a distress call . . .' He grinned slightly and the sardonic look flickered back into the white face. 'The bloody bang'll wake me if you don't!'

I came to a decision, subject to the Old Man's approval. I suppose it could have been construed as selfish in one way, because I didn't fancy having to slow down or stop, even for long enough to transfer a rating from *Mallard*. Seventeen knots was a better insurance against torpedoes than a dead ship in the water at the wrong place. I nodded. 'O.K., Larabee. You're on your own until Cape Town. Then we try and pick up a replacement for Alf whether you like it or not.'

As I slipped through the door, stepping over the coaming into the velvety blackness of the night, I caught a glimpse of him lifting his feet back up on to the desk and I wondered what it was that I didn't like about him. I shrugged. At least he was honest enough to let you know if he didn't like you, not like some others I could think of who did everything right yet still managed to leave you with a feeling that they couldn't care less whether you vanished on the spot. Curtis, for instance, the Third Mate; quiet, well mannered and thoroughly efficient, but indefinably aloof, almost mysterious. Like the *Kent Star* message that still nagged away at the back of my mind. I shook my head and climbed slowly down the ladder to the well deck. *Mallard* had picked her signal up too, so there couldn't be any mistake . . .

Athenian slipped quietly along on our flank. Even without lights her great hull showed black against the faint line of the horizon. To a waiting Kapitan-Lieutnant she was as clear a target as a Celluloid rabbit in a shooting gallery—which meant we were as well!

The stars looked very bright above my head, but I didn't think the night was still lovely—not anymore.

I got nearly a whole hour's sleep before the thunder woke me. I stretched out an arm and, switching the light on, tried to focus on my watch through the white glare in my gummed eyelids. Two a.m., four bells in the middle watch. I rolled over with a lazy groan and buried my head in the pillow. Still two more hours of blessed sleep before the duty quartermaster called me with a cup of stewed tea and an ingratiating smile.

Thunder though? The ship felt steady as a rock. Surprising . . . Thunder, with no sea running . . . ?

Oh, Jesus!

My feet were already running as they hit the deck. One hand clutched at the cord on my pyjamas while the other grabbed my cap off the hook as I went through the door. I skidded to a stop in the alleyway, looked down at my bare feet and shot back into the cabin to slip into my deck shoes. Then back out again to collide with an equally fast-moving Third Mate Curtis, also in gaily striped pyjama bottoms but without even the dignity of a hat. As we tangled with each other I couldn't figure for a moment in my sleep-dulled mind why he looked so like a pregnant woman, then I realised he had his bright blue and orange Board of Trade lifejacket on. But Curtis always was a pessimist—and maybe a lifejacket *was* more use than a hat for a swim in the South Atlantic.

He dodged from side to side and yelled, 'Gunfire!' while I tried to make it past him like a scrum-half with no one to pass the ball to, and roared, 'I know, so gerrout the bloody way youstupidbastard!' then, breaking through, pounded up the old familiar trail to the bridge.

The Old Man was up there before me this time, though it took me a few moments of night blindness before my eyes adjusted from the glare of the accommodation lights to the blanketing solidity of the night, and I could see him properly. It wasn't all darkness though. Not on the horizon.

Evans was fully dressed and, together, we stood silently watching the fantastic display of pyrotechnics ahead. Red and green flares swarmed slowly into the night sky, while the steely blue-white of tracer shells streaked almost flat along the line of the distant sea one moment, then curved lazily and nearly vertical the next. All the time, rolling towards us over the sparkling reflections in the glassy water, came the sullen thunder of gunfire punctuated by the sharper cracks of light weapon bursts.

And we were heading almost directly into it.

'Gunpowder, treason and plot . . .' murmured the Second Mate as he stood slightly behind us.

The Captain swivelled, 'Keep an eye on *Mallard*, Mister Shell. If she doesn't give us a course alteration away from that bloody Brock's benefit within three minutes either Braid's a fool or they're all dead on the fancy boat.'

'Aye, aye, Sir.'

Evans turned to me worriedly and the flashes ahead illuminated his lined features. 'What the hell is it, Mister Kent? There doesn't seem to be any sense to it. Look!'

I saw what he meant. There was no apparent pattern in the lines of fire as you'd expect from two ships which were, presumably, firing at each other. Instead, the vari-coloured streamers seemed to sprout from one central core, fanning out as they rose into a gigantic, exploding vase of flowers.

'Maybe the war's over and we're celebrating,' I said,

trying to be dryly British and humorous in the face of fear.

The Old Man wasn't laughing very hard. 'Or perhaps the war's over and the bloody *Nazis* are celebrating,' he answered grimly, still trying to focus his Barr and Stroud 8×50's on the source of the display.

He let them go in disgust and they fell down on the straps to swing against the barrel chest. 'Goddam fools doing that must be well below the horizon—say ten, fifteen miles? I can't see a blasted thing other than the Fifth of November stuff going up.'

'Should I get a man up to the masthead, Sir?'

He considered for a moment, then shook his head. 'No, Mister Kent. He wouldn't see much anyway and I have no intentions of steaming very much farther on this heading, either with or without the Royal Navy's permission.'

I began to feel a bit better. It was reassuring to think there were at least two cowards on board, and we carried the rank. I knew, though, that Evans wasn't scared for himself—not in the way I was. It was just that he intended to carry out his duty with the minimum possible hazard to ship and crew. My train of thought was interrupted by Charlie Shell lifting the Aldis expectantly, 'Escort's signalling, Sir.'

We watched the tiny, flickering light from the black sliver that was *Mallard*. It was very dim, shaded for obvious reasons. Braid must have been dead worried to have risked showing a light at all, even though the illuminations lit up the seascape for miles around. It was fast, too. The signalman was in a hurry this time, but it didn't bother me. My morse was nearly up to professional operator standards as it was one accomplishment I'd always been interested enough in to practise rather more thoroughly than the average merchant navy officer.

The rumble of the guns was getting louder and I had to raise my voice slightly. 'COMESCORT TO MASTER CYCLOPS: REPEAT TO MASTER ATHENIAN: SUGGEST THIS IS ONE PARTY WE DON'T GATECRASH COURSE ALTERATION PORT TEN DEG TO 143 DEG T REPEAT 143 DEG ON MY EXECUTE SIGNED BRAID END.'

Evans wasn't any more impressed at the Commander's attempt at dry British humour than he had been with mine. He looked at me expressionlessly and the peak of his cap threw flickering shadows across his eyes. 'We're bearing farther east at last, Mister Kent.'

I nodded silently, not sure whether to be pleased or sorry. We had to try for the African coast some time and the way we were heading meant we should hit New Schwabenland in the South Polar Regions in about two weeks. I didn't relish the thought of trying to skin past the U-boats that were reckoned to be between us and Cape Town, and we still weren't all that far past the area where the unlucky *Kent Star* had screamed from, but what was the alternative? To keep on veering west until we either ran out of fuel or, at the very best, lost so much time and distance that the critically important cargo in the strongroom ceased to have any value in terms of lives saved and ships kept clear of our own minefields?

Another blip from *Mallard* and the Second Mate said sharply, 'Execute, Sir.'

Evans nodded. 'You have the watch, Mister Shell.'

'Aye, aye, Sir.' Charlie Shell stepped into the wheelhouse and we felt the ship heel over to starboard as we swung on to the new course. I was watching the pretty lights as the black silhouettes of the foremost mast cut across them when suddenly, without the slightest warning or even a gradual diminishing of intensity, the thunder stopped and they went out. Just like that! As if someone had switched them off. It was bloody crazy, the whole thing.

The blackness seemed very intense after that but, despite the unknown hazards it concealed, I felt a sense of greater security. Then *Mallard* spoiled the whole thing by going into competition with whatever had been on the horizon. Her shaded Aldis now seemed like a searchlight, beckoning U-boats like some lantern left in a window to entice a recalcitrant lover. Braid cut out the flannel this time, though. Just a few quick A's to catch our attention, then INCREASE TO EMERGENCY REVOLUTIONS END.

I wasn't much of an asset up there in my pyjama bottoms so I tactfully asked the Old Man's permission and scuttled down the ladder, leaving him to do the dirty work and tell the Chief about the new increase in speed. It was going to be like asking him to volunteer as a blood donor in vampire country.

This time I felt the vibration under my feet creeping up so grudgingly slowly it was almost painful.

I had just got back to my cabin, and was inhaling my first mouthful of much-needed tobacco smoke, when the gunfire rumble started again.

This time the Third Mate stood well back in anticipation as I took off down the alleyway—and without my bloody hat. If the Company wanted to fire me for such an extreme breach of etiquette then that was O.K. by me. I was quite prepared to leave the ship immediately, with or without references.

At the top of the bridge ladder I ground to a halt and stared at the sky ahead in baffled horror. Almost dead in line with the bows, practically bisected by the jackstaff up in the eyes of the ship, the same crazy carnival of spraying lights and colour was being re-enacted on the black edge of the horizon. The blazing illuminations were almost an exact second-house showing of the pyrotechnics that had chased us off course half an hour before.

But we were *still* headed straight for them.

This time it seemed that every officer aboard had found his way to the bridge for a grandstand seat, and Curtis wasn't the only one wearing a lifejacket either. I shouldered my way through the silent silhouettes, feeling the soft breast of kapok nudging me as they stood back, still perplexedly staring ahead. In the wheelhouse I stopped beside the nervously gum-chewing quartermaster at the wheel and peered anxiously at the course board, praying to God we'd changed back to our original heading for some reason while I was below. But we hadn't.

'How's her head?' I asked sharply.

'Steady on 143, Sir,' the man at the wheel answered, confirming what I already knew. I glimpsed his white, scared eyes shining in the green-washed face as I turned sharply to meet the Old Man who had entered the wheelhouse behind me.

'Aye, Mister Kent . . . It's a different bloody ship that's doing that little lot,' he said quietly.

I nodded numbly. For the original firework exhibitionist to have moved through a ten-degree arc from us to the horizon meant the anonymous ship travelling some twenty-five to thirty miles in half an hour, or at sixty knots, which was impossible. Ergo—there were two separate ships. At least! My stomach started to churn acidly as I realised the implications. Our gateway to Cape Town, continuing from our present position, was clamped firmly shut.

'I wonder what funny remark Mister Braid's going to have up his sleeve this time?' Evans grunted sourly, turning to face the corvette running slightly ahead of us, lit up like a Christmas tree in the glare from the distant spectacular. He didn't have to wait long to find out.

COMESCORT TO . . . PARDON MY SLIP IS SHOWING COURSE ALTERATION STARBOARD TWO FIVE DEG TO 168 DEG T REPEAT 168 DEG BEING WEST LEG OF REPETITIVE ZIG-ZAG PATTERN STANDBY FOR FURTHER FIVE DEG PORT ALTERATION EIGHT MINUTES FROM NOW EXECUTE IMMEDIATELY SIGNED BRAID END.

Which meant that, instead of using any fancy zig-zag plan involving several alternate headings at varying, pre-determined intervals we were settling for a happy medium by sailing a compensating zig-zag with only five-degree swings at firm, eight-minute intervals. We would lose less ground but the safety factor was proportionately smaller. In the chartroom the Old Man braced himself against the vicious heel of the ship as we tore round in a wide, twopoint arc and settled on the new course. He deftly snatched the pencil up as it rolled across the chart and, using the parallel rules, drew a faint line from our present dead reckoning position along 170 degrees, this being the approximate mean of our new heading. We were now running well away from the West African coast, with our only possible landfall several thousand miles ahead in the region of the Norwegian island of Bouvet, around 54 degrees south. I looked gloomily over his shoulder. In the glaring light of the Anglepoise lamp our marked course over the past twenty-four hours looked like a deformed dog's hindleg.

Evans threw down the pencil irritably and glared at the chart for a long time without speaking. Then he looked up and shook his head. 'It's not bloody good enough, John. A few more hours on this heading and we'll be so far out we'll never make good the time lost.' He shrugged. 'And there's another factor to consider . . . Any extension of our sea time automatically increases our risk. Commander Braid may be wrong in his assumption that all the danger lies between us and the coast.'

I looked as I felt—dubious. 'I suppose there is a time when the advantages of steering away are outweighed by the disadvantages, Sir, but . . . ?'

He waved his hand at the chart. 'Look at our track, man. We're buggering about over the ocean like a man who's scared stiff of his own shadow. Nearly every time something's happened it's forced us to swing farther west. Another few imagined ghosts like those and we'll end up in bloody South America!'

'Those lights we saw out there weren't imagination, Sir, I said anxiously. 'They gave us one solid, incontrovertible fact . . . that there are at least two, maybe even more, ships between us and the coast. We can't pretend it didn't happen. If it had been a Royal Navy stunt we'd have been informed. Merchantmen just don't carry that kind of illumination, so . . .'

He switched the light off and opened the door. The horizon had reverted to a dim, black, unbroken line on the edge of the world again, while the unexplained cascade of colour had died away as suddenly as its predecessor, leaving the darkness of the night and the twinkling stars and the only sound the rush of water past our vibrating hull. We stepped back inside and Evans switched on the Anglepoise again. He tapped the pencil thoughtfully against his teeth as I reached up and brought two cigarettes out of the old tar's tin.

The smoke tasted good on my palate as Evans looked at me strangely and snapped the match in two. 'Has it ever occurred to you, John, that there seems to be some kind of pattern to what's happened recently?'

I frowned, 'Pattern?'

'Some form of intent, of deliberate provocation, to drive us farther and farther west. Away from the coast.'

It didn't make any sense. 'Why?' I said, inhaling nervously. 'What possible reason could anyone—the Germans, presumably—have for doing that? I mean, even if they can anticipate our movements, which that would presuppose, then surely it would be as easy for them to sink us here and now.'

I couldn't see it but, at the same time, something Larabee had said in another context back in the radio room
after old Foley had died, jumped into my mind. I looked at
the curving, erratic line on the chart again. Larabee had
used the word 'Sheepdog' and, from the way the lines had
almost continuously veered westwards, they could be construed as the tracks of an animal being driven deliberately
along some pre-determined track. We were the sheep, and
the assorted U-boat scares, the *Kent Star* message and the
mysterious displays of distant lights the collie dogs.

'No, Sir,' I said again, shaking my head with a certainty
I didn't feel, 'it looks more like coincidence to me. I can't
see it as being anything deliberate, I can't even begin to
imagine any reason behind it, for a start.'

'Neither can I, John. Not one that stands up, anyway.
But, in that event, surely it's equally likely that there
could be ships farther to the south-east as well? It indi-
cates to my mind, that all we're doing is chasing round
in circles putting off what will eventually be inevitable—
the need for a breakthrough to the Cape.'

I didn't like it but I couldn't disagree. The suggestion
of deliberate intent was obviously too far-fetched to be
considered seriously. He seemed to come to a decision
and reached for a message pad. I watched silently as he
furrowed his brow then, suddenly, slid open a drawer
under the table and brought out a tattered, thick old book.
My eyebrows shot up in involuntary surprise as I recog-
nised it. It was the Holy Bible.

He must have seen the look on my face because he
grinned, and the big red face crinkled up into little white
lines round the corners of his eyes. 'Our friends in the
Royal Navy don't have the monopoly on funny signals,
Mister Kent,' he murmured.

I watched him as he leafed through the pages with a
deft hand. 'I thought you said you weren't a religious
man, Captain.'

He smiled again, softly. 'I'm not . . . But the Bible
makes a bloody good story-book anyway, you know.
There's a lot of sense to it, even for an agnostic.'

He found what he wanted and, with a satisfied grunt,
picked up the pencil and started to write MASTER CYCLOPS

TO . . .

Then he hummed a bit and, crossing out the line, started again. I smiled this time despite myself. The message read COMCONVOY TO COMESCORT: SUGGEST YOU CONSULT PROVERBS 28: 1 AND ACT ACCORDINGLY WITH COURSE ALTERATION EAST SIGNED EVANS END.

I picked up the heavy book and looked at it curiously. The small print jumped into sharp focus. '. . . the wicked flee when no man pursueth; but the righteous are bold as a lion.'

When a curious Charlie Shell handed the reply in it was with an alacrity which indicated that Evans wasn't the only skipper in the group who knew his way through the Good Book. The Old Man read it, frowning, then handed it to me and I frowned too. This ecclesiastical repartee was a bit above my head. COMESCORT TO COMCONVOY . . . The heavy irony of the first part didn't escape my notice . . . WHILE ACTING ON YOUR SUGGESTION ALSO CAME UPON PROVERBS 16: 28 PROPOSE MAINTAIN PRESENT ZIG-ZAG AND SPEED UNTIL DAYLIGHT SIGNED BRAID END.

The Old Man was thumbing back through the bible with a comical mixture of impatience and frustration on his face. 'Jesus Christ!' He gritted eventually, with a brutal irreverence that confirmed he was purely a reader and not a believer.

I watched with furtive interest, 'Sir?'

He glowered for a few moments, then started to grin at me. 'Cheeky bugger! It says—"A violent man enticeth his neighbour, and leadeth him into the way that is not good".'

CHAPTER THREE

At two bells in my watch I was on the bridge, talking in a low monotone to Brannigan as we watched the first streaks of reddish-coloured daylight exploring over the distant horizon. Aboard *Cyclops* it was still blackness broken only by the green glow in the wheelhouse and the occasional spark wafting back from the great funnel above and abaft the bridge deck. I hadn't bothered to use up the rest of my watch below trying to sleep, instead I'd just slipped down to my cabin to change my rather ill-used pyjama bottoms to a clean set of whites. When I came up again I hadn't forgotten to bring my lifejacket with me either.

Young Conway moved at my elbow and I jumped nervously. All through the past hour I'd been seeing U-boats move surreptitiously through the shadowy sea around us, only to find almost immediately that the threatening shadows were caused by sullenly rising waves. I noticed the wind had veered three points until it was blowing almost directly from aft and I groaned, now we weren't even going to have the consolation of a cool breeze fanning over us from the dodgers. Glancing at the cadet I could see, even in the darkness, that I wasn't the only one under strain, and I should have been better equipped to cope than a little boy who ought still to have been going walks with his Mum and Dad instead of scuttling about the Atlantic like a frightened mouse.

'Yes, Conway?' I asked softly.

'Coming up to zig-zag time, Sir,' he answered smartly.

I nodded to Brannigan and he moved off into the wheelhouse as I looked back to the lad. 'Thank you. Er, have you had a smoke yet, son?'

He shook his head, 'Not due 'til four bells, Sir.'

I jerked my chin aft, 'Nip off down to the half-deck for a few minutes. Put your feet up and relax.'

He stared at me for a moment as if I were some kind of reformed monster, then mumbled thank you and scuttled off down the ladder, no doubt to spend the next ten minutes trying to convince himself that I'd only slipped temporarily and was still the steel-hard bucko Mate of his story-books at home.

Brannigan's teeth flashed in the darkness as he came back out on to the wing. 'Wish I'd had a big softie like you for a boss when I was a cadet, Sir.'

I hitched my shorts up and glared at him severely. 'That would only have been about six months ago at that, wouldn't it, Mister Brannigan?'

The teeth sparkled again. 'Yeah. But us boys were men in those days.'

Leaving the irrepressible Fourth grinning after me, I

wandered into the wheelhouse and glanced into the binnacle. The floating card swung slightly with the slow
roll of the ship. 'Watch your head!' I said unnecessarily
to McRae, standing stolidly behind the wheel in a bright
check shirt and tight jeans—almost the universal dress of
British seamen on board—plus, of course, in inevitable
heavy leather belt with the traditional double sheath for
marline spike and knife.

'Aye, aye, Sir,' he muttered, resigned to the fact that
the only justification for having officers of the watch at all
was their capacity to issue non-essential cautions to a
craftsman like himself.

I turned away and leant on the mahogany window-
ledge, staring at the brightening line of the horizon through
the circular Kent clearview screen. McCrae shuffled a bit
behind me. 'I see we're still headin' south by east, Sir?'

'I hope so, McRae. I hope so,' I answered absently without turning.

There was a few seconds' silence, then he spoke again.
'The crowd was thinkin' we should have been alterin'
towards the coast by now, Mister Kent.'

I pushed myself upright and swivelled round, trying to
look casual. So the sailors had it figured too? They were
beginning to wonder why we were churning on into
nowhere instead of running for the Cape. A few months
ago I would have brought him up with a sharp round turn
for inferring that the Captain needed assistance from the
seamen, but now, with the war beginning to hot up and
most of us living on our nerves, ships did a hell of a lot of
odd things that required explanations. The trouble here
was that I, myself, couldn't really explain this headlong
dash right past our destination. Even if I could explain it—
could I justify it?

Doing the next best thing, I shrugged and tried to make
my voice sound bored. 'Admiralty instructions. Ours not
to reason why, McRae.'

'You what, Sir?' he asked vaguely and I knew he
wasn't convinced, then to my relief Brannigan stuck his
head in through the door and said, 'Zig-zag leg again,
Sir.'

'Carry on, Mister Brannigan,' I muttered, and left him
to it. As I stepped aft over the low coaming of the chart-

room I heard him issue the new course alteration to McRae
and the ship lay over fractionally as we adjusted.

In the discreet privacy of the chartroom the bearded
old sailor frowned down at me from wise brown eyes. I
accepted the invitation and lit up, thinking he'd seen a
lot of nervous anticipation and a lot of action too—him
and the dignified ironclad moored in the bay behind him.
I wondered who he had been, and whether he had ever
tried to run away instead of facing the enemy, and how
many hoary old bluejackets like him there were aboard
Mallard. The blue smoke from my cigarette hung suspended in the glare of the overhead light as I grinned
tightly up at the tin. Not many. Not many hard old shell-
backs like my friend up there. The only ones I'd seen
from the lofty *Cyclops's* bridge had been young, pink-faced
kids who didn't seem to fit in with the efficient image of
what was still the greatest navy in the world. Still, we'd
heard rumours about a great naval engagement taking place
off Cape Matapan a few weeks before and, if it were
true, there must have been a lot of young boys getting
suddenly older in that—or *never* getting any older!

I realise, now, that I should never have had that bloody
sandwich.

Every time I picked up a sandwich it seemed to activate
an explosion—like when the *Commandant Joffre* was hit.
But I never thought about it as I picked distastefully
through the box on the tray beside the chart table. Cheese
this time and, as usual, dry as a piece of cardboard between
two slices of melba toast. My teeth meeting for the first
bite was the signal for the detonation.

In actual fact there were two explosions, almost simulta-
neously. The first, a whiplash-like crack, seemed to come
from directly aft somewhere, followed only micro-seconds
later, by a deeper, reverberating boom rolling across the
sea from over on our starboard beam. Oh, dear God! Bill
Henderson's *Athenian* was out there! My nerves, this time,
were so tensed I didn't even have consciously to drop the
fatal sandwich—it was already on its way to the deck as
my shoes scraped over the coaming and I hurled myself
out on to the starboard wing.

I had to steel myself to peer through the darkness that

hit me. Even the bright edge of dawn was lost as my eyes fought for mastery over their previous immersion in the chartroom glare. I knew it was *Athenian* in trouble long before my blindness finally faded and I could see properly again. It had to be her, over on that side of us. I felt the sick surge of acid in my throat as I gazed fearfully out over the black water, expecting to see the great shape lurching out of control, maybe even now swinging suicidally across our bows to bring us both to a rending, screeching halt.

But no; there she was, still racing stolidly alongside our protective flank and showing no apparent signs of damage.

Then slowly, but with relentless persistence, a little flickering light appeared on the after end of her boat deck. Gradually it seemed to expand like some enormous, swelling glow-worm, until the dazed Brannigan and I could see it was composed of individual licks of flame. The fire grew in intensity until the whole after end of *Athenian*'s centrecastle jetted long tongues of white-hot fire, fanning back over her after-well deck while leaping, crackling sparks flew erratically upwards to be lost in the darkness of her wake.

I swung round on the Fourth Mate, my voice high-pitched and vicious in its anxiety, 'Torpedo? . . . For Christ's sake, man, was it a torpedo?'

He shook his head, still not taking his eyes off the burning *Athenian*. All the bounce had gone from his shoulders and he seemed to droop. I suddenly realised he was as scared as me. 'My dear God! Oh, my dear God!' he kept saying, almost to himself, over and over again.

Then the Old Man arrived on the run, took one look across the water and *he* said, 'My God!' which seemed to indicate that He was much in demand by all of us that morning!

I took a grip of myself and, trying to forget Chief Officer Henderson five cables away, grabbed Brannigan's arm tightly. 'I asked you what happened, Mister Brannigan.'

He swallowed and took a deep breath. He must have got a whiff of new courage with it because the young face cleared and I got a frown instead of the wild stare he'd afforded *Athenian*. When he spoke I found out why he'd been so shocked in the first place.

'We fired at her, Sir,' he said simply.

It was my turn, and the Captain's, to stare in shattered disbelief. Evans found his voice just before me. 'What did you say, Brannigan? *Who* did you say had . . . fired?'

The Fourth Mate shrugged helplessly. 'We did, Sir. It . . . The shot must've come from our poop gun. I heard the bang and even saw the flash from aft.' He hesitated as though we'd caught him out telling a lie, then ploughed on determinedly, 'I'd swear it came from us. It wasn't a bloody torpedo, I'm positive of that.'

Evans swung round on me. The red face was working savagely as he realised the implications of what Brannigan was saying. 'Did you see anything, Mister Kent? Did you?'

I felt the crimson flush rising above my collar, 'Er . . . No, Sir. I was in the chartroom when I heard the explosion.'

I hoped he wasn't going to ask me exactly what I was doing sitting around in the chartroom but, on reflection, realised that he didn't have any reason to. Chief Officers aren't exactly unfamiliar with that little retreat, especially during the early hours of the morning watch, otherwise why have a cadet and a fourth mate up there too? It was a bit like having a dog and barking yourself.

Evans turned and faced *Athenian* again. Even in the few minutes we'd been out there the early dawn light had blossomed into a canopy of pale yellow and red tinted sky and every detail could be seen of the frenzied activity aboard our sister ship. We were so close we felt we could almost jump aboard and lend a hand. The feeling became so overpowering that I had to grip the smooth teak rail tightly to fight it off.

The searching eyes of daylight seemed to some extent to reduce the apparent damage. Clouds of thick, oily smoke now replaced what had originally looked like a solid mass of flame from well deck to boat deck, and we could see that the main outbreak was concentrated in the area of the wireless cabin and officers' smoke-room situated on the after end of the boat deck. They must have had nearly every member of the deck crowd fighting the outbreak and, already, the white threadlines of hoses webbed the deck from all available hydrants. If Bill was still alive—and assuming he'd been on the bridge as I was when the shell hit, he should be—then he'd done a pretty

smart job of organising his damage control parties. I resolved to have a word with the Bosun about our own drill
as soon as possible.

The Old Man was still simmering with barely sup-
pressed raged. By the grace of God, Athenian hadn't suffered
much hull damage but, judging by the twisted steel and
smoking wreckage they were jettisoning from the boat
deck, anyone in the region of the radio room or after-
accommodation must have suffered severely. I knew one
Sparks must have had the watch, while the other one
would have been turned in in the same cabin.

Evans pivoted to face me and his eyes were very hard.
'Get aft to the poop, Mister Kent. I want the man
responsible for this, and by God I want him badly!'

'Aye, aye, Sir,' I answered, feeling bloody glad it wasn't
anything to do with me.

He stopped me again at the top of the ladder. 'It must
have been one of those D.E.M.S. buggers. If it was, I want
them too . . . Especially them.'

The army gun crew we carried aboard to serve the
venerable 4.7 mounted on our specially strengthened poop
had somehow managed to develop into one of the Old
Man's pet hates. There were only three of them altogether
—two gunners and a Bombardier Allen of the newly
formed Maritime Artillery. This was their first trip with
us and they superseded the elderly naval reservist who
had been previously posted to us as a D.E.M.S. rating.
He had come from what was laughingly known as the
Defensively Equipped Merchant Ship organisation and had
actually fulfilled the duties of an instructor to the gun's
crew itself, made up from the *Cyclops*'s normal complement and headed by Mister Shell, our Second Mate.

The Old Man had been very proud indeed of His Fighting Lads as he liked to think of them. It was commonly
agreed that a place on the gun, which was never seriously
expected to have to fire a real shell, was a dead cushy
number and the current 'price' charged by the ship's fixers
—at least before the arrival of the disgruntled soldiery—
was reckoned to be in the region of fifty bob for a place
on the outward leg, plus another fifty bob when homeward
bound. Evans used to take great delight in gun drill and
would call them away from the most unpleasant jobs

regularly, just for the pleasure of watching the, on the surface, practised ease with which they traversed and loaded and almost pulled the firing lever. Personally I had grave misgivings about whether the bloody thing would actually fire or just blow up there and then and save the Germans a job.

At the beginning of this month, just before the ship sailed, the three pongoes had marched disconsolately aboard with orders stating that they were members of the Royal Artillery's newest off-shoot, the Maritime A.A., and, as such, were to replace the ship's own gallant Fighting Lads —the latter to be relegated to the status of common ammunition carriers and oddsbodies. Our frustrated potential Nelson of a master immediately blamed the poor bloody gunners personally for what he considered a slight on his ship and had refused to have anything further to do with what had suddenly become 'the blasted spit tube,' other than broadcasting gloomy prophecies of disaster to all and sundry.

And now it looked as though he was right.

I gathered a nervously returning Conway in my wake as I hurried aft along the boat deck. *Mallard* was now running close alongside *Athenian* and I could see the flat white caps on her bridge tilted back as her officers stared anxiously up at the looming cargo ship's upperworks. I couldn't remember having heard it, but someone must have pressed the tit on her attack alarm bell because her crew were all stood to at Action Stations. A steel-helmeted figure was moving among the depth-charge racks again, occasionally bending down to make adjustments, and I hoped like hell he knew what he was doing. Braid must have been fit to be tied right then and it was going to be an interesting and colourful conversation between him, Bert Samson, *Athenian*'s Master, and our Old Man when they got round to discussing whose fault it had been.

Larabee was hanging over the rail outside the radio room when I arrived at the after end of the boat deck. He looked red-eyed and tired and I noticed his whites were badly in need of a dhobey. As we approached he turned, and the thin face looked inquisitively over at *Athenian*. 'What happened, Mate?' he said.

I looked closely at him. It was gratifying to note that

even he seemed to be feeling the strain by now. A nervous flicker jumped in the wasted muscles of his cheek as he stared defiantly back. Had it been anyone else I'd have felt pretty concerned for them, but the sardonic Sparks was different. He'd asked for a load of extra tension anyway, after the way he'd flown off the handle about my offer of a replacement for old Foley. I glanced briefly over at our sister and was greatly relieved to see that the smoke had almost died away, though they were still playing the hoses on to the blackened shell of the W.T. cabin and smoke-room. A very appropriate description—smoke-room.

'I dunno, Larabee,' I said, trying to be as unhelpful as possible. 'Someone put a shell into her, looks like.'

I didn't stop but I could feel his eyes on the back of my head as I swung down the well deck ladder. He would never forgive, nor forget, what I'd done to him in the radio room the previous night. Larabee wasn't the forgiving type. I shrugged inwardly—I should worry. Second wireless operators didn't bat in the same league as chief officers, and Larabee wasn't even a regular Company man, he'd only come aboard as a temporary replacement himself because our original Second had been seriously injured by a Corporation tramcar, of all things, while crossing the road from one pub to another back in Liverpool. The chances were I'd never have to see the skinny little cynic again after this trip.

I met the Third Mate at the bottom of the after centre-castle ladder. He glanced almost guiltily at me as I frowned queryingly. He wasn't due to relieve me from the bridge until 0800 and Curtis normally clung to his bunk right up to the last minute.

'Couldn't sleep,' he mumbled, and judging by the white creases of strain flecking the sunburn round his mouth, I half guessed the reason why—his nerves were taking a beating. That made him a candidate to join the John Kent Coward's Club too. He said he'd just come aft when he heard the bang so I pushed past him and didn't think any more of it at the time.

It *was* a bit odd, though.

The long barrel of the 4.7 was still pointing forlornly to starboard as I reached the poop, with the three D.E.M.S. blokes gathered in a huddle behind the oildrum-shaped breech. The bombardier, Allen, came nervously to attention as I approached, and the two other soldiers shuffled uncomfortably. They looked an odd crowd as they stood there watching me with resigned anticipation, what with the two gunners being big and tall while the gun commander was a little, fat, dumpy character. They looked a lot stranger by virtue of the fact that they were all standing in their issue underwear. This made me even more bloody angry because, as I've already said, we were pretty careful about how we looked aboard *Cyclops* and I wasn't prepared to allow any goddamn' pongoes to come on board and act like a lot of casual layabouts.

I ground to a halt in front of the fat little bombardier. 'Right, Soldier! Who did it? . . . Who bloody did it?'

His round, chubby face screwed up and I could see he was nearly in tears. I didn't give a damn for their feelings, though. It only needed a glance at *Athenian* to know that men had died violently over there, and the tell-tale traverse of the gun confirmed what Brannigan had already said —that this was the weapon responsible. The bombardier started to shake and the identity discs round his neck clinked together over the khaki vest. He didn't seem able to speak with the fear of retribution inside him, but I was in no mood to be sympathetic with a man whose mistake must have cost irreplaceable lives.

I smashed the flat of my hand down on the barrel of the gun and gritted, 'Which one of you bastards is responsible for firing this?'

When the bombardier's voice came it was only a cracked, almost indistinguishable, whisper. 'None of us, Sir. There weren't none of us up here when she fired.'

It was a day for surprises. I stared at him disbelievingly. 'It must have been one of you . . . Allen, is it? Or are you trying to say the bloody gun just fired itself, with no one up here?'

He shook his head numbly. 'No, Sir. No, it couldn't fire off its own bat. Not without someone to load it for a start.'

His two mates just stared stolidly ahead with regimented, unseeing eyes, offering no help to the floundering bombardier. I glanced at Conway, but he was staring across at the other ships, watching as *Mallard* sheared away from

C

Athenian and, with a sudden splurge of white water under her stern, pulled rapidly ahead of the formation. The ratings on her foredeck were trooping back aft and I supposed Braid had called them from Action Stations on the assumption that we had finished shooting at our opposite number for the time being.

I turned back to Allen in frustration. 'Now, listen to me, Corporal . . .'

'Bombardier, Sir,' he muttered, sniffing.

I felt my jaw tightening. '*Bombardier* . . . I want to know who fired this gun a few minutes ago, and I want to know *now*! I want the man whose bloody criminal stupidity caused that . . .' I waved my hand, 'to happen aboard *Athenian*.'

The rounded cheeks quivered. 'I dunno, Sir. We was all in our kips downstairs when it happened.'

I blinked. 'You mean you were all below? None of you were up here on the poop?'

He shook his head positively. 'None of us, Sir. Like I said, we was all sleeping when we heard the shot over our 'eads. We tumbled out pretty sharpish but, when we got up 'ere, Phyllis was pokin' her nose at that ship there and there wasn't a soul near her. Mind, it was pretty dark at that time, an' all.'

'Phyllis?' I queried, trying desperately to think.

'The gun, Sir. We call it Phyllis . . . after my old woman.'

I tilted my cap back, feeling the sun's rays starting to beat down on my shoulder blades. One or two of the sailors were clustered inquisitively round the top of the ladder but, when they saw me glancing towards them, they quickly disappeared in case I remembered day-work men turned to at four bells and it was now well past that. I didn't bother right then, though—I had another problem to solve before I concentrated on the domestic running of the ship.

I looked suspiciously at the little bombardier. It didn't make sense . . . No one else aboard would want to play around with the gun on their own, and certainly not in what was damned near the middle of the night, and in the pitch dark . . .

Allen went over to the after end of the 4.7 and pulled a lever. The shining brass cartridge case slid out through a puff curl of spent smoke and fell with a clang on to the freshly caulked wooden deck sheathing. An acrid whiff of burnt powder caught my throat as we bent forward to inspect the softly gleaming shell case.

'Check the ready-use locker, Ewing,' said the bombardier, with surprising authority in his voice. He nodded at the spent case and looked up at me. 'Fixed H.E., Sir. Looks like our usual ammo.'

One of the big gunners turned round from the locker where the immediate supply of ammunition for the gun was kept. 'One round missing, Bomb.'

Allen seemed to have regained his confidence now, and shrugged as he caught my eye. 'That's it then, Sir. Some bastard's been interferin' with Phyllis, and it weren't none of my blokes. I'd swear to it.'

The way he said it gave me the impression that he wouldn't have been half so upset if the Phyllis in question had been the real one and not the mechanical monster sitting so oddly out of place on our stern. I started to get a tight feeling in my belly as I got up and walked slowly aft to the taffrail, stopping under the big Red Ensign that whipped and cracked above me. Leaning on the rail, I stared moodily into the boiling tumult of white foam under our counter, trying desperately to figure out who could possibly have wanted to do such a bloody stupid act in the first place. If it wasn't the army crew—then it must have been one of the ship's complement.

A tinny, rattling sound made me look down and I realised that the metal band of my watch strap was vibrating against the metal of the rail. I became aware of the tremendous shudder caused by the threshing of the twin screws underneath me as they twisted against the water pressure at what was, for us, excessively high revolutions. We were still on emergency speed and running away . . . from what? The whole voyage was turning out to be a succession of nightmare mysteries, of effects without apparent causes, of ships sinking so quickly that they didn't have time to get off more than an indication of their positions, and of Brock's benefit displays in the middle of the night in an area where even a cigarette glowing in the dark could invite, a sudden, choking death. And now . . . the gun.

A bloody silly gun called Phyllis.

I swung round and found the little bombardier's eyes fixed firmly on me as the other two soldiers hovered almost protectively behind him, and I knew Allen was telling the truth. Whoever had fired that gun hadn't been among the D.E.M.S. crowd. The Old Man wasn't even going to have that slender crumb of comfort to sustain him.

'It wasn't us,' the bombardier repeated earnestly.

I nodded and saw the look of relief in his eyes. 'I know, Bombardier. But I'm damned if I know who else would want to play silly buggers up here in the middle of the night.'

He glanced at me strangely. 'How d'you know they was . . . well . . . *playin'*, Sir?'

I stared back, feeling the knot in my belly tighten even more. 'What do you mean?' I asked hollowly.

He shrugged again and the I.D. discs clinked faintly. 'I dunno that I mean anything, Sir. But these guns ain't easy to fire by accident. The drill's pretty complicated, if you see what I'm gettin' at.'

'You're suggesting that the gun was fired deliberately?'

He swallowed nervously. 'I think so, Sir. But I can't see no reason for anyone to do it, mind.'

Neither could I. But if . . . *if* . . . the shot had been fired deliberately, then the second question was obvious—had it been fired *at Athenian*, or . . . ?

I jerked my chin at the long barrel. 'How accurate is it, Bombardier?'

'Theoretical range, 'bout ten thousand yards, Sir. But I wouldn't like to bet on hittin' anythin' at much over half that.'

I glanced over at *Athenian*, noting at the same time that the smoke had almost completely ceased to issue from her wounds. The hoses still snaked over her decks like long white tapeworms, but her crowd were now busy rolling them up and stowing them away. Several figures seemed to be moving into the burnt-out wireless room. I was damned glad I wasn't one of them. Mentally I estimated the distance between us—still about five cables, roughly one thousand yards. She was so close we could have damaged her with spit.

I pointed. 'How close could you place a shell on *Athenian*, Bombardier? Could you be fairly sure of hitting, say, an area the size of her wheelhouse with reasonable accuracy?'

He spat contemptuously to windward, then brushed the khaki vest vigorously as he found there was more to seamanship than a vague knowledge of how to tie knots. 'At this range, Sir? An' without the boat goin' up an' down? . . . I could put a shot through one of them little round windows on one side, then out the other without scratchin' the paint.'

I nodded. It was a reassuring thought, if it were true, for when we ever met a U-boat but, at the same time, it told me something else. Hitting the *Athenian*'s radio room hadn't been a pure mischance. I thought back to the big, black silhouette riding alongside us during the night, every detail picked out against the stars behind. The acute angle of the after end of her centrecastle standing out as stark and clear cut as any naval gunnery target, and less than one-fifth of the distance away. Always assuming the unknown marksman knew how to fire the gun, of course.

The docking telephone secured to the rail behind me buzzed angrily like a captive wasp. Conway quickly opened the door of its protective cabinet and answered. I could hear the Donald Duck voice even from where I stood. The cadet went a bit whiter and, standing back, pushed the receiver anxiously at me.

'The Captain, Sir,' he said, unnecessarily.

I lifted the phone gingerly. 'Chief Officer, Sir.'

The chipped metal receiver spat back at me immediately. 'Have you got the bloody madman that did it yet, Mister? I've just had a signal from *Mallard* and another one from Bert Samson over there. Now you just bring the murderin' bugger up to the bridge this minute do you hear- Right away, Mister Kent!'

I winced. 'I'll come right up, Sir.'

As I hung the phone back inside its box I caught a glimpse of young Conway watching me with a strange, almost understanding expression on his face. Maybe, now, he was beginning to find that bucko mates weren't the only anti-social bullies aboard ship.

It took quite a time to convince Evans that the R.A. gunners weren't the people responsible for what had happened.

Finally, he quietened down enough to listen to me and
looked pretty disappointed and shaken about it too. I read
the signals he handed me with an even sicker knot expand-
ing in my belly. The first was from *Athenian* . . . BOTH
RADIO OFFICERS ALSO CADET SIMPSON D KILLED TWO RATINGS
SERIOUSLY WOUNDED ALL WT EQUIP DESTROYED WHAT
HAPPENED QUERY SIGNED SAMSON END.

The second message was from Braid. COMESCORT TO
MASTER CYCLOPS: . . . No fancy titles this time! . . .
PLEASE INVESTIGATE CAUSE OF MISFIRE YOUR VESSEL SUG-
GEST YOU USE APPROPRIATE PRACTICE BLANK SHOT FOR
FURTHER DRILLS SIGNED BRAID END.

I bit my lip and looked up at the Captain. He'd got
over his blood lust it seemed, or maybe he wasn't so keen
on finding the anonymous culprit now that he knew it
wasn't the army personnel? But no—I was being unfair
to Evans. I realised his problem, but I didn't know what
advice to proffer either. If the guilty party was one of the
crew then how did we even start to find out who? Did we
hold a full-scale investigation into the movements of every
man on board and break out a list of those without an
alibi? If that was the way to go about it then we could
start with the Old Man himself because he fitted into that
category—and so did at least another thirty men. So
what did we do?

'We could ask every member of the crew if they saw
anyone about on the poop at the time the gun was fired,
Sir?' I suggested, searching desperately for inspiration.

He looked at me and I could see the tiredness and strain
in his eyes. 'Do you really think it's likely that someone
saw something yet hasn't reported it, John?'

I shook my head. He was dead right and, apart from
that, the shot had been fired while it was still pitch dark.
The crew's quarters were aft, apart from the officers', and
anyone wanting to make himself scarce quickly just needed
to slide down the ladder and back into the poop housing.
He could have been back in his cabin before the boom of
the shot had died away and, with most of the sailors
bunked only two to a cabin in a modern ship like *Cyclops*,
the chances were he would have planned it for when his
oppo was on watch anyway.

I hesitated before asking myself the next obvious question. What if it had been one of the officers? But, even then, all they had to do was nip forward along the well deck and lose themselves in the shadowy anonymity of the centrecastle accommodation. Again no one would have been likely to have seen them in the darkness.

Oh, Hell! Supposing an officer *had* been seen then—what's so suspicious about a ship's officer being seen aboard a ship? I'd even seen one myself—Larabee, outside his W.T. Room. Wait! . . . I'd forgotten the Third Mate, Curtis. He was even farther aft, even closer to the gun platform *and* he looked like a man with a problem on his mind. Could it have been how to forget the deaths of three men by remote control . . . ? I struggled to get a grip on my imagination and looked at Evans helplessly.

Why? That was the question that was haunting both of us.

Why in God's name should any man aboard want to fire at our sister ship . . . ?

CHAPTER FOUR

Cadet Breedie bumped into me as I was leaving the saloon after another coffee-and-nothing-else breakfast. He skidded to a halt and waved an apologetic hand. 'Sorry, Sir! The Old . . . er . . . the Captain would like to see you in the radio room as soon as you can manage, Sir.'

I hauled my cap down over my eyes and nodded savagely. Everything seemed to be revolving round the radio officers right then, what with Foley's disappearance and now the recent—I shrank from the word 'Murder'—the recent deaths of *Athenian*'s Chief and Second Sparks. What else could have happened since then? The only slim consolation I had was in the thought that, if anything *had* gone wrong, then it had gone wrong with Larabee.

When I arrived at the after end of the boat deck the Second Operator looked pretty well as per normal, which meant still moody and sardonic. The Old Man was engaged in deep conversation with him and I noticed with a feeling of shock the tired creases seaming the normally smooth, ruddy face. He'd had a bad time of it in the past few months, like all of us, but on top of that was the fact that ship's masters carried a deeper responsibility which, with most of them anyway, seemed to erode their physical health even while they were snatching a few hours of precious sleep below. This current voyage wasn't being made any easier by the added burden of knowing what would happen should the three critical, secret bags fall into the wrong hands.

The door to the radio room was open behind them and the air was full of the hiss of static with the occasional twitter of rapid morse from some distant transmitter. Almost subconsciously, my ears tuned to the signals and I felt an inordinate sense of pride when I found I could distinguish the major part of the traffic, even from the nimble fingers of the professionals. I wondered how Larabee could possibly sleep through the jumble of noise yet remain alert to the slightest rattle of our own ship's call sign; but then, I could be fast asleep below yet be instantly wide awake and listening at any unexpected alteration of course. Our oil-hungry Chief Engineer was the same—any variation in the even throb of his giant diesels and he was out of his bunk and down below before the watch keeper himself realised it. We were, all of us, in some strange inexplicable way, tuned to the heartbeats and pulse of the ship. All of us like specialists round the bedside of a patient, each one alive to the faintest irregularity in his own field of responsibility. This facility could at times even be anticipatory. I remember once, several years ago aboard one of our old coal burners, the venerable 'Lamps', a hoary old seadog of a lamptrimmer, had actually appeared on deck during the middle watch and climbed the foremast just in time to replace the masthead light bulb as it went out.

Evans looked up as I approached. 'Mister Larabee seems to feel there may be some danger to him in his capacity as wireless operator, Mister Kent.'

I looked inquiringly at Larabee, who nodded, almost apologetically. 'Yes, Mate,' he muttered. 'I reckon there's something going on aboard this ship that we don't understand, and I'm not happy with it. Not now the Sparks over on *Athenian* have parted their cables.'

'That could have been an accident, Larabee,' I said, not very convincingly.

He shook his head for a change. 'And Alf Foley going over the wall? Was that an accident? In my book, Mate, two accidents make a conclusion . . . and my conclusion is that some bastard's out to clobber all the wireless ops for some reason.'

'What reason, Mister Larabee?' Evans asked sharply.

Larabee shrugged. 'I dunno, Sir. But I don't plan on finding out the hard way, if you see what I'm getting at?'

I lifted my chin at him. 'What exactly do you expect us to do, Larabee? You've already turned down the offer of a replacement for Alf. What else can we do—even admitting you may be right, that is?'

The Second Sparks touched the door behind him. 'I want a man outside this door twenty-four hours a day, Mister Mate. And armed, if possible. Like I said before, I don't need no one to help me do my job, but I'm bloody sure I'm not goin' to sit around waitin' for some crazy bastard to shove me over the side in the middle of the night. No thanks.'

'I'm not arming any seaman aboard this vessel, Mister,' Evans grunted. 'If Mister Kent feels it advisable, then we shall post a man up here, but he won't be carrying any weapons except his marline spike and his own two fists!'

He looked over at me and I nodded in agreement. It was going to look bad enough to the crew anyway, but start issuing them with weapons and they'd think there were Nazi spies round every corner. The ship's morale would plummet like an anchor on the run.

'O.K., Sparks,' I said. 'You'll get your bodyguard. But I don't want any scaremongering, understand. If I put a seaman on the door we'll say he's there as a messenger—not as a strong arm. I don't want you saying anything about our real reasons, imagined or otherwise.'

I glanced at Evans and saw that he concurred. Larabee nodded doubtfully but I wasn't prepared to make any further concessions to his rather out-of-character hysteria. In fact, as we walked away, I couldn't resist the childish impulse to turn back. 'Just hope, Larabee, that the man outside your door isn't the same bloke who put old Alf over the wall in the first place . . . or didn't you think about that?'

To my dissatisfaction he grinned. 'Strictly between you an' me, Kent . . . Maybe it's not the Jerries I'm wantin' protection from so much as a certain bucko Mate that's too bloody quick with his hands!'

I glared hard at him. There wasn't any humour in the smile, just a promise of something indefinable. It gave me an uncomfortable feeling, but I couldn't take it up with him right then, not with the Old Man waiting, and anyway, I'd asked for it with my snide remark. I hesitated another moment, trying to think of some cutting repartee, but nothing came.

Swinging round abruptly, I followed the Captain along the boat deck.

Twenty minutes later I was nearly running out of words again.

'Five million quid?' I exploded.

The Old Man nodded slowly. 'Five million pounds *Australian*, John . . . That's not as much as its equivalent in Sterling at the current rate of exchange, of course.'

'Five million quid Australian, then,' I said again. 'That, Sir, is big money in *any* national currency.'

Evans leaned forward and poured himself another cup from the big silver coffee pot on his dayroom table. The engraved Company crest flashed briefly as he replaced it on the tray and added milk. We had repaired to his cabin for a long overdue discussion on the normal work of the ship, a problem which was proving only too easy to ignore under the current conditions. Somehow I had this bad feeling about what was going to happen and that, in itself, made me want to postpone making decisions about mundane jobs like replacing wire ropes, paintwork and the thousand and one duties and responsibilities of a chief officer. It's funny how you can get an idea into your head and, subconsciously, it affects your whole attitude, although, at the time, you may not even be aware of it yourself. All I knew was that I felt a deep weariness, a sort of apathy which was slowly undermining my ability to plan ahead.

And now, the Old Man's bombshell about the value of

the currency we carried in the forward strong-room. I had guessed there was a lot of money from the capacity of those leather and steel-bound boxes that had come aboard, but five million . . . ! Evans looked at me over his cup. 'It's still not as important as the mail bags, John. Bank notes can be reprinted, given time—sunken wrecks can't be refloated from the bottom of the sea.'

I sucked a hollow tooth that had been nagging me for months but which I was too scared to admit to a dentist. 'Maybe, but that much money makes us a security risk in itself, Sir. It makes this ship a very desirable property to anyone who's interested.'

'Like who, for instance? The Germans?'

I shrugged. 'I don't know. Maybe they would like to get hold of five million to buy themselves another couple of U-boats. But, well . . . Oh hell! There's a lot of blokes on our own side would take a big chance for that kind of a return.'

Evans smiled. 'You think the mysterious fireworks last night were pirates then, John? That any time now we may be boarded by black-bearded sailormen with cutlasses and hooks for hands?'

While the idea was incongruous, it still didn't appeal to my rather depleted sense of humour. 'More like bristle-headed Huns with Schmeisser machine-guns and whips!' I muttered sourly.

'That,' said the Captain, 'could be rather more of a possibility. But not for a few million in banknotes which would only be of use to any agents they may have in Aussie. Even then, the notes will be serialised. It might be a worthwhile risk for a common criminal, but I can't imagine any spy worth his salt leaving a trail of banknotes known to be stolen from *Cyclops*, can you?'

I shook my head. Of course he was right.

'Well, it beats me,' I muttered, feeling one of my bloody-minded turns coming on but, even with that awareness, still wanting to pick flaws in somebody. 'Why in God's name did they send us out with only that . . . that elastic-driven bloody wood carving out there as an escort? If we're so important, then why didn't the Admiralty lay on a proper escort?'

The Old Man got to his feet and stared out of the port.

I caught a glimpse of the brass surround framing the heavy foremast of *Athenian*, swaying easily and reassuringly on our beam. He didn't turn as he spoke. 'We are important, John. Very important. You already know why. But don't let's delude ourselves into thinking we're the *only* people in this war. The Navy's got a big problem, and nowhere near enough ships to cope with it. Our speed is our greatest protection—our speed . . . and luck! Without luck I don't suppose an ocean full of escorts would be of much assistance. Just thank God for small mercies, John—at least we don't have any aircraft worries so far south.'

I sniffed. 'No, none at all . . . neither ours nor theirs. Surely they could have spared us a couple of planes for air cover? We're less than three hours' flying time away from the S.A.A.F. bases now.'

'Cover from what? Other planes? We're too far from the nearest Luftwaffe fields in North Africa. Apart from U-boats our only other danger could be from their surface raiders, and I understand this area is considered clear at present . . .' He saw the look of scepticism on my face and hurried on before I could get my protest assembled and fired. '. . . so what use is there in our having a Sunderland buzzing round and round above us, acting as a marker for every sub within thirty miles?'

'Sunderlands are *supposed* to be anti-submarine aircraft, aren't they, Sir?' I queried pointedly, still unconvinced. 'They carry depth charges or bombs, don't they?'

He swung round to face me and I could see the argument was nearly over. It would be 'Mister Kent' again this time. 'So does *Mallard*, Mister Kent—but you don't seem to go much on her as a form of protection. I have no doubt whatever that air cover could be provided if necessary, but the powers that be felt it better not to furnish us with an openly displayed invitation for the Huns to come and investigate *what* the planes were covering. They considered it more sensible for us to try and remain undetected, rather than to revenge themselves on the enemy while *we* cheer—from the lifeboats.'

His argument, based as it was on the lesser of two evils, was certainly sensible. It somewhat lost conviction regarding the 'detection' bit though as suddenly the cabin lurched hard over to starboard under the effects of an apparently massive helm alteration while, above us on the bridge, the ship's siren screamed two short warning blasts. The engraved coffee pot slid off the shiny silver tray with a crash and the Captain's best Egyptian Axminster soaked up the mess of spilt grains as we stared at each other in shocked, frozen silence.

Two blasts. The emergency signal to all other ships . . . 'I am directing my course to port!'

And whoever was at the wheel was directing us to port with an urgency which suggested we were under investigation—with or without air cover.

The third Mate was waiting for us at the top of the bridge ladder. The Captain made it one rung ahead of me, though I could have sworn I was first out of his cabin. Maybe I had a footprint on my back? Curtis waved an excited hand and his eyes were very bright in the flushed face. 'Torpedo, Sir! A bloody torpedo for Chrissake! I was jus' . . .'

Evans cut him savagely short. 'Whereaway, man?'

The ship's head was swinging really fast now. I glanced aft and saw our wake curving sharply round as the masts lay well over against the shimmering line of the horizon with the centrifugal pull of the turn. We were almost at right angles now to our original course. Curtis blinked vaguely at the Old Man for a moment, then swung round to get his bearings on the fast changing heading. 'It came from almost abeam, Sir. Port side. I swung her into it as I thought it would help kick our stern out of the way . . .'

'We must be practically heading for the sub now then, Three Oh?' I asked sharply.

His head bobbed violently. 'Yessir. More or less.'

'Good lad!' I yelled, as I ran into the wheelhouse. I'd have preferred it if we had been pulling away from the spot instead of heading right for the bastards, but a narrow bow shot was a lot more difficult for them than if we carried on swinging through a hundred and eighty-degree arc to present them with yet another five-hundred-foot-long beam target.

The helmsman's eyes were as big as saucers as he stared at me and I could see his hands white where he gripped the spokes of the big wheel. He must have been almost as scared as I was. 'Midships the wheel!' I shouted, grabbing for the engine room phone.

The spokes blurred under the release from the 'hard' position and, immediately, I felt the deck tilting back to the horizontal as the rudder pressure eased and our head steadied. 'Wheel's midships, Sir.'

'What was your zig-zag heading before the alteration?' I snapped urgently.

'168, Sir. We was on the port leg.'

'And now? What's your head now?'

He peered into the binnacle and I could see the glint of sweat on his brow as the sunlight struck through the open doorway. 'Er . . . Comin' up to 082, Sir, and still swingin' to port.'

I stabbed at the phone buzzer and tried to force my mind to think. We'd already swung through nearly a right-angle. Curtis had reckoned the torpedo had come from broad on our port beam, which meant that the sub was bearing approximately . . . 078 when it fired. Allow, say, another half point to compensate for our travelled distance from there and we should be just about right on the nose. Their nose! I heard the click as the phone came off the hook down below, but I covered the mouthpiece with my hand and jerked my chin at the helmsman. 'Steady on 073, Quartermaster . . .'

I took my hand away from the receiver. 'First Mate here.'

Someone, I don't know who, answered tinnily from the oil-gleaming depths. 'Aye, aye, Mister Kent.'

'I want maximum emergency revolutions . . . Every turn you can give me.'

The voice sounded hurt. 'Christ, Mate. We're already goin' like shit. The Chief'll have my guts with gravy if . . .'

My voice felt hoarse with savagery. 'The Chief'll have a bastard torpedo up his backside if you don't. Now you just get her opened up, Engineer. Right up!'

The pause was only fractional. 'Aye, aye, Mister Kent. She'll shake herself to bloody bits, though.'

'I don't give a monkey's ass if we bloody fly! Just do what you're told . . .' I slammed the phone back in its cradle, then started to look for *Athenian* and *Mallard* with a sudden sense of guilt. I'd clean forgotten them when I started giving the order for the Charge of the Light

Brigade to the man at the wheel. With relief I saw *Athenian* steaming half a mile ahead, over on our starboard quarter, the white water kicking high under her rounded counter as she slid away from us, going fast and still on her original course. A light was bleeping from her bridge structure and I just caught the end of her message . . . UT WE WOULD PREFER NOT TO BE SEEN WITH YOU. Hah, hah! Bloody funny to you too, Chief Officer Henderson.

The vibration under the deck crept up and up until I half expected the deckhead rivets to start popping. Whoever was below hadn't been joking about shaking ourselves to bits. We must have been working up to twenty knots now, probably the fastest she'd steamed since her speed trials when she was still in the builder's hands three years ago, in the palmy days of '38. I wondered where Henry McKenzie, the Chief, was and felt mildly surprised that he hadn't already presented himself on the bridge in irate, Celtic protest at the abuse of his beloved wee engines. Maybe, this time, Henry had just gone and had a stroke over the much abused carcase of his revered Company Fuel Log?

Or, on the other hand, maybe he'd just ignored the possibility of an agonising, oil-choked death in the velvety blackness of a torpedoed ship's bowels and had swung down the long, shiny, deathtrap handrails of the engine room ladders to be with his boys and his engines, and to do his duty?

I started to feel ridiculously melodramatic and, instead, tried to wrestle with a time and distance problem called 'Find the Submarine.' Glancing at the bulkhead clock, I guessed that we'd now been travelling down the track of the torpedo, or torpedoes for that matter, for approximately seven minutes. That meant we were roughly two and a half sea miles from where the coffee pot had spilled on to the Old Man's fancy carpet. I wished I knew how far a torpedo carried or what a U-boat's attacking range was. One mile? Two? Surely no more than two miles? That meant, then, that the bloody sub was now astern of us, that we'd already passed over the area in which she was lying. Perhaps we'd even passed over the very spot where she was submerged?

A tremendous explosion from aft shocked me into

realising I wasn't the only bloke who could do sums in his head. I threw myself out on to the starboard wing just in time to stare down our wake and see the green ocean astern erupting into mushroom after mushroom of dirty, yellow, contaminated water less than ten cables off our quarter. Then I saw the little *Mallard* screaming round with canted decks, White Ensign board taut, as she positioned herself for another depth-charge run over the spot. I was watching the spiralling shock waves of the first explosions skimming across the otherwise sullen flat calm of the sea when Evans came up behind me and raised his binoculars.

'The Grey Funnel Line signalled an Asdic contact, John,' he said with a satisfied, frighteningly pleased expression on his red face. 'I'd like fine to see one of those Nazi bastards with his guts spilling out in the bloody water, by God but I would.'

I stared at the Captain in shocked silence for a moment, still feeling *Cyclops* tremble like a fleeing animal beneath my feet. How could a professional seaman with a pretty, fair-haired daughter like he had—how could he possibly wish to see a fellow human being floating all splayed out in the silent water with his entrails waving around him, spewed from his gutted body by the terrifying force of those obscene weapons? A man who, only a few months ago, had pushed us at seventeen knots through some of the biggest seas I'd ever seen to go to the assistance of a small Arabian coaster which had screamed for help over its Heath Robinson radio through the howling frenzy of an Indian Ocean maelstrom. I hadn't been surprised then. Just scared as the great, green water smashed over our bows and leaped and roared aft to crash, with the force of an express train, against the break of our superstructure.

Then the terrible columns of atomised water hung in the air again in the wake of the racing, worrying little bulldog of an escort, and the blast from the charges beat on our eardrums, and I started to feel the same as Evans.

I felt an almost sexual blood lust with the excitement of it all. I *wanted* to see the signs of victory in the bloated, sundered corpses bobbing in the skin of oil and debris from the shattered hull of the U-boat. I wanted to see it so bad I could almost taste it. I wanted to see it because

I knew that those men—even though they were maybe fathers of little fair-haired girls themselves—were of the same kind as the animals who had sunk *Hesperia* without even giving her the chance to cry for help. These were the men who had killed big Eric Clint in the prime of his life and career . . . and had just tried to kill me, and Curtis, and the Old Man, and thin, nervous, first trip away from home Conway.

Brannigan came pounding up the ladder too, as *Mallard* skittered round in another of her sliding turns under full helm. I envied Commander Braid the exhilaration of handling a thoroughbred ship that could almost skim round in her own length like one of those funny little waterbug things you see on stagnant ponds back home. There was a brief flash of golden light from her foredeck and I realised it came from the brass shell casing held by one of her gun crew, stood to and waiting for the first signs of a break in the now subsiding water. That made me think of our own museum piece aft—I'd been forgetting a hell of a lot of things in my panic—and I dropped my eyes to our poop.

Yes! There she was, pointing hungrily over to where the U-boat lay. Phyllis! What a bloody silly name for a bloody silly gun. I noticed the glint of a white cap cover amongst the khaki-clad figures of Bombardier Allen and his comrades-in-arms and grinned to myself through the tension pulling at the corner of my mouth. Charlie Shell was still unable to keep away from his pride and joy, even though he'd had his nose pushed in by the army. He'd never fired it, not once, but to listen to him you'd have thought that he and that obsolete cannon were the only things keeping the *Bismarck* cowering in port.

And so we waited . . .

We waited with the sun beating down on our shoulders, and the sea burning almost yellow with the heat from it. No one moved and no one spoke, while the ship throbbed excitedly under our feet and the exhaust gases from the giant funnel above roared like some monstrous dragon into the burnished sky. The cordite-fouled cloud on the sea was very calm again, broken only by the splaying arrows of *Mallard*'s wake as she hovered hungrily, gun silently alert.

We waited, staring tensely at the stain on the water. My eyes ached with the strain of peering through the binoculars, but I couldn't look away. The knot was back in my stomach again, but this time it was sadistic anticipation that was causing it, a glorious hope of being able to hit back, with the cards stacked on our side for a change. A sense of appeasement after our constant fear, and our running eternally south. The sheep were now the wolves and, by God, we were getting our money's worth.

And then—like a brain that suddenly snaps—it was all savagery, and noise, and violence, and hate.

At my shoulder I heard the hiss of indrawn breath as Evans watched the yellow patch on the water slowly darkening. My hands holding the binoculars started to shake uncontrollably, so that I had to lean with my elbows on the teak rail to steady them. I knew that, for the first time, we were about to *see* the fear that haunted us.

The dark stain grew blacker and started to bubble like a witches' cauldon as oil seeped and rose from ruptured fuel tanks. German oil. Vulture's blood. Christ, how I wanted to see it turn into rich, red, satisfying plasma.

Then an obscene boil on the water. A bulge of whipped white foam and a belch of liberated air throwing great gouts of black liquid in high slashes against the burnt yellow sky. Someone was shouting behind me and I realised it was Brannigan trying to tell the duty-trapped quartermaster at the wheel what was happening. 'Yes! She's coming up . . . She's coming. Oh, the bastards, the beautiful bastards . . . There they come, right out of the bloody water . . . Oh, Jeeeeeesus!'

For a fleeting moment I was back five years to a big room in Port Said where I'd sheepishly paid a tin of fifty Gold Flake to watch two gigantic, sweat-shining black bucks doing unspeakable things to a slim, blonde White Russian kid with enormous breasts . . . She'd screamed just like the Fourth as she'd writhed in the supreme eroticism.

Then I forgot about everything as the huge, streaming hull rose nearly vertically from the sea. We heard the screech of her desperately venting air tanks as she hung, almost motionless, on her tail like some old sailor's nightmare dream of the terrible white whale. But she wasn't white, she was black. Death black. The black of oil-burnt lungs, with little red and pink scars where the rust showed through. Black like the colour of Eric Clint's drowned, suffocated face.

And, even in the milli-seconds while she was still suspended, a little man—a black little man—fell screaming from her conning tower. A little man like the star figure that had spiralled into the air from the *Commandant Joffre*'s funnel. And the guns opened up on her from *Mallard* as she slowly tilted, then came crashing faster and faster into the waiting sea.

I heard a throaty boom from our own poop and felt the deck shiver. Phyllis was firing . . . by God but she was firing! Even above the smash of the shells I could hear the fat little bombardier screaming his fire orders in a high-pitched but surprisingly controlled voice. 'Load! . . . On! . . . On! . . . On! . . . *Fire!* . . .', then Phyllis boomed again and the shell sounded like a Fifth of November rocket as it supersonicked through the heavy air. Then, 'Load! . . . On! . . . On! . . .'

The U-boat was lying low in the water by now, angled well over to port with her conning tower and gun platform almost brushing the water. I couldn't see the surface around her for the white-whipped foam as *Mallard* opened up with light weapons while, on the little warship's foredeck, her gun crew moved like well-lubricated machines and the empty brass cartridge cases sparkled in the sunlight.

The submarine's ratings were leaving her fast now. Half-naked men, some of them enormously distended under inflated life preservers, all terror stricken . . . except those who were already dead, ripped to bloody tatters before they even hit the water. I felt the shock-wave snap at my eardrums as our gun boomed again, then a tremendous explosion in the after part of the U-boat's conning tower sent her light ack-ack gun spiralling high into the air.

I saw a man run with the hopelessness of death along the bloated buoyancy tanks, tiny matchstick legs jerking desperately towards the comparative safety of the smoother water at her bow . . . Then the funny little Swan Vestas figure seemed to disintegrate as the sparking ricochets chased him along the black casing and overtook him. I watched an arm come off and still the legs kept on running for the impossible sanctuary ahead, then one of the legs came off too and the running corpse just fell apart, still travelling forward.

And suddenly I didn't want to see any more blood, and I didn't hate the Germans for what they did to Eric, and I wanted it all to stop . . . Please God, make it stop!

And the Old Man was still gripping his Barr and Strouds and saying over and over again, 'Oh, the bastards! . . . The bastards! . . .', and I really wasn't sure, this time, whether he meant Them or Us.

And Brannigan had stopped screaming his commentary to the helmsman and, instead, was heaving and sobbing over the wing of the bridge as he spewed his guts up beside a curiously silent, thoughtful Curtis.

And Phyllis shouted hate again from the poop, and . .

. . . and, just as suddenly, it was all over.

The mess in the water was quite a long way astern of us by the time the Lewis guns stopped chattering and the ugly, pink-tinged foam ceased spurting round the shattered hull. The steel-helmeted ratings round her four-inch were still, too, standing motionless and inspecting the havoc they'd wreaked on their enemy. I wondered how they felt right then. Had any of their flushed young faces gone a shade paler? Or wasn't that allowed when you wore the uniform of one of the fighting services? Despite the sickness in my stomach I felt a grudging surge of respect for Braid and the smooth Admiralty machine which he manipulated.

Phyllis coughed once again from our poop and we felt the shiver in the deck as a last blossom of flame and black smoke bloomed at the base of the German's conning tower, now lying flat on the water. Typical bloody woman, Phyllis—always had to have the last word. Then the bombardier's almost girlish voice yelled, 'Check! Check! Check!' as the cigar-shaped corpse of the enemy reared up slightly, silhouetting a skeletal jumble of rudder, hydroplanes and propeller against the shimmering, burnished horizon.

Maybe it would have been more appropriate if she'd

blown up then. Disintegrated in a million spiteful fragments of Nazi steel and Nazi men as a last Teutonic blast of hate—a threat of what might be waiting for us, too, her murderers. But she didn't. She just slid silently away from the surface, leaving only a few blisters of bursting air and half a dozen black-humped shapes face down in the gory, diesel scum.

The last glimpse I caught before I turned to look for *Athenian* was the little grey *Mallard* dropping more yellow canisters off her stern. Life-rafts this time, like she did for the Frenchman. She must have had a nest of them below somewhere and I wondered if she would have enough of them left for us, if we ever needed them. She didn't stop, though—the orders said 'No survivors.' I don't really think she had any need to anyway. Not that time.

In the wheelhouse I glimpsed the flash of white teeth as the quartermaster grinned fiercely at me, but it vanished quickly when he saw the look on my face. I ordered a full ninety-degree alteration to bring us back on an overtaking course with our sister, now several miles ahead and still going like a racehorse, then reached wearily for the engine room telephone.

The receiver was snatched off below when I'd hardly touched the call button. It was the Chief himself. 'Whit?' he yelled above the pounding background of the machinery.

'Kent here, Chief. You can take the kettle off the gas now.'

McKenzie sounded aggrieved. 'Aye? And about bluidy time too, man. We're havin' tae haud the engines together wi' rubber bands doon here.'

I grinned without humour. 'Put 'em back in the box again then, Henry. Maybe one day we'll want you to go really fast.'

There was a pregnant silence down below and I thought for a moment he'd hung up on me. Then the broad accent came back, tinged with grudging curiosity. 'Did we sink the bastards, John? Did we nab them good and bluidy proper?'

I looked at the phone, then back out to where Curtis was wiping his mouth thoughtfully with a stained hankie. 'Oh, we nabbed them, Henry,' I said quietly. 'We nabbed them good and proper, all right!'

The answering screech of Highland joy and satisfaction rebounded round the wheelhouse as I gently put the receiver back on its hook and stepped out to the wing in time to meet Charlie Shell rushing up the ladder followed by an almost hysterical Cadet Breedie.

'Did you see us perform back there?' screamed Charlie in flushed excitement. 'Oh, Jesus, but did you? Were you watchin'?'

The Third Mate excused himself abruptly and hurried into the chartroom, leaving Shell standing there in his filthy, oil-grimed white shirt and shorts, with the grey stains of cordite smearing his sweating red face. I nodded and tried to look suitably impressed, though, by this time, my head was splitting and the bile in my stomach felt as if it were eating its way through the very lining. 'You did a bloody good job, Charles. You and the army both.'

He grinned like a Cheshire cat. 'Yeah? You really think so?' He turned to the Old Man. 'Now can we paint a little U-boat on the side of the funnel, eh Sir? Like they do on the Raff planes when they bag a Jerry.'

I saw the Captain hiding a smile. He was looking pretty sick too, but Charlie was just like a kid at a Christmas party. It was dead funny, even to us on the bridge who'd had to stand and watch, and suddenly go off war, and killing, and bestiality, 'Not on the funnel, perhaps, Mister Shell,' Evans said solemnly. 'But I don't suppose a small, discreet one on the side of the monkey island would harm anyone, do you, Mister Kent?'

I shook my head. No, it wouldn't do any harm. Anyway, it wasn't the little painted U-boats I was worried about, it was the big, black, real ones. Maybe, one day soon, some leather-jacketed Kapitan-Lieutnant would be painting a little white *Cyclops* on the side of his conning tower. But, every dog has its day . . .

'Breedie can nip down for some paint and a brush, Two Oh,' I said, smiling at the pleased look on Charlie's face. 'But only a small one, mind.'

I glanced aft at our curving wake. It lay behind us like a great question mark. It suddenly struck me that, for a short time, we had been heading almost directly towards our destination for a change. Now we were running away again, steaming practically due south. It couldn't go on for ever, sometime soon we were going to have to stop avoiding trouble and just go straight into it. Very soon.

A few minutes later Breedie came back with the paint and the Second Mate was climbing the vertical ladder to the top of the wheelhouse. I wondered perhaps if he shouldn't put a long line of hump-backed, face-down little men up there too.

With a tiny, matchstick half-man running frantically at the end of it.

CHAPTER FIVE

It took us over two hours to catch up with *Athenian*, and only then after we'd flashed her a sarcastic signal advising her that THE BADDIE HAS BEEN SMACKED YOU CAN STOP RUNNING NOW DEAR END, followed on a rather sourer note from *Mallard* asking DO YOU RUN YOUR ENGINES ON FEAR OIL QUERY PLEASE REDUCE TO FIFTEEN KNOTS CONTINUE ZIG-ZAG FORTY DEGREES EVERY SEVEN MINUTES SIGNED BRAID END.

Which meant that Bill Henderson's crowd had to spend the next two hours swanning about like a drunk in an earthquake and getting nowhere fast. One thing for sure— no ambushing U-boat crew would ever figure out an attack plan for a ship behaving as irresponsibly as she was right then.

The Old Man couldn't resist a crack at Bert Samson when finally we drew up on her beam and she was able to settle back into a somewhat less gyrating passage through the water. Our Aldis flashed again from the wing, COMCONVOY TO MASTER ATHENIAN: RESPECTFULLY SUGGEST YOU KEEP BONDED LIQUOR STORE LOCKED FOR REMAINDER OF VOYAGE SIGNED EVANS END.

He grinned as wide as Charlie Shell with his painted submarine when he read the reply. MY WATCHKEEPERS TOO USED TO KEEPING STATION WITH CYCLOPS TO KNOW WHAT STRAIGHT COURSE IS ALSO REF BONDED STORE IF COM-CONVOY WOULD CARE TO BOARD FOR MASTERS CONFERENCE NO DOUBT LIQUOR PROBLEM WILL CEASE TO EXIST SIGNED

SAMSON END.

Evans and Bert Samson were professional enemies of long standing but, unlike Bill Henderson and me, they didn't exactly hit it off on a social level either. As with Evans and *Cyclops*, Captain Samson had been master of *Athenian* since he'd taken her over from the builders and, also like Evans, he was a tough, iron-hard, first-class seaman. Actually, if anyone ever belied his name from a purely physical point of view, it was Bert Samson. At first sight he was a tiny, wispy, almost cadaverous man who even had to stand on a little wooden platform when the ship was docking so that he could get high enough to see over the dodgers. I sailed with him once and I'll never forget standing on the foc'slehead as we berthed and, looking aft, seeing Bert Samson up on his little box peering down suspiciously at me from the vast height of the bridge— all one could see was a great, flat, wide-brimmed cap over the grey canvas screen with just the merest slit between the two for eyes. It was only when you spoke to him that you realised the tremendous force of personality behind the frail exterior, the stubborn, go to hell if you don't like it attitude. A very irascible little seadog was Samson of *Athenian*.

At precisely 1526 hours we altered course again. The two merchantmen, followed motheringly by the skipping *Mallard*, swung round together and, when our bows had settled on the new heading, we were at last homing on a course for the Cape. It was do or die now. Had it been pure coincidence that, so far, all signs of enemy activity had emanated from the area into which we were now steaming? If not, then should we have stuck to our original routing, even after the death of the *Commandant Joffre*, even if it would have meant refusing to shy away from those mysterious pyrotechnic displays on the horizon? I still didn't know. All I was sure of was that we'd been lucky so far. Very lucky. If Curtis hadn't seen those tell-tale tracks earlier on . . . If . . . If . . .

I watched as Charlie Shell, now the officer of the watch, chalked up the complex system of courses, times and alterations on the blackboard in front of the helmsman. Not for us any more of that ordinary 'straight' zigzag—now we were to run on a complex, pre-planned pattern devised with the express purpose of making it as difficult as possible for any waiting submarine to anticipate our course as we closed on them. It was nerve-racking, it was dangerous, but by God it was damned reassuring to me.

The signal from *Mallard* lay on the flag locker before me. COMESCORT TO MASTER CYCLOPS: REPEAT TO MASTER ATHENIAN: . . . The signal branches were having a busy time today . . . COMMENCE ZIG-ZAG PATTERN THREE SEVEN REPEAT PATTERN THREE SEVEN MEAN COURSE 085 DEGREES T REPEAT 085 DEG SPEED EIGHTEEN KNOTS GOOD LUCK ALL SHIPS SIGNED BRAID END.

Zig-zag pattern thirty-seven. Braid was really taking precautions after our last brush with the, that time, un-fortunate enemy. All merchantmen of our type carried several plans of the compensating alternate headings I've described, and the pattern we were about to embark upon was one of the most complicated. I smiled ironically to myself—the fancy new zig-zag schedules were probably included among the contents of the three bags we carried, the bags this was all about. So far on this voyage we hadn't wasted a lot of time on deviating from our straight route other than in the frightened little squiggles we'd been performing over the past twenty-four hours which, nevertheless, cumulatively were carrying us farther and farther from the original. Now we were heading inshore, however, we were really going to weave as we went.

I glanced again at the course board. We'd all be certi-fiable before this trip was over—first a 25-degree alteration to port with a run of six minutes at eighteen knots, then a 10-degree swing to starboard, two subsequent small altera-tions of 5 degrees port for eight and five minutes respec-tively, then a massive, hair-raising, starboard turn through 60 degrees, and so on. If the watchkeeper was a genius and the helmsman could steer as straight as a tram driver, the legs would in theory compensate themselves and we could start all over again forty-seven minutes later. And incidentally, while all this was going on, we would have covered a lateral sea distance between the outer extreme legs of some two miles. A U-boat commander didn't need a periscope to plot his attack—he needed a crystal ball.

The Second Mate stepped back and grinned wryly at

me as he admired his handiwork, then the zig-zag clock, a sort of alarm present to ring in time for each leg and vital in such a complex manœuvre, gave a sharp 'ding' and the quartermaster put the wheel over after a nod from Shell and a glance up at the new heading. Charlie Shell watched as the bow bore round—we were now coming up on to the big, sixty-degree swing—while I peered nervously over to see how *Athenian* was doing.

We were swinging fast now and I bit my lip as the sea room between us and *Athenian* closed rapidly. Charlie came out and stood beside me watching anxiously as we drew together. Obviously they hadn't started their turn on her bridge yet. Shell blinked at me queryingly, the distance was down to less than four cables and still narrowing. There wasn't a soul to be seen on her bridge wing. What the hell were they doing aboard Bert Samson's boat?

Charlie shuffled nervously. Even though I was up there with him, unless I relieved him it was still his watch and his was the primary responsibility. Four cables was quite a good distance, still two-fifths of a nautical mile, but on a collision course like this is wasn't nearly far enough for peace of mind. Collision at sea is one of the nightmares we all had to live with, so much so that, until one was actually in a position like this with two great ships in close proximity, one just tried not to think about it. All one could do was study the antiquated and obsolete 'Regulations for Preventing Collisions at Sea,' which in theory should but, in actual practice, just didn't seem to. Anyway, who had the responsibility for keeping clear in a crazy, wartime set-up like this?

Shell couldn't stand it any longer and started to walk across to the wheelhouse, presumably to wake them up over there with a series of short blasts on the whistle. I heard him tell the quartermaster to ease the helm and slow the swing down, then, as I lifted the binoculars, I saw the after end of *Athenian*'s smoke-blackened centrecastle start to widen as her stern came round and she, too, commenced her alteration. I called to Charlie and he came back in relief. Together, we watched as the gap between us steadied to an even closer three and a half cables.

For anyone who doesn't know the sea I suppose it's

easy to frown and wonder what all the fuss and nerves
are about, to ask how two modern ships with highly
competent officers and in full sight of each other, both
steaming on the same mean course, could possibly run
the risk of collision. But it's happened before, too often,
even without the added stresses and strains of a critical
zig-zag plan such as we were involved with. It'll happen
again when this war's finished—maybe even more often
as, presumably, merchant shipping increases in numbers
and density. If there are any of us left to increase upon.

No doubt after the disaster it's comparatively simple for
a Court of Inquiry to pronounce learned judgment, following months of deliberation, on what should have been
the correct actions—to be decided in *split-seconds* by the
various watchkeepers involved—taken to avert a maritime
collision. No doubt it's also easy to overlook such intang-
ibles as the fact that a ship travelling over shoal water
tends to sheer into the deeper, adjacent channel. Or that
there is an undoubted form of magnetism acting between
two converging hulls knowns as 'inter-action,' which appears
to have the contradictory effect in that, from the bows to
midships, they tend to repel each other, while from midships
to aft they seem to draw together. And finally, that there is
such a thing as the human element—the fact that no two
minds can work in complete sympathy and understanding
when viewing the same problem from different angles.

As a further example of how everyone could assume that
they, themselves, were in the right and that it was up to
the other bloke to give way, *Athenian*'s second mate came
wandering out on their port wing, took one look at us—
which, to my biased mind, he should have done a bloody
sight farther back—then grabbed for his Aldis. GO AWAY
CHARLIE I GET NERVOUS WHEN I'M ACCOSTED.

I left it to Charlie Shell to deal with his opposite
number across the water, which he did with an aggressive
GET KNOTTED IT'S YOU WHO ARE SOLICITING US.

Then *Mallard*, carrying out an optimistic Asdic sweep
ahead of us, had to join in the act too. Braid had obviously
seen the incident and wasted no time in admonishments.
COMESCORT TO MASTER ATHENIAN: SUGGEST YOU DROP
FIVE CABLES ASTERN CYCLOPS TO AVOID PHYSICAL VIOLENCE

BETWEEN WATCHKEEPERS IF NOT BETWEEN VESSELS SIGNED
BRAID END.

Larabee was leaning over the rail at the top of the boat
deck ladder as I climbed it, having just completed my
after-dinner rounds of the ship. His private bodyguard, a
bored-looking able seaman, lounged at the entrance to
the wireless room, which also annoyed me—if he hadn't
been up there then the Bosun would sure as hell have had
him chipping rust or up to his elbows in soojee. Then I
remembered that the daywork men would have been finished for the night by now anyway, so I didn't say anything.

The Second Sparks grinned faintly as I pulled myself up
to deck level. 'Evenin', Mate.'

I nodded coldly and hoped he wasn't going to start
talking about what a hot-shot radioman he was. He seemed
to have other things on his mind, though. 'I see we're
headin' east now, then.'

I nodded again. At this time of night, and with the
setting sun almost burning our tails off, it didn't need a
Vasco da Gama to figure that one out. He pursed his
lips thoughtfully. 'Yeah, well I still think we should've
gone farther south before we headed for the Cape.'

He must have been the only man on board who wasn't
damned glad to be heading for Africa for a change, even
despite the possible hazards that lay ahead. I still couldn't
bring myself to be nice to him, though. 'If we went much
farther south, Larabee, we'd be in more danger from
bloody icebergs than U-boats.'

He grinned sardonically. 'Come off it, Mate. We can't
be all that far past the Cape? What's a few more miles
between friends?'

I ignored the 'friend' bit. 'It's more days and more
exposure to risk, for a start.'

'Aye, but we'd maybe stand a better chance of gettin'
round the back of the Jerries doin' it my way.'

I was interested despite my aversion to the man. Anything that suggested greater safety was of interest right
now. 'And what's your way, *Mister* Larabee?'

He shrugged. 'Roughly speakin' I say we should head
due south for, maybe, two hundred miles past the Cape

to avoid all the convergin' shipping lanes into Cape Town
—they're dead naturals for any U-boat waitin' for a target
—cut east till we have Port Elizabeth broad on our beam,
then right round an' flat out on zero, zero, zero. Like cutting round three sides of a box if you see what I'm getting
at. They're bound to have bunkering facilities in Elizabeth
any road, Mate, What do we want goin' to a big place like
Cape Town, apart from to attract attention to ourselves?'

He was dead right there, to my mind anyway. Publicity
was the one thing we didn't need right now, and the
bigger the port, presumably the more comprehensive the
screen of U-boats around it. In fact, everything he said
made sense in a way, if you ignored the extra steaming
time involved. But then, Larabee didn't know what we
carried in our strong-room. Or did he? Otherwise why
should he assume we were something special?

Something in the way he had this all figured made me
glance at him suspiciously. 'What makes you so sure all
our trouble lies the way we're heading, Larabee? We're
already well to the sou'west of the normal lanes . . . Why
should the Germans be expecting us to come into the Cape
from where we are now, never mind from even farther
south?'

He seemed to shift uncomfortably, or maybe it was just
my imagination. Then his frown cleared and he winked
knowingly. 'Who are you tryin' to kid, Mate? I've got
eyes the same as everyone else on this bucket. I saw the
fancy illuminations out there last night, same as you and
the Captain did. And that sub this morning. Are you
tryin' to pretend it was coincidence that she was where
she happened to be? She'd have been wasted down here
if she hadn't been waitin' for us. There's not another
allied boat for miles.'

I still wasn't happy but I couldn't quite put my finger
on why. 'You seem to be very keen to go farther south,
that's all I know, Larabee. There've been a lot of funny
things happening on this trip and *all* of them have tended
to make us follow exactly the same plan you've suggested.
The *Commandant* whatsit—the Froggie—she was hit from
the port side . . .'

He shook his head, still smiling, but the hooded little
eyes looked very bright as he stared at me. 'So she had

to get it from one side or the other. Where's the big conclusion in that?'

'There isn't! But if you add the call from the *Kent Star* and those fancy lights you mentioned, and that sub this morning. Add them together and you're getting some kind of pattern, Larabee. Pressure to do exactly what you're proposing we should compound. Like grab for more and more southing . . .'

As I spoke it all started to fit together. I could also see that Larabee and I were due for another big blow-up, we seemed to act on each other like gunpowder and flame. Was he just getting mad because he could see that I was setting out to needle him, or was I genuinely rubbing on some secret nerve that he'd unwittingly exposed?

He started to smack one hand in the palm of the other. 'What the bloody hell are you suggestin', Kent? That I'm some kind of super magic spy or somethin'? Those lights in the night . . . Did I háve some kind of speed boat that could whip me out there, set them off, then sneak back fifteen miles with no one to see me? Did I? . . . And that *Kent Star* signal you're so hot on . . . Listen, Mate, I wasn't even on *watch* when that came through. Foley got it, for Christ's sake! Foley *and* the Navy boat, they both picked it up. You're off your bastard chump, you're so bloody scared an' suspicious, that's what . . .'

He stopped suddenly when he saw me staring at him. I'd expected, in fact invited, him to haul off at me, but never quite as violently as that. For a few moments then he'd acted like he did that night in the radio room, like someone crazy with strain . . . or guilt!

There was still someone aboard *Cyclops* who pushed men over the side and who fired guns at other ships in the middle of the night, that was one thing Larabee couldn't pretend didn't happen. I was going to open my mouth when Larabee forestalled me angrily. 'Yeah, I know. Now you're goin' to say it was me pushed that old bastard Foley over the wall, aren't you?'

I didn't say yes, but then again I didn't deny it. I just stood and looked at him and maybe enjoyed myself a little, feeling about him the way I did. He glared at me tight-lipped for a moment then, disconcertingly, smiled and nodded knowledgeably. 'O.K., O.K., if that's what you think, Kent, then jus' you go ahead an' do two things . . . One. Try an' bloody prove it. And two. Just ask yourself, if I'm such a spooky character in your book, then why it is that I've got the Old Man to put a strong-arm zombie like *him*,' he jerked his head contemptuously at the still lounging and apparently indifferent A.B., 'right outside my bloody door?'

I blinked. I hadn't thought of that. Perhaps *I* was the one who was suffering from the strains of fear and no sleep? Perhaps, as Larabee had said, I was so scared that I was seeing something to suspect in everything that happened round me? What fifth columnist would invite—no, positively demand—a witness to his every movement? And anyway, surely no trained agent could be quite as bloody objectionable as Larabee? A professional would fit in unobtrusively, not stand out like a skyscraper in a desert.

Of course there was no pattern, no purpose, behind the events of the past two days . . .

By then I was so convinced it was all in my mind that I nearly said sorry to the still white-lipped Sparks. I didn't, though. Instead I forced a sneer on my face and tried to sound like a tough, bucko mate. 'So you haven't been slammed on the skull an' shoved over the wall yet then, Larabee?'

I heard his cutting sneer as I turned away triumphantly towards the bridge. The hard voice was full of malice. 'No . . . But then again, I haven't seen the fuggin' Mate of this crap boat when I've been left on my own, so far!'

And, as usual, I couldn't think of a thing that was sharp enough to retort.

The Old Man was stamping back and forward out on the starboard wing when I arrived on the bridge. His cap was crammed well down over his eyes, and the way he paced out there, like a caged lion, hands clasped grimly behind his back, made me shoot a guilty glance at Brannigan as I entered the wheelhouse. Evans had been standing my watch while I had dinner and did my rounds and, judging by the glare in his eyes, I'd been too long away. I stole a quick look at the stolid quartermaster behind the wheel—it was McRae—and tiptoed over to the Fourth Mate.

'What's the Captain so raised about, Four Oh?' I whispered apprehensively.

He jerked a casual thumb at the sea, out past the threatening figure of the Master. 'The escort, Sir. She's been swanning around under our bows for the past half-hour. Dropping back, then surging up alongside us like she doesn't know what she's doing.'

I felt distinctly relieved. At least it wasn't me who was incurring the Old Man's wrath this time. The zig-zag clock dinged for the next leg and Brannigan turned to McRae. 'Five more to port, McRae.'

The blue-jeaned sailor put her two spokes down and watched the lubber line on the gyro compass. The ship's head had hardly moved across the now darkening horizon before he was bringing the helm back amidships, stopping her dead on her new course. 'Steady on 060, Sir.'

I glanced up at the course board. We were now running at twenty-five degrees to port of our mean course, with that big, scary sixty-degree swing to starboard as the next leg. It was starting to get dark quickly too, as it always did in these latitudes, then we'd really have to be on our toes. I sort of hoped that Braid over on *Mallard* would decide to change the zig-zag pattern during the night. Even with the apparently adequate distance between us and *Athenian*, it was only too easy to creep up five cables on the ship ahead of you when they weren't showing any stern lights. I decided to do something about it and gestured to young Conway who was standing out in the solitude of the port wing, keeping as far away from the Captain as possible.

'Nip down and tell the Bosun to prepare a barrel for streaming astern during the night,' I said, as the kid came over.

He nodded, looking intelligent. 'Aye, aye, Sir,' then moved away on the run. I stopped him before he slid down the ladder. 'Conway.'

'Sir?' he blinked at me.

'Do you know *why* I want a barrel streamed aft?'

He frowned in concentration, then shook his head. 'No, Sir.'

I didn't think so. Why was it that all cadets were the same? None of them ever had the sense to know that, unless they asked questions, they never learnt anything about what was supposed to be their chosen profession. Or was I too much of a spectral, ogre-like figure for a scared young kid like Conway to approach? I didn't want to be.

I tried to look patient and understanding, though I suppose, to him, I just looked bloody bad-tempered. 'I want a barrel streamed over the stern, Conway, because when it gets dark it will be extremely difficult for the watchkeepers on *Athenian* to know exactly where we are. We aren't showing any lights, there may not be a moon like there was last night, God be pleased, so if we allow a barrel to drag along the surface of the water about a cable astern of us . . .'

He looked bright. 'Then the spray it kicks up will help them keep their distance, Sir?'

I nodded. Thank heaven for small mercies. 'Right, lad. You'll probably find the Bosun having a last pipe on number five hatch.'

He dashed off and Brannigan said, 'Now, when *I* was a cadet . . .'

'. . . which was only a spit ago, Mister Brannigan,' I finished for him, 'you still didn't know anything. Like now.'

He beamed cheerily as I decided to face the storm and stepped out on to the starboard wing. Evans met me with a growl of rage directed, however, at the little *Mallard*, now less than two cables off our beam. She was so close I could almost see the features of the two officers and the ratings on her bridge.

'What the bloody hell do they think they're playing at?' the Old Man gritted. 'They've been buggering round under our bows like this was some kind of fancy fleet exercise we're on!'

I leaned over and looked down at the corvette. When you really saw her up close she seemed to be all depthcharges and White Ensign aft while, farther forward, there was just a miniature superstructure that could have sat on our smallest hatch cover with room to spare, then a slip of a foredeck to provide a platform for the gun. She was smart, though. Everything was either smooth black or smooth grey with hardly a scratch or flaw to be seen in the paintwork. Wooden hulled, of course, which helped to avoid rusty streaks.

D

I shook myself suddenly and realised that I'd been looking at her with the critical eye of a ship's husband and not as a navigator viewing a potential hazard. I started to get an uneasy feeling myself about the way she was seemingly ignoring our proximity. If it had been me down there with all the South Atlantic to play with I'd have been a good half-mile away at the least.

Why *was* she so bloody near?

The binoculars were in the box in front of me so I lifted them and had a good look at the men on her bridge. One of the white-shirted officers was a midshipman and the other didn't look very much older, come to that. Probably the First Mate or Lieutenant or whatever it was they had in the R.N. The silly bastards seemed to be just watching us and grinning as if this was some kind of game we were playing. Chicken. That was the name of it . . . Chicken! See who gave way first. Obviously Commander Braid wasn't up there or they wouldn't be arsing around like that.

Beside me Evans still seemed to be more angry than concerned so I decided to act. It was my watch anyway, even though I hadn't formally relieved the Old Man again. I moved over to the wheelhouse and told Brannigan to get the Aldis out on the wing, then I ordered McCrae at the helm to ease her a little to port to give us a bit more room. Stepping back out to the wing, I sighted the Aldis on her bridge and commenced signalling irritably. GET OFF MY BACK IMMEDIATELY YOU ARE MUCH TOO CLOSE FOR SAFETY.

One of the white shirts on her control platform raised an arm in careless salute and her lamp flashed stutteringly, SORRY WE WERE JUST ADMIRING YOUR FIGURE. Then the white cap cover flashed briefly in the last rays of the setting sun as the watchkeeper bent over the row of voice pipes under her glass windscreens, and the foam at her counter kicked higher as she started to draw ahead with an acceleration that made me green with envy.

Suddenly, from inside the wheelhouse, our zig-zag clock dinged again, signalling time for the next leg. I still didn't like *Mallard*'s proximity, so I lifted a warning hand to Brannigan who'd already started to give the new helm order to McRae at the wheel. Like me not so long ago, he'd also forgotten to check first on where the other ships in the group lay. The Captain hadn't moved all this time from his stolid, legs apart stance, but when he saw me gesture he looked round. 'That was the bell, Mister Kent.'

I looked at him a bit surprised, then jerked my chin at the escort, by now about three cables ahead and to starboard of our flared bow. 'Yes, Sir. But the next leg's the big one . . . to starb'd!'

Evans sniffed bad-temperedly. 'Aye? Well then?'

By God but he was needled with the way *Mallard* had come in so close. I didn't really blame him, but . . . 'I'm sorry, Sir, but I don't consider the escort to be far enough ahead to make a sixty-degree turn across her stern.'

He glanced forward and seemed to consider for a moment, then the aggressive jaw hardened almost petulantly. 'Bugger them! They started this bloody chasing round in circles, Mister. As the escort it's their duty to keep clear of us.'

I weighed her relative position again. She certainly seemed far enough ahead by now to be clear of our turning circle, assuming that nothing went wrong. But could we be sure? It was almost twilight, the bad time of evening to see perfectly. The time when big ships only a few hundred yards away in reality look small and insignificant. And another thing . . . *Mallard* was still the stand-on ship, irrespective of whether she was our escort or not. According to the B.O.T. regulations we, as the overtaking vessel, still had the responsibility to keep clear.

It was obvious that the Old Man didn't subscribe to the rule of the road when it came to escorts, though. He wasn't alone in this feeling either, come to that. A lot of merchant masters I'd met felt that, with the added strains of zig-zag routing to contend with, it was the responsibility of the Royal Navy to give us the sea room required especially when there were several thousand square miles of it as in this case. Still, I had to have one more try.

'We could delay the turn a few more minutes, Sir. Give her more time to draw ahead of us,' I ventured.

To give him his due, he didn't just haul off at me as he could have done. Instead, he glowered critically over at *Mallard* yet again before he answered. 'She seems to have settled down for the bloody night where she is,' he grunted irritably. 'No, Mister Kent, starboard your helm or we'll never turn at all. If she doesn't shift when she sees us yawing towards her, then we'll wake the blighters up with a blast or two on the horn.'

He was certainly right in one way. *Mallard* didn't seem to be moving any farther away after her first debonair spurt of acceleration and, if she *was* keeping permanent station so close under our bows, then we'd never be able to turn in safety. The minutes were ticking past quickly, and on our present leg we were already well to port of our proper heading. I turned into the wheelhouse and crooked a finger at Brannigan.

He came over inquiringly and I jerked my thumb towards the foc's'lehead where the small, black shape could be dimly seen cutting ahead of us. 'The fancy boat's still close under us, Mister Brannigan. I want you to stand by the whistle lanyard to wake 'em up if necessary. Right?'

He nodded, 'Right, Sir.'

I stepped over to McRae at the wheel. For some reason I suddenly found I was whispering, which was bloody silly but, somehow, it just seemed so quiet up there right then. McRae glanced pointedly at the green glowing dial of the zig-zag clock in silent admonishment and I saw we were now four minutes past the pre-arranged zig-zag point.

For some reason I didn't give him the new course and leave him to it—maybe, subconsciously, I still felt there was something wrong. Instead, I just said, 'Starboard your helm ten, McRae,' meaning him to put the wheel over until the 'Tell-tale' pointer of the telemotor showed we had a constant ten degrees of rudder. Then I walked forward to the window and watched as we started to swing, slowly at first, then faster and faster.

'Sing out our heading every ten degrees, Quartermaster,' I said without turning, eyes fixed on the blob that was *Mallard*.

'Aye, aye, Sir,' McRae answered phlegmatically behind me, then, almost immediately, started calling out the changing course bearings. '050, Sir . . . 060 . . .'

She was swinging really fast now so I called out to McRae as I turned, 'Ease the helm,' to slow us down a bit. If *Mallard* wasn't watching at precisely this moment, then I didn't want to come round on her too quickly.

'070, Sir,' sang McRae, and I could hear the gyro clicking off the points as the lubberline on the card swung in its mounting. The Captain was still a silent, unmoving figure out on the wing.

Suddenly, as I turned back to the window and looked out again for the corvette, I started to get uneasy. Well, I'd been uneasy all the time—now I was plain scared. *Mallard* had apparently vanished. One minute she was there, steaming ahead and to starboard . . . now she was gone! Perhaps it was a trick of the half-light. It was getting dark very quickly and the sea seemed to heave sullenly like black, billowing glass.

God! Where the hell was she? I swung round on Brannigan.

'Short blasts, Fourth Mate. And keep on blowing till I tell you to stop!' I yelled as I headed for the wheelhouse door. Then I saw we were still swinging too fast against the fuzzy grey shading of the horizon. Even if we'd been heading west instead of almost due east I would at least have had the blood-red crack of sky remaining to help me find that vanished escort.

'Midships the wheel,' I threw over my shoulder as I went through the door itself, eyes clawing for the dark sea ahead.

Then I saw the Old Man running towards me and, with a sick feeling in my guts, I knew it was too late.

Things had happened so slowly at first that it was confusingly unbelievable that they could be piling one on top of another with such terrifying speed. I suddenly realised that the reason I couldn't see the little *Mallard* was because she was already hidden from the bridge by the enormous flare of our bows. Already her officers and ratings were staring up in unbelieving horror at the overhang of steel looming over them like a Damoclesian sword. They were dead men, yet they were still able to scream.

I know, because I heard them.

And *Cyclops* was screaming, too, as the gravel-throated siren shrieked too late from our funnel abaft the bridge.

Captain Evans and I—I have to include myself—had both been trapped into misjudging our true distance from

Mallard as she sat out there on our bow. I found out later what had actually happened as he talked dazedly about it in his cabin.

At the start of our turn, as our high stem had started to bear round on them, they must have thought for a few crucial moments that we were only yawing through the inattention of our helmsman. Probably her First Lieutenant had been too sure of his right of way as the 'Stand on' ship to worry overmuch at that stage. Then, as they realised with what must have been incredulously dawning horror that we were actually turning into our sixty-degree leg alteration, her officers had acted in a way which should still have saved them. According to Evans, the white water had boiled under her counter as she went to Emergency Full Ahead, while at the same time, presumably in an attempt to kick her after-end away from our bows, she had suddenly leaned over under full starboard helm. Then, just as he thought everything was clear, the mysterious forces of water pressure had taken over.

Mallard was a little ship. She was so light that she didn't so much sit in the water as on it. I suppose a plain view of the relative positions of the two ships just before the moment of impact would have shown *Mallard*—under full starboard helm and ahead power—pulling across our bows from left to right. *Cyclops,* on the other hand, had already started to slow her swing due to my order to 'Ease the helm' a few seconds previously. At that time we were still roughly one cable, or six hundred feet, away from her. Both Evans and I later agreed that she had done the right thing in starboarding as that way, in theory, she should still have stayed ahead of us and eventually drawn out of the radius of our swing. But then, as I've already said, no doubt a Court of Law could have pronounced learned judgment, given time to debate, but could an officer have acted any differently with the shadow of twelve thousand tons of rushing, juggernauting steel looming over his tiny cockleshell?

The bulge of water beyond our forefoot had hit *Mallard* first at her stern. When a big ship is travelling at speed a mass of displaced water is pushed ahead of her, acting with indescribable force on any object in its path. *Mallard* was such an object, sitting light on the surface as she was.

The racing, compacting mass of our bow wave had caught her—already under full starboard helm—and pushed her stern farther and farther round like a cork thrown into a weir. The effects were disastrous. Round had swept her bows, round, round, round until, still under full emergency power, she had practically been facing us stem to stem. Then the force of her own engines had driven her remorselessly back into our path . . . right into the welter of rushing, roaring water under our razor forefoot.

It shouldn't have happened. But then, theoretically, no collision at sea should. Collisions are invariably an accumulation of small, individually insignificant events which, if unnoticed, make up the formula for disaster. Like this one where the corvette watchkeeper's irritating elan had needled Evans into a disgruntled attitude towards his Royal Navy counterparts. Where *Mallard*'s inexplicable insistence on remaining so close off our bow had been further compounded by our misjudgment of her true distance in the waning light. Where the nebulous forces of water pressure, of 'Interaction,' had combined with the already exerted helm action to swing the escort's bow through a fatally over-extended arc. Where . . .

Oh, what the hell's the use? The dead, drowned Navymen didn't care how it happened.

Yet, strangely, it was what occurred *after* the impact that I remember most of all . . .

I remember standing searching frantically in the half light for the vanished corvette. Then the Captain came running across the wing and, seizing my shoulder, literally dragged me away from the wheelhouse door to allow him passage. I heard him bellowing to the man at the wheel while a dazed, petrified Brannigan still clung desperately to the whistle lanyard.

'Hard a port!' Evans screamed, lunging for the engine room telegraphs. The brass handles flashed in the last rays of the dying sun as he swung them back and forward, then back again to 'Full Astern.' By this time I, too, was in the confused terror of the wheelhouse as the wheel blurred under McRae's spinning hands. We had just commenced to heel over when the shudder came from the bows, and the shrieking and tearing of wood and metal and men came sweeping back over the canvas dodgers.

Something else was shrieking too, with the agony cries of a wounded monster, and I realised it was that bloody siren on the funnel, still operated by an almost zombie-like Fourth Mate. It was eerie, the way he kept on pulling and pulling at the lanyard. Suddenly I couldn't stand it any longer and smashed his arm down violently, yelling that it was too goddamned late for that. Then I felt guilty at the look on his shocked features as I remembered I'd told him to keep on till I said to stop.

The bows seemed to ride up slightly as we cut into *Mallard* abaft her ridiculous little funnel, then the line of the horizon jumped as our full, ponderous weight took over and we sliced down, down and through her galley and mess decks. Our carnivorous forefoot smashed into her engine room, tons of water-streaming rusty steel impacting down on them from the collapsing deckhead being the very last sensation her engineers must have felt as they stood before their shiny brass wheels and gauges. Then on and on, down and down even farther, through her oil-filled double bottoms and keel until, in a matter of fleeting, devastating seconds, *Cyclops* had ripped her completely in two, yet feeling only an irritating little jolt to mark her passing . . .

The Captain ran past me again, face white as death, to the extreme starboard wing. I saw him leaning so far out over the sea that, for a sickeningly frightening moment, I thought he was going to overbalance and fall into the rushing black water below. Then he ripped his cap off and started beating the rail with it in an agony of frustration at our inability to repair the havoc we'd created. What made it even worse was that he wasn't swearing or shouting—just smashing and smashing with the crumpled, braided cap, smashing down on the rail as though belabouring his own conscience through the medium of the ship.

We had started to shudder violently ourselves now. Every window frame and loose object in the wheelhouse was chattering and jumping excitedly. It was the torque effect of our propellor shafts suddenly thrown under full astern power. They must have felt it too, down below, to have hit the engine controls so quickly . . . Oh, Christ! The screws. They were still spinning and by now the shattered bulk of *Mallard* must be sliding slowly aft along our flank. If one of our churning phosphor-bronze propellors even touched her . . . I threw myself at the telegraph and swung it desperately to 'Stop Engines' . . . The jolting vibration ceased almost as soon as I took my hand away and the silence clamped down on the darkened wheelhouse with an almost physical grip.

Then McRae at the wheel said, 'Wheel's still hard to port, Mister Kent, Sir,' in a shocked, quiet voice, and I shook myself free of the dazed horror that threatened to paralyse me. I saw them both, Brannigan and McRae, watching me dumbly and I knew I had to do something to break the sick tension.

'Midships the wheel,' I said, forcing my voice to remain as icy cold as I could. Then, to Brannigan, 'Get down below . . . Take the carpenter and sound the forepeak. Sound the forra'd bilges too, then report back here.'

The Fourth Mate blinked, then nodded and almost ran from the bridge. I glanced at the clock—only a few seconds had actually passed since the start of the nightmare . . . Where in God's name was *Athenian*? She was still slamming up astern of us. Maybe they hadn't seen anything to account for our crazy, gyrating course. Maybe she was still on a heading to bear down on us and anything that was left of the corvette. I ran out to the bridge wing and skidded to a halt.

Evans was already signalling to her. Thank heavens he'd not slipped into a dazed trance as a host of masters might have done in the appalling circumstances. Subconsciously I listened to the clicks of the shutter as he slowly, unpractisedly, spelt ATHENIAN . . . U . . . U . . . U . . . U . . . the International Code warning—'You are standing into danger' . . . KEEP WELL TO STARBOARD MY TRACK.

And, suddenly, another noise. A strange sound coming from somewhere below our feet. Where? What was it? The silence on the bridge still blanketed down, only broken by the purr of the muffled exhaust from our funnel, the laboured clicks of the Aldis in the Old Man's hands, and the swish of the sea along our smooth hull . . . And the noise.

A sort of soft whup! Whup! Whup! . . . getting louder

and louder as we slid quietly through the black water. A sound like the steady flagellation of an already dead corpse. Louder and louder . . .

Then I knew what it was. I rushed to the rail and looked out and down, out over the green-painted sidelight screens and down into the sea below, and I saw it. I saw the ship we'd just murdered.

Or . . . part of it.

I found myself staring down on the after part of *Mallard*. Slowly, ever so slowly, it was passing down the length of our towering sides. The impact of the collision must have slowed us down more than I had at first estimated—that and the throbbing braking power of our engines during the short time they were full astern.

There was still the sound of engines, though . . . *Mallard*'s engines. That was the noise I had heard—the slash of her still spinning propellers, driving the half ship against our side in a futile attempt to bury herself into our inch-thick steel plating. Almost as a last, defiant gesture of mutual destruction.

My hands gripped the rail in front of me as I stared, frozen to the spot while the eviscerated corpse of the corvette tried to push into us as, at the same time, she bumped and grated blindly aft, shedding bits and pieces of ship and fittings into the hungry sea between us.

I remember seeing her White Ensign still streaming proudly from her box-like counter, and watching men jumping from under it with an unspeakable, goddamned unbelievingly disciplined silence, into the oil-fouled water. I remember watching an elderly petty officer moving methodically among the rows of black canisters on the depth-charge racks, moving almost as if he wasn't aware of the horror around him, sparing us not a glance as he bent over the ugly drums, each packed with three hundred pounds of high explosive, and calmly removed the primers from as many as he could before . . .

Before . . .? Oh, dear Jesus! The depth-charges! I swung round and found the Old Man beside me, staring down too, with a terrible look of sadness on his suddenly much older face. His eyes caught mine and held for a long moment, then I said simply, 'Her depth-charges, Captain?'

I saw the lined features age even more in those few seconds as we stood there over the cadavar of a dying ship. There was only one decision he *could* take—we both knew that—but I had to leave it to him to make. I didn't have the courage to accept responsibility for an act I knew would make me die a little more for every day I had left to live.

We could save a lot of those silent, jumping, fresh-faced seamen if we stayed. Already I could see our own crowd down on the after-well duck urgently preparing ropes to drop down to the oil-blackened survivors. But with thousands of pounds of high explosive liable to detonate under our keel at any second, could we really have extended their hold on life for more than another few, precious moments? And what about our cargo forward? Had Braid risked *that* when the *Commandant Joffre* had leaned over on her crewmen?

At my side the drooping shoulders squared resolutely and, turning quickly away, Evans strode deliberately to the wheelhouse. Behind me I heard the sharp clang of the telegraphs moving over to 'Full ahead,' then, from the depths below, the muffled acknowledgement. The first rope snaked over into the water from our well deck as the placid water under our stern suddenly whipped into a surging white froth and, slowly at first, we started to forge ahead with the throbbing, whirring after part of *Mallard* still almost pleadingly forcing into our side.

I saw a young, black-faced kid in the water grab imploringly at the rope's end and hang on with the terror of death strengthening his grip; I saw three of our blokes trying to stop a fourth merchant sailor from climbing over the side to help before they all fell back struggling and cursing to the deck; I saw the bobbing heads in the water staring up at us as we surged faster and faster away from them, then, as they realised we were leaving them to die alone, the white eyes and the red mouths screaming hate and filth at our anonymous bulk; I saw the young kid on the end of the rope still hanging on as the force of the water smashed him time and time again into our steel plates until, almost drowned and terribly battered, he fell away in the welter of white water under our stern.

I saw the old sailor on *Mallard*'s after end look up momentarily from his crouch over the depth-charge primers as the half ship fell away astern. His arm went up briefly to the lowering sky, then he bent back down again to his self-imposed task. Was it a gesture of supplication . . .? No. I closed my eyes in silent prayer as I realised he had been saluting us—a final absolution from a man who knew what it was all about . . . A Royal Navyman!

And I knew, too late, there was no room for the contempt of differences between Us and Them.

Evans was standing beside me again and, together, we watched numbly as the forepart of *Mallard* slid into view from the previous shield of our port side. We didn't speak as the two halves of the little ship almost incredibly met again in our wake. For one unbelievable moment it looked, in the distorted half light, as though she was about to rise whole from the waiting sea, to resurrect her cloven hull and her already dead, trapped, mangled sailors.

Then suddenly, without warning, the stern section seemed to fall forward, the still whirring propellers bit hard into the water, and the whole after end—with the old torpedoman still working under her White Ensign—drove down and down into the black depths below.

And, even yet, she wasn't completely dead. I heard someone sobbing great gouts of indrawn breath until I realised that it was I who was crying, and then, fantastically, the bright stuttering beam of her Aldis blinked for the last time from the doomed forepart. GOODBYE DO NOT STOP TO RESCUE SURV . . .

And the shadowy white columns of water rose high in the air as the smashing blast of the explosions thundered across the water towards us. Time after time the flashes spread through the sea, first the milli-second of bright yellow incandescence from the depths, then a sudden contraction of the brilliance followed by the terrible mushrooms of atomised spray climbing higher and higher. Then another convulsion, and another, and another, until the whole sea between us and the black horizon seemed to be tortured and ripped by the hellish firestorm. I caught a never-forgotten glimpse of *Athenian*, a long grey bulk on our starboard quarter, flickering and illuminated by the awesome light while, all the time, the explosions went on and on and on.

Then, suddenly, the submarine holocaust ceased and the last mountain of spray fell back to the surface with an eerie, audible hiss, and everything was quiet again aboard *Cyclops*. It was completely dark now, with the pupils of our eyes contracted by the glare of *Mallard*'s funeral pyres, so we just stood there, staring blindly aft, for a very long time. We didn't even move when there was the sound of a scuffle from the after well deck and a hysterical voice screamed, 'Bugger you, Evans, you bloody murderin' gutless bastard!', then the sound of a man sobbing as he was forcibly led below . . .

Finally, the Old Man turned to me and I saw that his eyes were full of moisture. I drew myself up and bit my lip as we faced each other. In the wheelhouse the zig-zag clock dinged again, and Evans lifted his chin.

'You have the watch, Mister Kent,' he said.

Very softly.

CHAPTER SIX

It was well past midnight before we were finally squared away after the collision. I'd gone forward to join the Fourth Mate and Chippie as they sounded the wells, finding our forepeak was making water fairly fast. *Mallard* obviously hadn't gone down without any protest as, somewhere below our waterline, she'd lain us open too. This, in itself, wasn't too serious and, after discovering all our other forward compartments were dry, I reckoned we'd been lucky. Thank God the corvette had been a wooden ship . . .

Still more than two days out of Cape Town. Another fifty hours of running the gauntlet of whatever lay ahead. Another fifty hours of walking the decks, subconsciously keeping your knees slightly bent in case the sudden vertical lift of the ship over the smash of a torpedo shattered your hip joints.

I knew then that it was unreasonable—that the death of *Mallard* had nothing to do with the enemy—but suddenly I became certain that they were watching us. Watching and waiting and, somehow, shepherding us into an area of their own choosing. That we weren't a group anymore—we were a flock. A flock of ships.

But why? Why, in that case, didn't they just sink us? They couldn't possibly hope to capture our precious confidential bags without the Admiralty taking immediate steps to render the information valueless. Hadn't the Old Man said that, even if we *were* sunk without trace, the information would still be regarded as captured? The questions battered unceasingly at my strained mind.

I brought it up again with Evans after we'd settled down on zig-zag three seven again, this time with *Athenian* steaming a good, safe, mile astern, and both of us going like bats out of hell. It was two a.m. and the night, for a blessed change, was as black as the inside of a tar barrel. Charlie Shell had the watch, with Cadet Breedie and an extra hand as lookouts on the bridge. They were tired— we all were—but they were scared too, and fear provides its own adrenalin. Any one of the officers would have stayed up there for the next fifty hours if need be.

I was in the master's cabin where we had gone to decide our next move. I knew Evans would dearly have liked a discussion with Bert Samson, but Bert was ten cables away on *Athenian*, so he had to settle for me.

He didn't laugh when I told him of my suspcions, but I could see he didn't agree with me either. Shaking his head slowly he dismissed my argument, 'Damn it all, why, John? Why should they want us farther south? Any plan they may have could equally well be carried out here, at this spot.'

Which was just what I'd been asking myself. Nothing made sense any more. I shrugged worriedly. 'I don't know. But there *were* those bloody queer lights, and the shot into *Athenian*. And that U-boat we sank. She was well south of where we might have expected her—usually they hang around the regular shipping lanes.'

He shook his head again. 'Coincidence, John. And lack of sleep, eh? Strain makes you start thinking out of all proportion.'

I still felt doubtful. 'Maybe.' Then I grinned wryly, 'It's ironical, but I guess the best thing that's happened so far is that *we* were the target for that torpedo. Otherwise

I'd probably be seeing a deep plot to dispose of the other
ships first and isolate *Cyclops*—perhaps so as to get at those
bags in the strong-room.'

The Old Man paced the carpet thoughtfully for a few
moments, then swung round abruptly. 'Did you notice
where the escort was lying at the time those torpedoes
were fired, John?'

Frowning, I thought back to our mad scramble up the
bridge ladder as *Cyclops* heeled over under her emergency
turn. The only thing I really remembered seeing was
Curtis's excited white face waiting for us, and our swinging
masts broadside across the horizon.

'*Mallard*, Sir?' I queried doubtfully. 'No, I can't say
I noticed her right then. Why, does it matter?'

Evans shrugged. 'I don't know. But I registered, as we
arrived topside, that she was broad on our port bow—and
we were turning to port.'

I stared at him miserably, suddenly seeing it all again.
The Third Mate's incredulous, 'A torpedo, Sir. A bloody
torpedo for Chrissake,' and the helmsman's hands still
spinning the wheel as we careered crazily round, and the
corvette—also swinging hard—well out in a line with the
break of our foc'sle. But if she'd been in that position
relative to us at *that* stage of the manœuvre, then . . .?

'The escort was steaming abeam of us when the attack
came, wasn't she?' I muttered, starting to feel sick again.
'Which means she was smack between us and the U-boat.
That bloody torpedo was fired at her, not us.'

So we were back to square one—and I'd invented another possibility. That we were now a target ship. But a
target for what? If they didn't mean to sink us, then
what? I couldn't see them boarding us before we could
destroy the bags. The crew, then; could some of them be
in on it? Impossible. The Old Man thought so too when I
diffidently suggested it.

'The crowd, John?' He shook his head positively. 'They've
nearly all been with us since '38. This is a happy ship,
man, we don't lose our sailors every pay-off like some.
They're British to the last man.'

But someone had still fired that bloody gun back there.
Someone who wasn't quite as British as Evans liked to
think, so who had joined us only recently. Who? . . .

Larabee! That obnoxious little cretin Larabee.

I must have said it out loud because the Old Man looked at me in surprise. 'Larabee?' he said, raising his bushy eyebrows. 'What's the Second Operator got to do with it, Mister Kent?'

I noticed the disapproving 'Mister,' but I was committed now. 'Larabee, Sir? Well, there's just something about the man—he joined just before we sailed, he's not an old hand like the rest . . .'

'Somebody had to replace Buxton, Mister.'

That was true, anyway. Buxton had been our previous Second, and he'd certainly needed replacing having taken a dive under a Liverpool Corporation tramcar while navigating from one pub to another, but . . .

I shrugged. 'Larabee also seemed to have a lot of sympathy with the idea of our heading farther south when I spoke to him . . .'

Evans cut me short. 'You spoke to him? When? By God, but you didn't talk about what we have in the strong-room, man? If I . . .'

But my nerves were in tatters as well. It was my turn to break in angrily, 'No, Sir, I did not. And you've no goddamned right to suggest that I'd act in breach of your confidence, or the Official bloody Secrets Act. But I'll tell you one thing now, and that's that Larabee seems to be a helluva sight more interested in where we're going than a second sparks should be . . . Sir!'

For a moment I thought he was going to blow his top, then he got a grip on his frayed nerves and, this time, his voice was very soft. 'I apologise, John. You'll perhaps understand.'

I nodded, feeling a bit ashamed. I didn't have to bear the final responsibility for what had happened a few hours before. I hadn't had to ring for 'Full Ahead' while men died horribly in the water alongside us. I also remembered that Germany had been preparing for this war for a long time. Their agents must have been infiltrating our society for years, insidiously blending into all our spheres of life— and, whatever else, Larabee just didn't blend.

Suddenly a memory of Curtis flashed into my mind. An image of the Third Mate's face when he had realised that some U-boat was actually trying to torpedo us. But why? Why the surprise? This was a war we were in, the enemy could be expected to shoot at us—or, in the Third Mate's case, was it the *enemy* who were shooting? If I was a German agent I guess I'd have been a bit shattered too if I had suddenly found my oppos were trying to cancel my contract with a torpedo. I swallowed and, clutching desperately to reason, forced a change of subject before I landed myself with a defamation of character case as well.

'Now we've lost the escort, couldn't we radio the Navy at Simonstown, Sir? Ask for instructions and another escort?' I suggested tentatively.

He shook his head slowly. 'We're under strict radio silence, you know that. If we risked transmitting even one short message it could home every U-boat within a hundred miles.'

I looked at him. There were two ways of arguing that one. 'But if I'm right, Sir? If the Jerries already *know* where we are? Then we're a sitting duck that our own Navy haven't even got marked on the chart. None of us— *Mallard* included—sent out our positions over the past few days *because* of radio silence, which means we're so far south-west of our expected course that the Admiralty wouldn't even know where to start looking.' I sat forward and stared at him earnestly, willing him to understand. 'It could be that the U-boats already have our exact position plotted, while our own people don't even know if we're still afloat.'

He looked at me thoughtfully, then opened his mouth to speak, but I never did find out what he would have done had the situation remained as it was up to that moment.

Because the sullen rumble of distant gunfire ahead started us running for the bridge again without even picking up our caps.

The distant, inexplicable pyrotechnics looked even more impressive this time, reflecting as they did from the low cloud ceiling that had formed in the early hours of the night.

We stood gazing over the bows for what seemed a very long time, watching silently as the multi-coloured streamers climbed gracefully into the black sky almost directly in line with our foremast. It was mad. It was sheer crazy improbability that a thing like this could be happening—but it *was* happening, and in less than an hour we would be right there with it.

Unless . . .

The Captain turned slowly away from the silent group of officers and stepped into the chartroom. I followed and shut the door softly. As he looked up at me the glare from the Anglepoise threw his lined, exhausted old face into sharp, craggy relief. I didn't say anything, just reached up and handed him a cigarette from the Old Tar tin, then lit it for him as he leaned over and listlessly dragged the signal pad towards him.

I still didn't say anything as he started to write, but what I read made me feel a bit better. The lights out there had convinced me finally, and I think him too, that we were under constant observation—that the enemy alone knew our every move and were waiting. Just waiting. Dear God, please let the Navy get to us first.

The pencil moved slowly across the paper and I noticed the blue veins standing out on the backs of the Captain's hands—old man's hands. Tired, almost defeated old hands. Occasionally he stopped writing to check the chart, twice he twirled the brass dividers as he marked off various positions. When he'd finished he picked what was left of his cigarette out of the ashtray and pushed the pad across to me.

It read COMCONVOYH24S (our N.C.S. group designation) TO COMSAW (Commander-in-Chief, South Atlantic Waters, he was really going right to the top): COMMANDANT JOFFRE SUNK 0540 HRS 26 5 STOP ESCORT MALLARD SUNK 2120 HRS 28 5 STOP PRESUMED NO SURVIVORS OUR PRESENT POSITION P36 50S P2 45E COURSE 085 TRUE SPEED 19½ KNOTS STRONG ENEMY ACTIVITY SUSPECTED AHEAD PLEASE ADVISE YOUR INSTRUCTIONS QUERY URGENT URGENT URGENT SIGNED EVANS MASTER CYCLOPS.

He could have added 'Help' for my money.

The gunfire stopped as I finished reading the signal and we stepped outside into the cloying darkness. Evans spoke softly in my ear, almost as if he were afraid the U-boats might be listening too. 'I'll be down in my cabin encoding this, John. Send a quartermaster down in ten minutes to take it aft for transmission, please.'

'Aye, aye, Sir,' I said, then hesitated. 'The lights ahead. Do you want to continue on our present heading?'

I saw his mouth smile softly in the darkness. 'Not particularly, Mister Kent. Unless you're terribly curious yourself perhaps you could swing round and notify *Athenian* of the change. We should get an answer to this before very long, until then . . . let's hear all, see all, but do nowt.'

Which was just what I had hoped he would say.

I stayed up on the bridge until the answer came back less than an hour later. Thank God they weren't all in bed in Shipping Control H.Q. Larabee brought it up to the bridge himself and waved it at me. It was a long one and, in the form he'd received it, just a jumbled mass of coded letter groups. I frowned at him. 'You should be at your set, Larabee. There's blokes awake all over the ruddy ship right now for running messages.'

He grinned in the dim light of the wheelhouse. 'I jus' couldn't live a minute longer without seein' you, Mister Mate.'

I felt my nerve ends grate together like the jagged edges of a torn tin can, but I just grabbed the signal form out of his white, delicate operator's fingers and pushed past him to the ladder. Larabee and I, we'd said it all before and I was too anxious to know what hopes of salvation we had to pray for, hidden as it was in the untidy mass of code in my hand.

'You have the watch, Mister Shell,' I flung over my shoulder as I slid down the sloping handrails to the master's cabin, knocked on the door, then entered without waiting. As I closed the door behind me and pushed through the green black-out curtain I still felt Larabee's eyes somehow penetrating the thick cabin steel, digging and boring into my back. I shivered involuntarily, it was an eerie sensation, especially when connected with such a scruffy, unprepossessing little bastard. God, but my imagination was really extending itself this trip.

Evans was in the middle of an early morning shave as I entered his day room. He struck his head round the bathroom door and I held the signal form up to him while noticing, somewhat ironically, that he didn't always shave with his hat on, after all, and he wasn't in the nude this time either. He'd only been half-way through the operation but, right away, he came out of the little tiled area and wiped the flecks of lather from his face with a big, fluffy Company towel.

'In code, I hope?' he grunted through the enveloping white folds.

'Yessir,' I nodded. He grunted and, walking over to the master's small safe in the corner of the cabin, patted the pocket of his baggy shorts, pulled out a bunch of keys and opened it. While he brought the lead-covered code book over to the desk—lead-covered in case we had to ditch it quickly—I noticed his orange and blue life-jacket lying on the settee instead of gathering dust in its usual place under the bunk.

Did that make him a coward too? I remember my first captain watching me cynically during lifeboat drill in Singapore Roads many years ago. I was sweating and red-faced with embarrassment at struggling with the awkward cork things we had in those days. 'I feel such a fool, wearing this in a boat, Sir,' I'd muttered self-consciously. He'd grinned softly and, getting up from the tiller, had slipped into his own. 'You'd feel a bigger bloody fool without it, lad . . . in the water,' he'd answered.

No, Evans wasn't a coward. He just had good sense.

It took quite a long time for the Old Man to decode the signal and, when he threw the pencil down, he sat looking at it and frowning. 'What the . . .?' he muttered, then he shoved it across the desk towards me. When I'd read it, I had to agree with him—it seemed one of the craziest ideas the Admiralty had had to date, and that was really saying something.

I lifted my eyes and started back at the beginning in case I'd missed something important. But I hadn't. Our future orders, planned out like a game of chess by some uninvolved desk sailor with little wooden ships on a shiny white plotting-table five thousand miles away, were all there in the Old Man's spidery scrawl.

COMSAW TO COMCONVOY H 24 S: REPLY YOUR MESSAGE TIMED 0235 HRS 29 5: YOU WILL PROCEED QUICKEST ROUTE QUINTANILHA DE ALMEIDA ISLAND PER ADMIRALTY CHART NO. 1369ZB HEAVY ESCORT WILL RENDEZVOUS WITH YOU

ETA 1530 HRS 1 6 AT POSIT FIVE MILES DUE WEST OF ISLAND
UNTIL THEN YOU WILL WAIT REPEAT WAIT IN IMMEDIATE
AREA DESIGNATED YOU ARE ADVISED POSSIBILITY OF CON-
CEALED ANCHORAGE CENTRE QUINTANILHA DE ALMEIDA
LIMITED PILOTAGE INSTRUCTIONS AVAILABLE 1927 ISSUE
SOUTH AND WEST AFRICA NAVIGATOR BUT CAUTION NO RECENT
SURVEY DETAILS TO HAND WOULD STRONGLY ADVISE YOUR
ENTERING ANCHORAGE IF POSSIBLE BUT REQUEST YOU USE
OWN DISCRETION HOWEVER MASTERS CYCLOPS STROKE
ATHENIAN ARE ADVISED THEY ARE COMPLETELY ABSOLVED
RESPONSIBILITY FOR MISHAPS INCURRED SHOULD THEY
EXECUTE ABOVE SUGGESTION FINAL WARNING DO NOT REPEAT
DO NOT MAKE ANY FURTHER NORTHING OR WESTING YOUR
PRESENT POSITION DUE TO SUBSTANTIAL ENEMY SUBMARINE
ACTIVITY CONFIRMED THAT AREA GOOD LUCK AND GOOD
HIDING SIGNED TRYST REAR ADMIRAL END.

And that was that!

'Good God,' I whispered, starting to feel numb all over.

'Aye, you'll do well to flatter Him, John,' said the
Old Man slowly. ''Cause we'll be needing His presence
on the bridge pretty steady for the next three days.'

He pushed his chair back from the desk and walked
over to the bridge voice pipe hooked above the bunk.
'Send me down chart number 1369ZB please, Mister
Shell . . . And ask my tiger to bring coffee for two to my
cabin, will you?'

While we were waiting for the chart and coffee he
went over to the little bookshelf on the after bulkhead and
lifted down a heavy, red-bound volume. I glanced at it
as it lay on the desk—the ship's copy of the *South and
West Africa Navigator*. Then he flopped back in his chair
and looked at me. 'And precisely what does that signal
suggest to you, John?'

I pulled a face. 'It suggests we're going to have a
proper bloody sweat trying to keep out of the way of the
U-boats for the next eighty-four hours, for a start. *And* if
we can't get into that island the Navy talks about, then
we won't even have the advantage of being able to leave
the Hun behind. If we've got to cruise round waiting for
the new escorts then if they don't get us the first time we
pass they'll have plenty more chances before the afternoon
of the first of June.'

'You seem to be in sympathy with my own summing-up.'

'It'll be like driving a scheduled bus on a circular route past a homicidal maniac with a shotgun and a bloody timetable!' I affirmed emphatically.

Then the chart and the coffee arrived together and we sat in thoughtful silence as the Old Man's Chinese steward poured the coffee. I remember hoping apprehensively that, this time, the shiny silver pot wouldn't finish up on Evans's fancy Egyptian carpet while we finished up on the bridge . . . Or in the water! It was very warm in the cabin and my eyelids started to droop until I came round with a nasty, shivery start to find the tiger gone and the Captain immersed in the big book. I leaned forward and searched vainly for the sugar—damn! I'd forgotten we'd run out of that, too—while Evans ran his finger across the chart, then looked up.

'It's more like a bloody sixth-form history book than a navigational aid, this,' he muttered, then stabbed his finger irritably at the chart again. 'According to our three a.m. position the island lies roughly one twenty miles sou' sou' west of us . . . say about six hours' steaming.'

I glanced at my watch. 'Giving us an E.T.A. around 0930? We should pick it up about one bell in the Third Mate's watch.'

I drank the coffee and pulled another face as he tapped the open book with his knuckle. 'Did you know there was land that close to us? Before the signal, I mean?'

I nodded. I'd seen it often enough on the chart. In fact, on the small-scale projection it was often mistaken for a spot where someone had dropped their pencil point by mistake. 'I wouldn't really call it "land," though. More a spit of rock a couple of miles wide from the look of it on the chart. They say Tristan da Cunha isn't much more than that, and even it's a lot bigger.'

He seemed lost in thought for a few moments, then, lifting his eyes, he said, 'Well, John? What do you think we should do?'

I shrugged. 'We don't seem to have much choice, Sir. That signal doesn't leave any room for doubt. Presumably, they have a more accurate appreciation of the situation ahead of us . . . Though I still think it's bloody crazy to go right down there, farther south. As far as I can see, we're doing exactly what the enemy are trying to push us into.'

He got up and paced a few steps, then swung round. 'But we still have no *proof*, John. It's all assumption, everything. At least we have only another hundred odd miles to run doing it the Navy way, then we just wait around for the escorts. To me the risk seems very much less going for the island.'

I bowed to his decision, after all, he *was* the Captain. 'Aye, aye, Sir. But I still wouldn't like to put money on our chances, cruising round and round our own tails for three days. Maybe we ought to look at the pilotage instructions first, then decide if we can risk entering this anchorage the signal mentions?'

He picked up a pencil and bent over the chart, laying off a course to the tiny speck that marked the mysterious and, apparently, little-known island of Quintanilha de Almeida. 'Maybe we ought to get there first, eh, John?' he murmured softly.

Five minutes later he had blown Charlie Shell up on the voice pipe and given him the new heading. I guessed the Second Mate must have been beside himself with curiosity as he swung the ship through yet another sweeping turn and the compass settled back in its, by now, almost permanent state of southerliness.

Evans was reading his book, which suited me down to the deck. The chair was lovely and comfy and I didn't want to go back on the bridge. In actual fact it was still my watch below, but . . . the Old Man looked up from his reading. 'It's interesting that you should have compared the two, John.'

I blinked, 'Sir?'

'Tristan da Cunha with this . . . er . . . Quintanilha Island. Tristan was actually discovered by a Portuguese Admiral in 1506, a voyager called Tristao da Cunha, believe it or not. There are four islands, or groups of islands actually—Tristan itself, Nightingale, Gough and a cheery-sounding place called Inaccessible. Or did you know already?'

I didn't as it so happened, and now I did I still wasn't

much better off as far as I could see. I'd heard somewhere that people lived on Tristan, but anyone with an inclination to maroon themselves on a rock in the middle of the South Atlantic came well outside my sphere of understanding.

But then again, perhaps to the Tristan Islanders the idea of steaming around the ocean aimlessly butting at invisible barriers and going nowhere fast, may have had its macabre side. Hell—not only to the bloody islanders! And presumably, like us, the black teeth which marked Tristan formed the only legacies of an earlier submarine cataclysm. So were we really any different then?

The Old Man seemed to have relaxed considerably now that the responsibility for our next move was lifted from his shoulders, so I just poured myself another coffee, searched forgetfully for the non-existent sugar, then sat back and let him ramble on. 'Yes, well, apparently, when Almirante da Cunha finished discovering the Tristan Group which, incidentally, we British annexed in 1816 . . .'

'A good old sovereign tradition!' I murmured, not really listening too hard.

'. . . the admiral sailed on south, presumably giving the Cape a wide berth. In doing so he came across another island. He described it in his log as a "Bleak, inhospitable hoof of stone at first sight, and extending to some two and one half thousand hectares, but of value to the mariner by reason of its central lake, affording as it does a protection from the tempests met in the great sea around".'

He looked up and I jumped self-consciously. The comfort of the chair had finally overwhelmed me and I could feel great waves of lassitude blurring my mind. After no sleep for three days other than a few hastily stolen cat naps, I could well have spent this time more profitably in my bunk.

'Yeah? But does it say if that . . . that Quintel place affords protection from the U-boats met in the great seas around?' I inquired guiltily.

The grey eyes stared at me suspiciously from under the bushy brows. 'Quintanilha de Almeida,' he grunted finally. 'The admiral ran out of his own names by that time so he called it after his sailing master and dear friend, Almeida.'

'A nice, easy-to-remember name, Sir,' I ventured, trying to appear interested.

'And nice, easy-to-remember pilotage instructions too, seeing there aren't more than a couple of sentences of them.'

I sat up as he carried on. This *was* important. If we could find a way into that 'Central lake' of the old admiral's, then we'd be a damn' sight safer than swanning around in a permanent orbit of the island like a giant-sized German Navy torpedo range target. I leaned over to look at the chart again but it wasn't of much help, all it showed was an irregular blob shaped rather like a small-case letter 'd' with a tiny gap where the top of the circle didn't quite return to the vertical stem. This, presumably, was the entrance.

'Quintanilha has never been inhabited since its discovery,' Evans frowned, 'and apart from occasional visits from before she could despatch the results of her survey to the eighteenth century, has very seldom been landed on, or examined. It was surveyed by a Royal Navy ship, H.M.S. *Cilicia*, in 1868 . . .'

'Good God. That was the year before the Suez Canal was opened,' I murmured, snatching at a long-forgotten splinter of school memory.

'. . . which was, however, wrecked off Madagascar before she could despatch the results of her survey to the Admiralty.' He glared up at me in angry frustration. 'Silly bastards!'

'So we're not much better off now than we were before, Sir?'

He looked doubtful. 'It says that, while none of the *Cilicia*'s officers were saved from the wreck, some of her ratings survived and, according to statements from them, "It appears that a passage into the central anchorage is clear to ships with a draught of up to some twelve feet—this being the survey vessel's draught at the time of her entering—and navigators so doing are advised to keep well to the larboard side of the rocky fault forming the opening, but are further warned that an almost vertical submerged shelf, or reef, prevents direct access to the enclosed waters and necessitates a sudden turn to starboard just after the vessel's counter clears the inner periphery of the natural breakwater thus formed".'

'And that's all we have to go on?'

He nodded. 'Unless you're interested in the fact that the last recorded persons to land on Quintanilha de Almeida were the survivors of the German *Keil-Sud Afrika Linie* steamer *Darmstadt* in 1903? And they got fed up with waiting for no one to call so, after four months of living on seabirds' eggs and rainwater, seven men left again in a fifteen-foot boat. Two of them were still alive when they reached Africa.'

'Sounds like a bustling, friendly little place,' I muttered, trying to sound optimistic.

He closed the book with a snap. 'Let's hope like hell it's not. Bustling places might be bustling with the wrong kind of people.'

'Do you intend to try for the anchorage, Sir?'

The Old Man levered himself out of his chair and paced slowly up and down, hands clasped behind his back. 'I don't know. We don't have much practical information, just a lot of bloody silly history. And what we do have doesn't make me any keener to try.'

'At least we know the Royal Navy man went in.'

'Aye, with a twelve-foot draught . . . What was our mark when we sailed, John?'

'Twenty-eight feet, Sir.'

He turned the corners of his mouth down sourly. 'So where's the help in that? And another thing, they apparently made a sudden turn to starboard just when their stern cleared the inner rocks of the entrance. In those days, seventy years ago, she'd have been a big boat if she was three hundred feet long . . . we're what? Four eighty overall?'

I nodded and got stiffly to my feet. I needed a shower and a shave before I went on watch. 'So we'll be feeling our way in completely blind, Sir?'

He smiled fractionally and, for a fleeting moment, I got the impression he was actually looking forward to it. 'If I decide to go in at all, Mister Kent, we'll feel our way in as thoroughly as a virgin with his first lay.'

We picked up the island as I'd predicted—at about 8.40 in the morning watch. The low cloud had disintegrated under the onslaught of the sun's return, and already it was getting hot. To be on the safe side I'd posted a mast-head lookout an hour before our E.T.A. as well as a man up in the eyes of the ship. The Captain was already on the bridge, standing in the chartroom wading through a pile of breakfast sandwiches, when the call floated down from aloft, 'Laaaand fine on the starb'd bow!'

I hadn't bothered going below for breakfast, eating was a habit I seemed to be rapidly giving up. Maybe it was just nerves but, as soon as I saw food, I stopped feeling hungry and settled for a cup of coffee.

The Fourth Mate had stayed up on the bridge too, so the three of us, Brannigan, Curtis and myself, hung over the fore-end and allowed the cool draught to swamp over us as we watched the island grow, hazy and shimmering in the heat-distorted atmosphere at first, then slowly becoming more black and solid as we approached.

Occasionally I glanced aft to watch *Athenian* ploughing stolidly along just to the right of our, for a change, ruler-straight wake. Once a brief flash from her bridge showed that someone was laying their binoculars on the island and I wondered if it was Bill Henderson. Maybe, with luck, if we went in and anchored I would get the oppor-tunity for a chat with him. That was the trouble with being at sea, though we passed each other almost invari-ably twice a trip—once outward and once homeward-bound—very seldom did we actually have the chance to meet one another except through the medium of a hasty Aldis stutter.

Still, she looked good, did *Athenian*, with the high flare of her bows raising a sparkling hump of blue water as she cut through the glassy sea astern. One thing we'd been lucky in so far was the weather. Or had we? A force nine gale was uncomfortable but, at the same time, it dis-couraged U-boat activity. There was a snag in everything when you were at war.

Evans stepped out of the chartroom, brushing crumbs from the front of his barrel chest, and came and stood beside us. Curtis and Brannigan moved discreetly away, but I gestured to the Third Mate as he disappeared into the wheelhouse. 'Have Breedie go aft with the stand-by quartermaster and bring in the log, Mister Curtis.'

We were almost there, time to get the crowd moving to their stations. I pulled my whistle out of my pocket and glanced inquiringly at the Old Man. 'Blow stand by, Sir?'

He nodded, so, stepping to the after-end, I blew one long blast, then moved back beside Evans to watch as the anchor party ambled forward and climbed the ladders at the break of the foc'sle. The Old Man cupped his hands and leaned over the dodger. 'Make both cables ready, Chippie!' he roared, then, turning back to me, 'We'll let go the starboard anchor, Mister, but I want you ready with your other hook if necessary.'

'Aye, aye, Sir.'

I glanced at my watch. It was just coming up to two bells and we were less than three miles off the land now. It looked bleak and forbidding, bigger than I'd really expected, but somehow unfriendly with the oily sea breaking sullenly at the base of the near vertical cliffs. At first glance it appeared there was snow lying on the rocky outcrops, but it was only guano, acrid bird deposits left by generation upon generation of the seabirds that wheeled eternally above, hovering and swooping in the slight upcurrents of air from the black cliff faces. I shivered slightly and started to feel cold even though the steel of the well deck was now shimmering in the heat.

'I'll get down forr'ad then,' I said unenthusiastically.

Evans lifted the binoculars, searching for the entrance so much depended on. He spoke without lowering them. 'You have someone in the chains, Mister Kent?'

'The Bosun,' I answered, leaning out over the wing and looking almost vertically down on the small platform that had been lowered into place for the leadsman. Maybe, one day, we would get one of the new echo-sounding machines the Navy had, similar to their Asdic equipment, where you just listened into a headphone and heard the vibrations being returned to indicate the depth of the sea bed. I didn't think we would for a long time yet, though— things like that were far too fancy for merchantmen.

Evans lowered the binoculars and pulled a face. 'I can't see anything that looks like a passage yet. Mister Curtis!'

The Third Mate came out of the wheelhouse, 'Sir?'

'Will you stand by the telegraphs, Mister Curtis? And

ask the engine room to stand to on the platform and reduce to twelve knots if you would be so good.'

Curtis went on the engine room phone and I heard him telling them to stand by down below. Evans grinned unexpectedly at me and chuckled. 'Quite a change from picking up a wog pilot and letting him take you into a place prickling with buoys and navigation marks, eh, John?'

I smiled back uncertainly. Personally I preferred the less romantic approach to seafaring but . . . I realised that the old devil was in his element. 'Absolved responsibility for mishaps,' the Admiralty signal had said, and both Evans and Bert Samson on _Athenian_ were just the kind of bloody-minded old dogs to take their freedom from Board of Trade consequences in the strictest spirit. If there was a passage into Quintanilha de Almeida just one inch wider than our beam, then we were in. Then all we had to do was get out again when the Navy arrived.

I turned back at the top of the ladder, struck by a sudden thought. 'What about _Athenian_? Is she going to be right on our tail when we go in?'

Evans chewed his bottom lip. 'Better not. If we go aground or get into trouble she'd never be able to pull astern in time . . . Mister Brannigan. Get the Aldis out here if you please, and the Very pistol from the chartroom.'

Brannigan looked surprised for a moment, probably thinking it was a bit early to start sending distress calls before we even smelt the land, then the Captain helped to ease his mind a bit. 'Send to _Athenian_ . . . ANCHORAGE AND ENTRANCE APPARENTLY OBSCURED FROM SEAWARD SUGGEST YOU ZIG-ZAG ROUND PRESENT POSITION WHILE I FEEL MY WAY IN IF SUCCESSFUL WILL SIGNAL YOU TO FOLLOW WITH TWO RED FLARES REPEAT TWO REDS IF NOT WILL ATTEMPT LAND BOAT PARTY TO COMMUNICATE FROM TOP OF CLIFFS SIGNED EVANS MASTER.

The reply came quickly back from Bert. ACKNOWLEDGE BUT DISAPPOINTED YOU DON'T ALLOW PROPER SAILORS FIRST CRACK BEST OF LUCK SIGNED SAMSON MASTER.

We were less than a mile off the old admiral's island now and I could feel the tension building up around me on the bridge. The only man who seemed at ease was the

Captain himself, but I could see the grey eyes probing keenly for the first signs of a break in the looming rock ahead. I knew I should have been on my way forward to my station in the bows, but I didn't want to leave before I had to. Something—some comforting aura of competency—seemed to exude from the stolid bulk of Evans which helped to compensate for my uneasiness.

Then, suddenly, it was time to go whatever I felt like. We knew there was deep water right up to the base of the cliffs, the chart had told us that at least, so we hadn't slowed all that much until we had to. Five cables, half a mile, and the Old man said quietly, 'Slow speed, Mister Curtis.'

The throbbing under the deck died away to a barely perceptible murmur and the bows fell slightly as they adjusted the engine governors below. The exhaust note from the funnel softened to a muted whisper and we seemed to be gliding through the still water. For the second time I said reluctantly, 'Well, I'll get off forr'ad, Sir.'

Evans was still standing, hands behind his back, staring ahead. Without turning he said, 'Take Brannigan with you, John. The water should be fairly clear as the ground shoals . . . Keep a good lookout under the bow if you can. Don't forget, the Bosun with his lead is a good distance aft from where you are. He could still be getting a fair depth of water while the forefoot goes aground on that shelf the book talks about.'

I jerked my head at the hovering Brannigan. 'Aye, aye, Sir. We'll sing out if we have to.'

Sliding down the ladder with the Fourth Mate at my heels, I saw Charlie Shell and his crowd aft at their standby stations on the poop. The army bombardier, Allen, and his gun crew, looking very spruce now in khaki shirts and shorts, stood jealously round the long-snouted Phyllis, almost as if they half expected Charlie to steal it when they weren't looking. He might have done, too, if the damned thing hadn't been bolted to the deck.

The Old Man leaned over the after-end of the bridge. 'Ask the Bosun to start soundings as soon as he can, please, Mister Kent.'

I noticed how the Red Ensign drooped listlessly from

our stern as the telegraphs jangled for 'Dead slow ahead.'

Quintanilha de Almeida Island looked even more soulless when seen at close range.

From my station up in the bow, thirty feet above the slowly moving water, I watched apprehensively as the black cliffs loomed closer. The entrance was plain now, just a jagged slash in the rocks, veering slightly to port at first, then with a gradual sheer to starboard, almost like the opening to a small Norwegian fiord. Approximately one hundred feet wide at what appeared to be its narrowest point some two hundred and fifty feet ahead . . . So far, so good. Our beam was sixty-two so we didn't run any risk of jamming like a wedge in a crack. All we had to worry about was the depth of water under our keel. Brannigan and I craned over, staring tautly down into the still dark-green water. Below me the huge starboard anchor hung, almost brushing the surface, ready to let go at the first shout from the bridge.

The Bosun had started to find bottom almost as soon as our bow nosed into the space between the two seaward promontories. I could hear his throaty voice calling the sounding every few moments as he leaned well out against the chains and, with a beautifully controlled swing of the heavy lead, sent it snaking out to splash in the water well ahead of his perch. As the ship passed the point where the line stood vertically, he dunked it up and down to make sure it was bottoming properly and started to haul it in, coiling it in his horny left hand as he went.

It was a piece of white linen just touching the surface this time and, 'By the mark . . . fifteen,' sang the Bosun, reading and sounding from the material spliced into the line—cabalistic symbols of leather with a hole in it, or a twist of red bunting or blue serge or white linen, identical in every respect to that ritual tool used by the sealers visiting this island so long ago.

Then another mighty swing, the flutter of white farther above the surface this time, and the gravelly voice booming, 'And a half . . . thirteen.' Thirteen and a half fathoms, just about eighty feet of water, say fifty actually below our keel, but shoaling fast and with the narrowest point still a good two hundred feet ahead of our bow.

And still green, frightening water under the forefoot. Suddenly, without warning, the scene darkened as though a shutter had been drawn. I looked up, startled, to see that the high black cliffs had blanked off the sun completely. I saw Brannigan shiver and rub his forearms—when a deep-sea sailorman gets that close to land, then it's time to pray.

None of us spoke, standing there nervously on the foc'sle head. I could see the sailors staring silently up at the hanging, guano-layered rocks above us. Once, when I risked a sharp glance too, I caught an unsettling vision of myriads of cold, beady eyes glowering back as the seabirds resentfully watched us sliding below their domain. Ahead, a tempting glimpse of blue water and clear sun-slashed sky framed in the macabre irregularity of the channel buttresses.

We were hugging the left-hand side now, keeping so close to the slime-covered rocks that you felt you could almost stretch out a hand and pick yourself a bunch of seaweed. A glint from the high bridge made me turn in time to see the braided cap of the Old Man as he stood isolated on the port wing.

'By the mark . . . seven.'

God! Forty-two feet, and we were drawing twenty-eight.

What kind of bottom was it? Maybe there were massive spikes of rock projecting upwards through the green water, reaching hungrily for our double bottoms this very second —lethal weapons undetectable by the Bosun's lead before the deck leaped and we swung broadside to smash finally and irrevocably against the vast clubs of stone that awaited us.

The jangle of the telegraphs seemed very loud, even at this distance, funnelled as it was down to us through the gorge. 'Stop engines!' Almost immediately the faint tremor under the deck faded and we slid, now completely silent, towards the blessed light ahead.

'By the deep . . . six.'

'Jesus!' Brannigan whispered.

I couldn't even whisper, my mouth was too dry. Six fathoms . . . we needed nearly five to float us.

What was that . . .? Yes, there were dark, dim shapes

moving slowly aft under our bow. The bottom. Oh, please God, make them go away, make them sink back down into the anonymity of deep water. I felt the flakes of rust spearing into my fingertips as I convulsively clenched at the black-painted rail. I swung round to scream aft at the flat, white cap on the bridge. To warn him . . .

'And a quarter . . . seven.'

Forty-four feet? Wait! The shapes had gone . . . and only seventy feet to the beckoning sunlight. I wanted to look ahead, to see what we were about to come out to, but I couldn't. I couldn't drag my eyes away from the still water under our slicing foot.

'By the deep . . . six.'

Shoalling again, but not too fast. We were nearly through. Forty feet to go. I glanced up momentarily. Sparkling, twinkling blue water and, behind? Sandy beaches yellow warm sand. Please . . .

'And a quarter less . . . seven.'

Only a spit to the big, black rock that seemed to mark the inner extremity of the entrance . . . and then we were looking down on it as the bright sunlight burst violently on to the foc'slehead again. Sunlight. Beautiful sunlight. A quick vision of a wide, welcoming sea loch surrounded by high, sheltering land, then the Old Man's voice booming down from the bridge, 'Mister Kent.'

I waved my arms back, feeling the hot fingers of the sun in my hair. The voice echoed again. 'Remember the rock shelf, Mister Kent!'

I swung round. Hell, I'd nearly forgotten the anticipated swing to starboard. Or was it to port? Keep looking, keep staring desperately into the suddenly clear water below. Brannigan was hanging over beside me with most of the crowd, showing a row of tight, blue-jeaned backsides as they, too, craned over the rails.

We were hardly moving at all now. Just drifting forward through the water fast enough to raise a little splurge of flashing glass round the rust-streaked and battered stem . . . battered where we'd knifed into, and through, the unsuspecting *Mallard* a million years ago. What was it the book had said? A sharp turn just as the after-end of the long-dead survey-ship's counter had cleared the inner-most periphery of the entrance? But Evans had said she

E

could only have been about three hundred feet long af the
most. We wouldn't have more than two-thirds of the ship's
length clear at that.

The forward break of the centrecastle was sliding past
the big rock now, the shadow of the bridge cutting across
the water towards it. We must be two hundred feet into
the lagoon already. A sudden dark shape to port. The
shelf? I felt the sweat trickling down the side of my nose
as the shadow—distorted and wavering under the crystal
clarity of the water—drew frenetically away. A giant Atlantic Manta ray. So that was the end of any ideas I might have
had about a quick swim off that golden beach.

'By the deep . . . eight.'

More depth under us. Good, maybe the book was wrong.
Slow, very slow . . . There's nothing ahead. We were
almost stopped now, have to give her a turn on the screw
or we'll lose steerage way completely. but Evans was
being careful, very careful. I couldn't even see the giant
rock now, it must have slid well aft. Thank you for being
good to . . .

'Good God Almighty!' Brannigan suddenly shouted,
drawing back involuntarily.

Then I drew back too as I saw deep down into the water
twenty feet from our already splintered forefoot. A great,
black, evil wall of stone rising sheer to a point just below
the surface . . . a solid, impenetrable barrier of nightmare
outcrops, the whole mass seeming to move gently under
its obscene growth of marine plants.

I whirled round with frantically cupped hands, retain-
ing a never-to-be-forgotten mental imprint of tiny, gaily
coloured fish nosing in and out of the floating fronds.
'Shelf dead ahead! The shelf . . .'

The Old Man's hand went up in an almost casual
acknowledgement, then immediately I heard the telegraphs jangle in the wheelhouse. Through the windows I
could see the quartermaster bending over the spinning
wheel as he gave her full helm, then the steel deck started
to bounce and throb under the power of our twin screws.
I knew right away what Evans was doing, the shaking
judder under my feet told me. Slow ahead port engine,
slow astern starboard. The shuddering grew more and
more violent as, terribly slowly, we started to swing.

Was our stern clear aft, or would the flashing screws strike the tail end of the submarine hazards of the entrance and disintegrate into spinning shards of phosphor-bronze scrap?

'By the mark . . . seven.' Oh, that bloody, phlegmatic old Bosun.

It was all rock and blackness under us now . . . Christ, we were on to it! The bow jumped under our feet and we braced ourselves for the shock. Almost stopped though. The plate below us screamed as the great bows ground into the weed-skirted stone, crushing and boring. I closed my eyes and listened to the ship's agony, while Brannigan kept on thumping at the steel rail, on and on and on, as Evans had done that time we ran the corvette down.

The water round the bows was cloudy now, the crystal purity contaminated by tons of ground pumice as we slowly swung to starboard. I ventured a glance aft. Evans still stood out there on the wing, unmoving and unflustered. The swing increased and the submarine grinding and splintering faltered, then stopped. Brannigan and I leaned well out. Yes! The flared steel below was broadsiding into clear, deep water. The Fourth Mate grinned idiotically at me in excited relief, while the sailors at the rail slapped each other on the back and swore as if they'd just found some new words. I forced myself to walk nonchalantly aft to the break of the foc'sle, feeling my legs tremble under me, and waved again to the solitary little figure above.

'All clear forr'ad, Sir!' I yelled, then, turning, made like a bucko mate again. 'Stop that bloody row there! . . . Chippie, stand by to let go starboard. All hands abaft the windlass.'

From the bridge came the jangle of the telegraphs again. 'Stop starboard engine.' The shuddering cut immediately, then the bells again, 'Dead slow ahead both engines,' and we steadied on a heading for the far end of the lake.

The Third Mate came out of the wheelhouse. I heard a soft cough and a red flare soared high into the royal blue sky to burst with a distant plop and a fuzzy puff of grey smoke. Then another went up to hang beside it.

And we'd arrived at Quintanilha de Almeida.

CHAPTER SEVEN

Bill Henderson met me at the top of *Athenian*'s accommodation ladder as I ran up from the waiting motor lifeboat we'd lowered to act as a ship-to-ship tender for the
next three days.

We shook hands, then just gazed at each other for a
few moments, grinning like idiots. He looked just as sun-
bronzed and fit as ever, did Bill, standing there in immaculate whites with his cap shoved jauntily on the back
of his head and the three tarnished gold straps of his
epaulettes sitting saltily on the broad shoulders.

Then he pretended to punch me and said, 'Come over
for a few lessons in ship-keeping then, John?'

I glanced round the spotless decks with an exaggerated
expression of distaste. 'Nope! Just thought maybe you'd
have a lot of problems you'd be too embarrassed to *ask*
me to solve for you.'

We laughed and climbed the ladders, identical in every
respect to *Cyclops*, to the boat deck and master's quarters
below the bridge. As we went I glanced around at the
island of Quintanilha de Almeida again. Probably about
four miles long by some two and a half wide. It wasn't
really so much an island as a natural funk hole from our
viewpoint, situated as we were at the extreme western end
of the deep-water lake, well away from the entrance.
Behind us the black cliffs dropped sheer into the water,
as they did on our adjacent sides but, almost two miles
away on the other side of the channel, the sun glinted on
the warm sand of the beach which I'd noticed as we
performed our gate-crash act. I'd rather fancied dropping
the hook there but the Old Man had said 'No.' He
wanted to stay as far away from the shallow ground as
possible in case the wind got up and backed farther to the
left as is normal in the southern hemisphere.

We planned to land a lookout party the next morning
to watch for any signs of seaward activity, enemy or otherwise—not that we could have done much about it, penned

in as we were by the protective, or imprisoning, natural breakwater around. I had the uncomfortable feeling that we were now more in affinity with the remote islanders of Tristan da Cunha, that this place too was the freak result of some long-forgotten disturbance underwater and that we were actually anchored in the maw of an enormous submarine volcano, thrust to the surface perhaps a million years before.

I hesitated a moment before the burnt-out carcase of the radio room, and Bill gestured to where our own shell had gone in, a great jagged gash in the thick steel plating. 'Who in God's name would want to do a hellish thing like that, John?'

I shook my head bitterly and told him as much as I knew. I could see he was as baffled as we were but he didn't look disapproving as he might have done under the circumstances. He just glanced at the mess of tortured steel and incinerated wireless equipment and said softly, 'Poor bastards never knew what hit them.'

I bit my lip, imagining what it must have been like. One minute everything quiet and dark with the ship ploughing steadily on its track, then a banshee scream out of the blackness and a holocaust of super-heated steel shards exploding through jetting white flames and frying, disintegrating corpses. 'What about the cadet who was killed, Bill? How come he was around this part of the ship at that time in the morning?'

'Mike Simpson,' Bill stubbed viciously at a blob of molten metal with the toe of his deck shoe, and I could see my question had shaken him badly. 'He was in my watch, John. I thought he looked kind of peaky so I was a good bloke and sent him down to the halfdeck for an extra smoke. The fuggin' bastard shell took his bloody head clean off as he went aft, past here.'

I gazed at the rusty smears on the charred wooden deck and felt sick. I'd tried to be decent like that to young Conway so I could imagine what Bill must be thinking. He moved away forward and I followed as he spoke over his shoulder. 'It was Mike's first trip. He was an only son. Doesn't the name ring a bell with you?'

I frowned. 'Simpson? No, should it?'

He stopped and turned in front of the cabin door that

said 'Master' on its little brass plate. 'His dad was chief engineer of *Hesperia*.'

Hesperia? Eric Clint's dead ship . . . Oh, Christ, the bloody war again, breaking up the happy family. Now a mother with both husband and son in the Company service, and both gone along with Big Eric and old Tom Everett. The bloody, bloody war!

Little Bert Samson stood up and held out his hand as we went in, taking our caps off. The hard little eyes weighed me up from under eyebrows that could have been a twin set with Evans's bushy growths. As soon as I stepped forward I could feel the dynamic personality exuding from the skinny, diminutive frame. The gruff, contrasting voice was exactly as I'd remembered it. 'Well, Mister Kent, and how are things aboard *Cyclops*?'

The hand gripped me firmly as we shook. 'Very well, thank you, Sir. Captain Evans sends his compliments and apologies for not visiting himself, but he feels he should stay aboard the ship under the circumstances. He's sure you'll understand.'

Bert waved to a chair behind me and smiled, letting the withered skin crinkle up surprisingly round the corners of the obstinate mouth. 'Aye? I can't say I'm really surprised after him bringing us into a bloody rat trap like this.'

I shrugged deferentially. 'The only alternative was to run the risk of chasing each other's tails for the next three days, Captain. If there *are* U-boats in this area they'd have thought it was Christmas.'

'And if they see us in here, or watched us squeeze through the entrance, then we're already gift-boxed and ready for collection, Mister.'

The bushy protrusions rose again. I could see that, despite first impressions, he was in one of his bloody-minded moods, so I tried to duck out gracefully. 'The Admiralty signal did advise us to attempt an entrance if at all possible . . . Sir.'

'Did you query it?' Sharp and cutting.

Bill shifted uncomfortably next to me as I answered, 'No, Sir. We wanted to keep radio transmissions to a minimum. The longer we emit traffic the better chance the enemy has of getting a D.F. fix on us.'

'You still should've queried it. Three bloody days without an escort . . . it's unreasonable.'

I could maybe have added that the whole goddam war was unreasonable, but I was over here to explain the details, not get involved in an inter-ship debate on the rights and wrongs of conforming to what were, in Samson's opinion anyway, ill-advised instructions. So I just nodded and said, 'Yessir.'

But he wasn't going to be pacified that easily. The withered old mouth turned down petulantly. '*No*, Sir, Mister Kent. I just about lost my bloody screws with that goddamned sheer to starboard as we came in. And how the hell do we get out, anyway? One touch of the props on that shelf and we're here till the brass goes rusty.'

I felt Bill grinning sardonically but didn't dare risk a grin back. We both knew that Bert Samson was as capable of taking *Athenian* out of Quintanilha as the average bloke is of getting his car out of the garage in the morning, but Bert was Bert. I tried to look subdued and solicitous. 'We thought . . . er, with *Cyclops* that is of course . . . that we might run a line ashore from our inside bow to hold her, then heave her stern round with a wire from the starboard quarter to the opposite knuckle of the channel. Sir. Then we wouldn't have to turn the shafts as she swung round against the shelf.'

Of course he knew that perfectly well, but he was laying the doggedness on thick this time. Perhaps this war of nerves was penetrating even his armour-plated skin. He stabbed a bony finger at the air around. 'That may be all right for *Cyclops*, Mister. For some reason you seem to be the star turn in this act. But then—you're not carrying ammunition, are you?'

I stared at him. No one ever told me anything. And he'd brought *Athenian* through that cleft without even turning one of the few hairs he'd got left. Did Evans know? Somehow I didn't think so, or he'd never have made the decision to come in here without consultation in the first place. But that was bloody typical of Bert Samson as well. Do it first, then moan like hell about it for the next six months.

Bill confirmed the news solemnly. 'Numbers two, three

and five holds, John. General cargo for Adelaide, then sea mines, cased grenades and ball ammunition for Sydney. Twelve hundred tons, roughly.'

I swallowed and suddenly felt a lot happier about being on *Cyclops*. If a torpedo hit us, all we could do was sink. If *Athenian* caught one, they'd be flying. Penetrating Quintanilha was, for us, the lesser of two evils, but for Bill Henderson and Bert Samson it was a deadly risk, scraping twelve hundred tons of high-explosive over those clutching shapes that had risen so terrifyingly towards me from the dark green water. I shivered, and that old bastard Samson grinned slyly. He had made his point.

'Perhaps you would be good enough to tell me why this farce is so necessary, Mister Kent?' he said, slightly mellowed. 'Please remember that restrictions on communications between our two vessels have, to this moment, prevented me from doing anything other than what I have been told. From now on, however, perhaps I may be considered as an equal partner? Along with my dear friend and colleague, Captain Evans.'

The sarcasm bit now. I didn't mind, though. The Old Man had given me complete freedom to tell Samson about our cargo in the *Cyclops*'s strong-room—not only the currency consignment but also the secret bags—and to explain as best I could why we were content to wait for an escort rather than try to run the blockade alone. They listened intently as I went on to say that, while we suspected an enemy plan to force us farther south, there was no real proof and we had decided to follow the distant Admiral Tryst's instructions accordingly.

When I'd finished Samson sat back in his chair and chewed pensively at his thin underlip. I watched and hoped he wasn't going to get all bloody-minded and independent again. Finally, he glanced at Bill and then at me. 'So your only reasons for suspecting an enemy plot were the angle of attack from the two U-boats and those bloody fireworks we saw ahead of us? Oh, plus the possibility that they might have been trying for the escort that time rather than what should normally have been their primary targets . . . us?'

I nodded, as he continued, 'On the other hand, you had certain proof of enemy activity *between* us and the

Cape through that message from the *Kent Star* . . . which couldn't have had any bearing on plots imagined or otherwise.'

I frowned. There was that strange, warning tinkle in my mind as soon as Samson mentioned the *Kent Star*. What *was* it that worried me? What was so unsettling about the name . . . the *Kent Star*? Kent? John Kent . . .? Here I was again on the vicious, negative circle that had kept recurring in my head since poor old Foley had brought that distress call to me on the bridge.

Bill was frowning inquiringly at me, 'What's wrong, John?'

'I don't quite know, Bill. It's just . . . Oh, probably nothing in it anyway.'

Samson leaned forward over his desk. 'If you have any doubts, Mister, then perhaps you'll be good enough to bring them to my attention.'

I looked at the little captain.

'I honestly don't know, sir,' I muttered.

The bony knuckles tapped the walnut desk top impatiently. 'Listen to me, Mister Kent. And you too, William. The whole conduct of this voyage has been based on assumptions regarding the disposition of the enemy in this area. Every time we have seen a sign of other activity we have scuttled away, usually farther south, with the utmost expedition. Am I correct so far?'

We both nodded obediently as he continued. 'Very well. Now, Mister Kent has a theory that we are unwittingly conforming to some, as yet obscure, plan of the enemy's to shepherd us into this immediate area . . .'

'But I've no *proof* that such an intention exists, Sir,' I broke in anxiously. 'Just a few lights in the night that seemed to be ahead of us whichever way we altered . . . except south.'

Samson looked at me probingly. 'Aye? And because the bloody Navy said to do the same thing we're here, in this rat trap. Now!'

Bill scratched his head uncomfortably. 'But, Sir . . . As John's just said—there's no evidence to show that we aren't doing the sensible thing. The lights were fact, after all, and the *Kent Star* sinking was fact. Solid, undeniable fact.'

The wrinkled brows clamped together in a frown. 'Oh aye? But *were* they, Mister?'

Bill and I looked at each other blankly. I was starting to get irritated but Bill couldn't even afford that luxury in front of Bert. What, in Heaven's name, was Samson getting at? He must have seen the glances passing between us.

'Mister Kent.' The stabbing finger was aimed at me like a loaded gun.

'Sir?'

'Let us assume, for the moment, that there is some rational explanation for the occurrences which took place aboard *Cyclops*. I refer, of course, to the inexplicable disappearance of your Chief Wireless Operator . . . er . . . Foley, and that shot at us from your stern chaser . . .' He held a warning hand up as he saw me opening my mouth. 'Wait, Mister. I don't propose to enlarge on that at this moment, I merely mention it in passing. Now— for the purpose of hypothesis—we shall forget them. Right?'

Dutiful, bored chorus, 'Aye, aye, Sir.'

'Which leaves us with the extraneous incidents only to analyse. The actual reasons for our coming here.' He was really getting into his stride now. I just wished Evans had come over himself and left me aboard *Cyclops*. Bert Samson in one of his analytical moods was more than I could face right then.

He started ticking off the facts on a skeletal hand. 'One —the *Kent Star* distress call. Two—the sinking, from the coastal side, of the Frog boat. Three—them buggers wi' their illuminations. Four—yon U-boat you were lucky enough to sink, Mister Kent. (The bushy eyes challenged me to take him up on that but I let it go.) And five, gentlemen, the orders from an admiral five thousand miles away.'

He sat back and stared at us penetratingly. We didn't say anything because neither of us could see what he was trying to prove. With a sigh and the patience of an elementary schoolmaster, he proceeded: 'Number five we can discount seeing the signal came from the Grey Funnel Line and they're supposed to be on our side. Numbers two to four inclusive could be attributed to purely coincidental enemy activity. What I mean is that those incidents in themselves could have happened to any ship at any time and do *not*, on their own, prove any ulterior motive. Do you still agree, both of you?'

I was beginning to catch up at last, 'Yes, Sir.'

He poised, ready for the Great Deduction. This was Bert in full cry. 'Which leaves us, therefore, with number one—the *Kent Star* call. The only factor which involves a . . . a third party. The only incident, prior to the Admiralty orders themselves, which is assumed to have a *British* source.'

He swivelled round to me. 'Do you see *now* why I consider the authenticity of the call from the *Kent Star* a matter of vital importance, Mister? Do you?'

And I did, too. The whole thing revolved round the garbled message poor old Foley had picked up from the allegedly sinking freighter. If its origin was genuine and my doubts about it unfounded, then we had probably done the right thing in coming to Quintanilha de Almeida. If, on the other hand, it was a fake . . . Samson saw the shock dawning in my face and nodded surprisingly gently. 'Aye, John. If the call from that ship of yours was bogus— then we've run just the way whoever put it out wants us to, and that means the bloody Hun.'

'And that, in its turn, means they could be right outside the entrance at this moment, Captain. Just waiting for us,' I muttered, feeling very, very frightened.

'With the best part of three days to go before the Navy arrives,' Bill summed up succinctly.

I tried to sound more optimistic. 'We could put a signal out to Admiralty, Sir? To request confirmation of the *Kent Star* sinking? You could give it to your Sparks right . . .' My voice trailed off as I remembered the twisted, superheated steel coffin on the after-end of the boat deck.

Bert Samson shook his head. 'This is something you'll have to decide after a discussion with David Evans, John. We must all discuss it. As you said earlier—even a short W.T. transmission could give them a fix and home them on to us.'

He pushed his chair back and stood up, gazing out of the port for a long time. The shrunken body looked even more pathetic in tropical rig, like an undersized boy in his first set of cricket whites. I wondered how he managed to radiate such energy. Then he turned to face us and I saw how intense his eyes were. 'No, gentlemen. We're atween the Devil and the deep blue sea. If we go out we may run smack into a wolf pack. If we stay in, then the enemy could be heading this way as we stand speaking . . .'

There was a knock on the cabin door. A signal from *Cyclops* . . . CAN I HAVE MY CHIEF OFFICER BACK QUERY HE'S NOT MUCH BUT HE'S MINE SIGNED EVANS MASTER.

Bert broke off, looking a bit frustrated, but he still accompanied me out to the boat deck and shook hands. As I turned to walk away, back to the boat with Bill, he smiled unexpectedly and said, 'Tell yon Comconvoy of yours I'll splice a bottle or two with him first night back in the shadow of the Liver Building, Mister.'

I grinned back and nodded. Mister . . . Mister Kent . . . Kent Star . . . Oh, to hell with it. Maybe I wouldn't have the opportunity to see Bill for a long . . . I stopped dead in my tracks. The Liver Building? Liverpool docks? I remembered them the last night before we sailed, the night the mysterious vans had arrived laden with boxes of currency and bags of top secret information. Standing there on the wet deck and seeing the relief on the faces of the two naval officers who delivered the cargo for the strong-room. Standing there and feeling the rain trickle down my collar as I stared miserably across the black, oily waters of the basin to where a newly arrived freighter was still making fast, laden to her marks with war cargo. Standing there feeling the sadness of a pre-sailing hour and idly noting the name on her bows, the name that made me take a silly, paternal interest in her because it was the same as mine . . . The *Kent Star* . . .

Kent Star? . . . Jesus! . . . The *Kent Star*!

I swung round with a terrible urgency. 'That "S" call was a phoney . . . The *Kent Star couldn't* have been in this area two days ago.'

Samson glanced at Bill, then back to me, 'Why, Mister?'

'Because I've remembered now where I'd seen the name before. She was berthing across the dock from us just before we sailed, loaded to her marks. They'd have taken three weeks to clear that lot out of her . . .'

The luxuriant eyebrows met ferociously. 'You're sure it was the *Kent Star*?'

I nodded emphatically, 'I'm certain of it, Captain.'

He didn't waste a moment. Half turning to Bill he spoke tightly. 'Ring "Stand by" on the telegraphs, Mister Henderson. Get the hands to stations immediately and test the steering gear. And a leadsman in the chains. I'll need a slip wire ready starboard side bow and have the Second Mate prepare a manilla for paying out over the port quarter.'

Bill was already moving, 'Aye, aye, Sir.'

'And when you weigh anchor don't screw the windlass up tight, Mister, I may need it again in an emergency. We'll need a boat in the water to tend the shore lines while we snub her round the corner.'

'You can leave that, Sir. I'll send the *Cyclops*'s boat ahead to serve both ships then we can hoist her inboard on the seaward side of the entrance,' I broke in.

He nodded. 'Thank you, Mister Kent.'

I hesitated for a moment. 'You intend to leave immediately then, Sir?'

Samson smiled sourly. 'You're very quick to catch up, Mister. Aye, *Athenian*'s going out whatever happens. We'll take our chances at twenty knots in the open sea. If *Cyclops* wants to wait here like a shrimp in a keep net that's up to you and David Evans, but I've got twelve hundred tons of explosives aboard that says bugger the Admiralty, and I'm not giving the U-boats any more time to get in position to pick us off as we come out of that entrance at dead slow speed.'

I glanced at my watch. 5.15 p.m., and we came in about 9.30 in the morning. 'If we're right in our assumptions, Sir—that they know we're in here, I mean—then it may be too late already. They'll have had over seven hours to set us up as it is.'

The little figure turned away to the bridge ladder, then stopped. 'Aye, Mister Kent. So if you hear a big bang from the other end of the channel you'll know to be careful, won't you?'

He swung away without another word and started to climb the ladder as casually as if he was going up to meet the pilot for an ordinary harbour manœuvre. I watched him go, feeling the sick clutch of apprehension back in my belly, then a piercing blast made me jerk round. Bill was standing there with the stand-by whistle dangling from his hand. He smiled softly and punched me gently on the shoulder. 'Staying aboard to finish the trip with real sailors, John?'

I forced a grin. 'I would if there were any on this old tin can of yours, Mate.'

We stood there awkwardly for a moment. We'd seen a lot together, Bill and I . . . and big Eric. But Eric was already gone from the family, floating face down with his hair waving gently in the green water. I shuddered. It was an image I was seeing too often for peace of mind.

Bill stuck his brown hand out. 'Time and tide, y'know . . . See you in Cape Town, John.'

I took it and squeezed. 'We'll wait for you to catch up, Bill. And . . . keep a weather eye open on the way, huh?'

Then he was gone and I was alone beside the obscene, gutted shell of the radio room. Time to go, chum. Like Bill said, time, tide and U-boats wait for no man. The gruff voice from the bridge stopped me momentarily. 'I'll run east and west till you come out, Mister Kent. Then I intend to zig-zag for the Cape even if I have to run right over the bastards. Tell Captain Evans I'll be obliged to have his company on the way.'

I waved in reply, then slid down the ladder. I knew Bert was needled about the 'Comconvoy' messages from Evans, this was his way of soothing his ruffled pride. For the rest of the trip *Cyclops* could accompany *Athenian*, but he was sailing independently anyway. Stuff the Admiralty, the German Navy, the Board of Trade *and* the Cabinet— Samson was sailing today.

The faces that met me at the top of the accommodation ladder were composed of baffled curiosity and subdued excitement. Glancing forward along the alleyway towards the foc'slehead, I could see Bill Henderson moving among the anchor party as the windlass turned slowly, heaving the heavy cable short in preparation for weighing on a signal from the bridge.

As soon as we had stepped off the platform into the boat, *Athenian*'s young Fourth Mate raised a hand in parting salute and the ladder rose jerkily while two A.B.s waited to lash it along the rails, ready for sea. I glanced at my watch again. 5.40. The U-boats had now been given eight hours to prepare.

It seemed to take a very long time to cross the water between the two ships.

The Old Man was waiting impatiently for me at the top of our own ladder as I ran up it, noting automatically that the rust streaks had started to blister the grey-painted surface of the hull. A pity about losing these three days— I could have had the Bosun's crowd over the side first thing in the morning, chipping and slapping on a new coat. Ship painting was the bane of my life, it was like living on the Forth Bridge—no sooner did you have everything shiny and Bristol fashion than you had to start all over again at the other end.

'Perhaps you would be good enough to explain just what that silly bugger Samson thinks he's doing, Mister Kent,' Evans demanded petulantly, his eyes fixed curiously on the busily moving figures on *Athenian*'s decks.

I swallowed. It was like trying to negotiate a friendly agreement between Churchill and Hitler, only more difficult. 'Perhaps we could go up to the bridge, Sir?' I muttered, noticing the eager stares from the gangway quartermaster.

Faintly across the water carried the distant tinkle as they tested the telegraphs while, on *Athenian*'s poop, we could see the khaki shapes as her gun's crew closed up. Samson wasn't leaving any more to chance than he had to. The Old Man watched a moment longer, then turned away sharply. 'Aye, Mister Kent. Maybe we'd better at that.'

It took only a few minutes to convince him too, though I could see he didn't like Bert Samson taking the initiative. As soon as he was satisfied that the *Kent Star* message had been a deliberate fake, he didn't waste any time in analysing our, or the Navy's, mistakes.

'Blow stand-by please, Mister Kent. Have the accommodation ladder brought inboard and tell the Fourth Mate to take the boat away down to the entrance to tend the lines. We'll pick him up outside the channel.'

I looked at my watch for the tenth time. Just on six

o'clock. Please God, I know I ask for a lot for a bloke who doesn't really believe, but I promise I will if you get us out of here in time. I hauled my whistle out of my pocket and blew a long blast, then turned to the ladder and nearly collided with Larabee as he came flying up it.

I stopped dead, stunned by the expression on the Second Sparks's thin features, too surprised even to be nasty about his unseemly haste and the fact that he should have been aft with his bodyguard and his wireless sets.

'*Athenian*'s going out, Mate,' he snarled accusingly, almost as if he were scared of something.

I glanced quickly round for the Old Man's support, but he'd gone into the wheelhouse. Then the telegraphs clanged as the engine room went on stand-by and I turned back to face Larabee. 'So are we, Sparks . . . which means you'd better get back to your set, doesn't it?'

The usually sardonic eyes were disturbed as they stared past me to where the clank of *Athenian*'s cable could be heard over the windlass. I turned and saw it was almost up and down, the heavy links leading very slightly forward from the hawse pipe. Her hook was nearly off the bottom and a sailor was leaning well over the flare of the bow, washing down the incoming cable with a high-pressure hose. Streams of cascading, muddy-coloured water disturbed the otherwise placid surface around her forefoot.

'Get back aft, Larabee,' I repeated irritably. 'We'll explain it to you when there's time. Until then, keep off the bridge.'

He stared uncomprehendingly at me for a moment, then shook his head fiercely. 'Not me, Kent! I'm not goin' out there again before the Navy gets here. We know the bloody sea's blistering with U-boats between here and the Cape . . .'

I gripped his shoulder roughly to pull him away from the top of the ladder. The bones moved under the thin shirt as though they were only covered by a skin of tissue paper. 'We're sailing just as soon as I get forr'ad, Larabee, but as far as I'm concerned you can stay as long as you like. The Fourth Mate can put you ashore with a bastard axe and a box of matches and we'll pick you up when the bloody war's over.'

I swung round sharply at the sound of Evans's voice

behind me, crisp and irritated. 'What the Devil's going on here, Mister?'

The Old Man was standing with one foot still in the wheelhouse doorway. Larabee cut in before I could speak. 'I say we should stop here till the Navy arrives, Captain.'

The bushy eyebrows met in an arc of surprise, top dead centre in the beefy red face. 'You say . . . Larabee? As the Master of this vessel *I* shall take any decisions I think fit to ensure her safety. Do you hear me, Mister Larabee?'

What the hell was up with the wireless operator? No one, not even a chief officer, stood on a master's bridge and told him what to do. I dug him in the ribs and jerked my head aft encouragingly. 'Come on, man. *Athenian*'s got no radio . . . If she's hit going through the entrance we'll need to get a message out bloody quick.'

I couldn't have said a worse thing. His face went as white as a sheet and the thin lips pulled back to show paradoxically firm, well-formed teeth. 'Not till the fuggin' Navy gets here, Mate. No bloody madman's going to make me stick my neck out of this bay.'

I stared apprehensively at Evans. What Larabee had said amounted to little short of mutiny—rank refusal to obey a lawful command. I can't say I felt sorry about it, in fact under rather different circumstances I would probably have taken a sadistic delight in watching the outcome, in seeing Larabee collecting what had been due to him since the start of this God-forsaken trip. But right then we had to get out fast.

Bill Henderson's arm went into the air in a signal from *Athenian*'s foc'sle. A palm held sideways and slashed up and down—they were clear of the ground. Then her telegraph tinkled faintly again and a splurge of white water under her counter showed she was under way, starting to move slowly through the water. The Red Ensign that, a moment before, had hung listlessly over her stern gave a slight flap, then another. The sparkle of water rose a few inches higher under her bow. She was going out.

By now the Old Man's brows had inverted into a ferocious V so that the grey eyes were almost lost behind the overhanging bristle. He looked as though he was going to have an apoplectic stroke and I tensed for the blast as he waved his hands angrily at Larabee.

Then, without warning, the hand froze in mid air and the red face went a different colour as he focused on a point past Larabee and myself. He stood like that for a long time, not moving, and when he did finally speak the voice was much quieter than I'd prepared for.

'The point at issue appears no longer to exist, Mister Larabee,' he said, so low that we could hardly hear him.

The frozen hand pointed behind us, over towards the entrance. 'The Navy *has* arrived.'

CHAPTER EIGHT

The first lean shape slid slowly into the inland sea from the cover of the entrance channel, then a second followed right astern. Long, low silhouettes seen as they were from almost two miles away, out past the bulk of the slowly moving *Athenian*. We watched in silence as the first warship seemed suddenly to telescope in length, then I realised she was swinging towards us, helm hard over to anticipate that waiting shelf, almost as if she already knew of its existence. Behind me I heard Evans draw a long, hissing breath. He was right. The Navy *had* arrived.

Except that it was the wrong Navy!

'Oh, hell!' I whispered, as we both grabbed for the binocular box. At the top of the ladder, Larabee stood unmoving, staring at the submarines as they steadied on a course to bring them up to our anchorage. I felt the dull bruise of pain as the eyepiece of the Barr and Strouds came up against the bony protrusion of my eyebrows, then forgot all about it again as the focusing wheel spun the ships into stark clarity. Two German Atlantic class ocean-going U-boats, still glistening with a varnish of seawater after their recent submerged passage. There were men on their casings, too, closed up round the wicked looking 4.1 inch guns on the narrow foredecks while, right in the bows, the serrated net cutters projected evilly like shark's teeth from the stems.

Someone said 'Bugger it!' in a shocked voice behind me and, swinging round, I saw we'd been joined by Curtis

and Brannigan. Then Charlie Shell came whistling cheerily up the ladder, took one incredulous look past *Athenian*,
shouted 'Christ Almighty!' at the top of his voice, and
tumbled back down the ladder to the boat deck en route
for his beloved gun on the poop.

The Old Man pushed past me to the after end of the
bridge and shouted after him, 'Mister Shell.'

The Second Mate skidded to a halt and swivelled back
nervously, ignoring his cap which had fallen off his head.
'Sir? Those are U-boats, Sir? I'd better get . . .'

Evans's voice was flat and emphatic. 'You will make no
move to man the gun until I give you an order, Mister
Shell.'

Charlie just stared at him in disbelief. 'But . . . they're
U-boats for Chrissake . . .'

We looked tensely at the Captain. This wasn't like him,
not even to attempt to fight. They had guns, all right, but
so did we and ours were bigger than theirs. He didn't keep
us in suspense long. 'You will have the gun crew assemble
under the break of the poop, Mister Shell, out of sight of
the enemy. No one is to be seen making any move to
attend the gun platform unless I send you a direct order
or they actually open fire on the ship. Do you understand?'

Shell stood looking very white for a moment, then kicked
his cap viciously, sending it high into the air to clear
the rails. This wasn't the Old Man's day for unquestioning
obedience. I hoped he wasn't going to forget the main issue
for the sake of having a go at the Second Mate but, to
my relief, Charlie gritted, 'Aye, aye, Sir,' through his
teeth and trailed disconsolately aft.

Evans turned back to me, looking grim. 'The bastards
are heading straight for us, Mister. If we make any attempt to fire on them they could put four torpedoes into
each of us just by pulling a lever. If we can wait till they
swing away even a couple of points, then we may possibly
have a chance.'

I had difficulty in suppressing the note of relief in my
voice. Over Evans's shoulder I caught a glimpse of Curtis
staring expressionlessly at the submarines . . . Or was it a
trace of relief I could detect in his brown eyes too? And,
if it was, did that mean he was a coward as well? Or
something deeper? I made like a frustrated martyr. 'Does

that mean we do nothing, Sir? Not a bloody thing?'

The Old Man seemed to sag for a moment, then he squared his shoulders and shook his head determinedly. 'No, by God it doesn't. But there are more than sixty men aboard this vessel. I don't intend to throw their lives away over a pointless gesture of defiance. Mister Curtis.'

The Third Mate blinked, 'Sir?'

'You will have all deck hands and any engine-room personnel not urgently required below assemble along the port side of the midships accommodation. Life jackets will be worn. If there is any gunfire they'll stand a better chance down there, away from the enemy.'

I heard the Third Mate clattering down the ladder behind me as I turned to take another look at the U-boats. The last one in appeared to have stopped behind to guard the entrance but the lead boat was much closer now, still bows on to us and about one and a half miles away. It was almost possible, through the binoculars, to see the blurred faces of her crewmen grouped around the deck gun. A movement on the conning tower of the leading submarine caught my attention and I felt my hands starting to shake—the bastards were rigging a heavy machine-gun in a mounting on the grey painted rails forward of the one-pounder A.A. gun. I started to lower the Barr and Strouds to quiet the growing acidity of despair in my belly. Then I froze. *Athenian*! What the . . .?

She was still moving, yawing round towards the exit channel as if the approaching U-boats didn't exist. I suddenly realised that only a very short time had passed since the long, predatory silhouettes had first appeared. But still . . . Samson had had plenty of time to stop engines and put the hook down again. The white water was kicking up high under her stern now as it swung towards us, showing the bright Red Ensign flapping more actively over her taffrail. When in God's name was Bert going to stop her?

Larabee found his voice at last and I glanced round in surprise as the thin features looked queryingly at the Old Man. 'I'll get out a distress call, Captain?'

I could see Evans was struggling with indecision. Whatever the U-boats intended they wouldn't relish our screaming for help while they were boxed in this bloody deathtrap of an island along with us. And Larabee? Now he was acting the hero again. Why? Where was the mutinous radioman of a few minutes before? The man who had refused point blank to venture out into the open sea was now volunteering to go to almost certain death in a steel box that was a one-off shot for any experienced gunner aboard the enemy vessel. I found myself unconsciously shaking my head as Larabee spoke again, the now animated face looking as keen as mustard on the chance to be a posthumous hero. 'I'll get aft to the shack, Captain. Put out an "all ships" call before they realise I'm on the key at all.'

The submarine was closing fast now. I felt the tension mounting on the sun-washed bridge. What was Evans going to do? I started to get sick spasms with fright. One bleep from our W.T. could bring the smashing fury of white-hot shells crashing into our superstructure, atomising the radio room and bridge. The bridge . . . where we were all standing. The primary target. I closed my eyes as I anticipated the shrieking hell of oblivion that would come. Please Captain. Please. Don't let Larabee be a martyr. Not when it means he'll have company.

Brannigan's excited voice cut through my fear. 'They're signalling, Sir! The nearest boat.'

We watched as the bright beam of her lamp flickered from the conning tower. Out of the corner of my eye I was dimly aware that *Athenian* was still moving but, right then, I was more anxious to know what those submarine wolves had in store for us. Behind me the now calm tones of the Second Sparks read out the slowly stuttered message. 'It's in English. More or less anyway . . . ACHTUNG . . . REMAIN WHERE YOU ARE . . . VESSEL UNDER WAY WILL STOP YOUR ENGINES IMMEDIATELY . . . DO NOT ATTEMPT TO TRANSMIT WITH WIRELESS BOTH SHIPS . . . GUN PLATFORMS MUST BE ABANDONED IMMEDIATELY . . .'

Someone seemed to be shouting down aft and I looked to see the distant figure of the Second Mate gesticulating vigorously at the dumpier shape of our army Bombardier, Allen. Apparently the gun commander wasn't taking too kindly to the idea of our giving up without even a bang from Phyllis. Then, to my relief, they both moved away under the shelter of the poop and I could concentrate on Larabee's voice again.

The tone was still flat and matter of fact. '. . . YOU ARE WARNED THAT NOT TO CONFORM WITH MY ORDERS IS VERBOTEN . . . I REPEAT ANY SHIP ISSUING WT TRANSMISSION OR ATTENDING ARMAMENTS WILL BE FIRED ON . . .' 'Mister Kent.'

I swung round startled, until I realised the Captain was speaking. He continued, without taking his eyes off the closing U-boat, 'A word with you, please.'

Turning abruptly he walked towards the wheelhouse, out of earshot of Larabee and Brannigan. I followed nervously, not liking to lose sight of the approaching guns even for a brief moment. When Evans stopped, his voice was low and urgent. 'The confidential bags, John.'

'I could get forr'ad to the strong-room and try to ditch them over the side,' I suggested, not feeling at all brave but having to make the gesture.

He shook his head. 'No good. Why do you think those U-boats are here? This is a deliberate trap, John, and we've run right into it like a flock of bloody sheep. Even the blasted Admiralty helped with their orders to shelter in here. My God, but if I didn't know any different I'd think that they *wanted* us to be captured.'

It was beginning to fit together now. Ever since I'd found that the *Kent Star* message was a phoney the pieces of the jigsaw had slowly been knitting together. First, the firm establishment of intent to drive us south, towards Quintanilha de Almeida, and then our own blind stupidity in not realising that we were penning ourselves in the one spot in almost the whole of the South Atlantic where we didn't have the advantage of speed over the U-boats. The one area where they could board and search us at their leisure instead of having to settle for a quick kill at sea along with the inevitable loss of the papers.

I prayed that Rear Admiral Tryst, R.N., would rot screaming in Hell. His orders had been the one, final clincher that not even the most optimistic member of the Nazi High Command could have hoped for.

Evans was peering down at the glassy water around us and I realised then what he'd meant by it being useless to jettison the bags over the wall. Only eight fathoms below the surface the wavering sea bed showed every detail as clearly as through a magnifying glass. Beautiful fronds of

varicoloured weed waved gently over the submarine con-
tours of the boulder-strewn bottom while myriads of tiny
fish darted all around like shooting stars. Any object
lying down there would be as obvious as a sequined dress
in a shop window—and just about as available to any
navy diver.

'We could try to burn them, Sir,' I muttered, racking
my brains desperately for ideas.

'We don't have enough time, John. And a lot of the
stuff will be in book form. Have you ever tried to burn
books? We could never be sure they were sufficiently
destroyed to be indecipherable, especially the centre pages
and down the spines. And another thing. If that *is* what
they're after, what do you think they'll do when they see
smoke?'

I could guess—Bang! So what the blazes were we going
to do about saving all those other ships that were depend-
ing on us? I shivered at the obvious thought, to send a
signal out to the Admiralty advising them of our capture
which would at least render them useless to the enemy
too. A trickle of sweat ran into my eye, making me blink
painfully. I couldn't bring myself to suggest committing
suicide. Maybe Larabee had found a hitherto dormant
source of courage but the sight of those wicked shapes
bearing down on us had made me lose any pretensions I'd
ever had to be a hero.

And then I said it anyway, hating myself all the time
for being such a goddamned fool. 'We have to get a
signal out, Sir. The Navy's got to know what's happened.'

He smiled grimly for a moment at my obvious lack of
enthusiasm. 'Don't be in too much of a sacrificial hurry,
John. You'll finish the war as a P.O.W. At least it's better
than being a name on a war memorial, I suppose. You've
forgotten that, in the event of no signal at all being received from us, the Admiralty will assume we've been
captured anyway. All we're surrendering is time . . . and
the *Cyclops*.'

I looked at him in relief, mixed with concern at the look
of defeat on the lined, tired face.

Then everything happened at once, and the real horror
had started.

Evans's eyes had strayed back towards the entrance and

suddenly he stiffened incredulously. I whirled round fast, then stood and stared along the line of the Old Man's gaze. I was barely aware of Evans's voice, even gruffer than before with the shock of disbelief. 'My God, John. What in hell's he trying to *do*?'

Athenian had veered right round on a direct heading for the entrance and the approaching U-boats. The white water under her overhanging stern had now increased to a boiling maelstrom streaming well astern of her while the blue-tinged diesel fumes from her tall funnel jetted high in the clear evening sky. Aft on her poop under the now wind-torn Ensign her gun crew were moving feverishly to traverse the antiquated 4.7—Phyllis's sister—as far forward as it could bear for the safety stops designed to prevent them from blowing their own bridge and funnel off in the excitement of battle. Swinging it to bear at the first opportunity on the enemy submarine closing on them and masked, at present, from their view by the centrecastle superstructure. She was already roughly midway between us and the leading Nazi, about three quarters of a mile each way, but the steadily increasing throb of her giant engines and the constant splash of her cooling discharges carried clearly through the enveloping silence of Quintanilha.

The Old Man said again, 'What in God's name's Bert trying to do?'

I knew, because I knew Bert Samson. I knew that defiant, bloody-minded individualist like I knew my own father. So did Evans but maybe he was too scared to say it out loud. We didn't speak again as we stood and watched the beautiful ship with the tension building up to screaming point inside us. Watched as she vibrated with the agony of being forced up to full speed under wide open valves, watched as the rushing wall of water built steadily higher and higher under the great, knife bows. The bows? Was Bill Henderson still up there in the eyes of the ship or had Bert had the mercy to call them aft, away from where they wouldn't stand a dog's chance if she hit. Suddenly I knew something else. I was never going to see Bill again. Drowned Eric would, though. Yeah, maybe big Eric Clint would, if there was a place where chief officers went when . . .

Larabee threw out an arm and shouted with a sort of taut excitement, not hushed and reverential as I'd have expected from a man witnessing the opening act of such a vast, Romanesque tragedy. 'Look! . . . The bastards are calling her.'

The lead U-boat was still in sight from where we lay, the signal light from her conning tower flickered urgently and menacingly, STOP YOUR ENGINES IMMEDIATELY OR I FIRE . . . STOP . . . STOP . . . STOP. Then, almost without pause, the big casing gun on the U-boat's foredeck boomed viciously, the smash of the distant shot echoing reverberatingly round the black cliffs of the anchorage.

They must have been temporarily unnerved on the German's deck because the first shell went wide of *Athenian* and I watched in terrified fascination as it literally skipped across the water towards us like a flat stone on a pond until, less than three cables from our starboard side, it detonated in a climbing fountain of yellow water that momentarily obscured the other combatants.

Then, crazily, I heard a great cheer from aft and swivelled round in time to see Charlie Shell and the army gunners swarming up the ladders towards the lonely Phyllis, snout still pointing dejectedly astern. 'Christ!' I screamed at Evans. 'They've taken that shot as a bloody excuse to fight.'

The beefy red face grinned back at me savagely. 'Well, Mister Kent? Do you want *Athenian*'s crowd to corner all the glory on that war memorial, dammit?'

I stared at him in bewilderment as he wiped the spray from his cheeks. Slowly I became aware of the madness that was growing around me. The Fourth Mate was taking his second turn to pulverise the teak rail of the bridge as he yelled in frustrated excitement, 'What can I do to help for Chrissake? . . . Oh, what the hell can I do to get back at the sods?'

Our gun was traversing now, veering round black and hungry as the fat little Bombardier crouched over the traverse handles with eyes glued to the sighting telescope. 'On! . . . On! . . . On! . . .' he was screaming while the ready-use ammo flashed in the sunlight as the soldiers worked feverishly behind the breech. A bony hand gripped my shoulder painfully and I was looking into Larabee's eyes, gleaming with some inner emotion.

'I'll get a signal out now, Mate,' he shouted, 'before anyone can . . .'

And a tremendous explosion from across the water stopped the hysteria dead as we saw *Athenian*'s funnel sail slowly high into the air like an empty toilet roll, then plummet with terrible accuracy on to the figures round the gun on her poop. When the unrecognisable mass finally rolled over her stern to fall with a colossal gout of foam into the boiling water of her wake the men had gone, the gun had gone . . . and our own fury had gone.

Evans acted immediately and grabbed the megaphone from the rack, aiming it towards the poop. 'Mister Shell . . . you have *not* received any orders to fire. You will clear the gun deck immediately, do you understand? Clear the gun area immediately!'

He didn't even wait to see if his orders were being obeyed, just turned back to me with that tired look on his face again and nodded sadly towards the still racing *Athenian*. 'I'm sorry, John. I was wrong. It's just . . . Perhaps Bert Samson out there sees his responsibilities in a different way to me.'

Less than four cables between *Athenian* and the first submarine now. The end was very near. Suddenly I realised that Bert Samson had no intentions of running for it, he could never have hoped to manœuvre round that deadly corner at the entrance at anything more than dead slow speed, controlled with the precision of a ballet dancer. Evans was right—no master was justified in throwing lives away so stupidly. Not unless . . .

Three cables left and both U-boats firing fast by now. From where we watched the damage wasn't easily apparent, as we could only see the after-end of her upperworks but she was on fire forward somewhere, the thick black smoke billowing aft over her bridge and superstructure and tumbling to the water to lie like some monstrous funeral shroud above the surface, hardly stirring with the complete absence of natural wind.

I dragged the binoculars up to apprehensive eyes for a last look and saw the port wing of her bridge disintegrate into a spinning scatter of torn wood and steel plates, then another shell burst right in her fore, lowermasthead and the whole topmast keeled over to avalanche down on to her forward hatch covers. She wasn't beautiful any more, now. Just a hurtling, ravaged shape under the command of a little, stubborn, angry old man.

'She's going to try to ram,' I muttered, almost to myself.

Evans stood very still beside me and I could hear his heavy breathing even over the sounds of gunfire. 'You old bugger, Bert,' he was whispering softly. 'You'll never make it. The bastards will slip out of your way before you can get there.'

I shook my head. 'They can't go all that far. Not with that shelf there, they can't.'

Almost on the lead boat now. Oh God! And I was right the submerged shelf ran right along, almost parallel with the screening cliffs, leaving little room even for those slender cigar-shapes to take avoiding action. All the same, the Commander of the first sub must have had nerves of stressed steel as he conned his ship into the most advantageous position to meet the looming bulk of the crazily careering, burning British freighter. I watched as if hypnotized while the slim hull pointed almost straight at *Athenian*'s slicing bow, two vessels end to end, one carrying twelve hundred tons of high-explosive cargo, the other laden with some of the most devastating weapons in the world—torpedoes.

Evans choked. 'God, but he'll never catch that boat . . . Not while she stays on that heading. It's too narrow a target, John. Bert'll lose sight of her under the flare of the bow . . .'

I didn't answer because the pain in my throat was too intense as I watched *Athenian* slowly breaking up into flaming, anonymous splinters. Maybe Bill was already dead, or crying with terror in some corner of the deck. Then I thought back to that old Petty Officer as he worked steadily over the depth-charges on the sinking *Mallard*'s after-part and I knew that, whatever else he was doing, Bill wasn't hiding. He was of the same mould as Bert Samson and Evans and Charlie Shell back there.

Then *Athenian* was right over the U-boat and we could see the gunnery ratings lying flat along her black, glistening casing, gripping desperately to the nearest handhold as they waited for the end while, high in her conning tower, a peaked white cap was inverted to judge the exact moment to act, to manœuvre for salvation. Just waiting coolly for the critical few seconds when his ship would be hidden from *Athenian*'s bridge. My God, but that U-boat commander must have been one hell of a man.

Then the moment came and the white cap bobbed sharply. A splurge of white behind the pointed stern and the submarine nosed slightly to port, then a quick helm correction to bring her exactly in line with *Athenian*'s axis again and her bow was rising swiftly, relentlessly, on the swollen belly of water surging ahead of the merchantman. Up, up, up rose the black cigar with the men glued fly-like to her decks, then slipping farther to port, away from *Athenian*'s seeking stem . . . and the huge, grey hull was slashing past with the white cap still staring up at the looming, torn bridge.

Someone behind me drew a shuddering, sobbing breath while the eyepiece of my binoculars grew suddenly opaque as a trickle of sweat ran into it from my brow. By the time I'd fumbled to wipe it off, Evans was saying in a shocked voice. 'They're clear, John. They're clear of Bert. The poor old devil's missed.'

But the most macabre incident of all occurred as I brought the glasses back to my eyes. While *Athenian*'s bridge was still sliding past the enemy submarine a diminutive figure appeared, leaning out over the still intact starboard wing. I saw Bert Samson—it could only have been Bert—either shake, or wave, a fist at the figure in the conning tower sixty feet below him, and then—with his own sailors still pinned to the deck in the attitudes of crucifixion—that calculating, white-capped man coolly raised an answering arm in a mockery of the Hitler salute. Then *Athenian* was past and the U-boat was left shaking herself viciously in the boiling water of her frustrated adversary's wake.

Still afloat, and still as lethal as ever.

As if to prove it her gunners scrambled to their feet and, almost before the stern of *Athenian* was clear, the foredeck gun slammed again and another column of dirty water rose, obscenely weed-flecked, from a point less than a cable's length from our bow while, at the same time, the one-pounder on the low platform at the rear of the German's conning tower opened up with a monotonous pom-pom of fire. We could see the ripples of flame sparkling as the light shells burst haphazardly among the lifeboats and ventilators on the after end of *Athenian*'s centrecastle. Those U-boat men were as tough and methodical as automatons, and about as merciful.

Evans muttered, 'She's signalling again, damn their eyes.'

The lamp bleeped from the U-boat's tower as casually as though *Athenian*, still less than two cables past her, had been a train running through a suburban station. YOU HAVE A CONVENIENT LENGTH FOR TORPEDOES CYCLOPS . . . TAKE MY SHOT AS A WARNING . . . ACKNOWLEDGE YOUR SURRENDER BY VISUAL MEANS ONLY . . . IMMEDIATE.

We looked at each other in utter defeat while all the time the rumbling thunder of the disintegrating but still driving *Athenian* continued to drift across the green and blue water. Only God knew how many men were already dead aboard her . . . Please make it stop now. And Bert? Was he torn to bloody tatters on his sacrosanct bridge, conscious only of failure in his last subborn moments of life? And Bill, my friend of many years of roaming the seas . . . Was he with big Eric yet? When was the once beautiful, proud ship going to die herself? The fires must be eating well down into her innards now, down to the tons of explosive in her belly, fanned into a howling fury by the wind of her last passage . . . When would she go . . .?

Evans said sickly, 'Mister Brannigan . . . Acknowledge.'

No one spoke as Brannigan slowly lifted the Aldis to his shoulder. He didn't grip the trigger for a moment, just turned and looked appealingly at Evans—then the U-boat spat again and another gout of water climbed in the air so close under our bow that tons of yellow putrescence smashed back down on our foc'slehead and cascaded through the scuppers with a malevolent hiss into the iridescent sea below. Everyone ducked nervously except the Old Man, but he just stood there gazing at his contemporary's funeral pyre with a look of terrible weariness and gritted, more bitterly this time, 'I said acknowledge, Mister Brannigan. Or do you want to kill more men just as bloody pointlessly?'

The Aldis clacked sharply and I saw the white cap on the U-boat nod, then the boat surged forward towards us leaving a trail of bubbles astern while the big foredeck gun traversed on an unwavering line dead centre with our bridge. She was about half a mile from us when Larabee suddenly grabbed the rail and pointed out past her to the now distant *Athenian*. 'Keerist, Captain, but she's got the other pig-boat right under her bow!'

Then everything was sick, hysterical excitement on the bridge again as we forgot about the closing menace to ourselves and watched the last act in the mammoth tragedy. Even through the binoculars it was difficult to see for the pall of oily, dead smoke that blanketed the far end of the anchorage but I could just make out the blazing bulk of our sister as she fast approached the entrance through which we had so carefully manœuvred. Then someone hit me on the shoulder and screamed in my ear, 'The second U-boat . . . Jesus, but she's broadside on in the channel. Bert's goin' to stamp right over her . . .'

I peered desperately through the smoke. Yes! . . . there she was. The other submarine. They'd been waiting to cover the entrance as *Athenian* started her mad rush but then, when they saw the great ship running amok, the German commander had tried to turn his boat too late and too hurriedly. Now she was stuck fast with the pointed bows dug into that underwater shelf and her whole length exposed to the approaching knife of *Athenian*'s cutwater, after nearly two miles of a run working up to maybe fifteen knots and still relentlessly increasing as her engineers remained grimly below, responsive only to the telegraphed commands from what must have been a blind skeleton of a bridge.

Evans was sobbing as he gripped his Barr and Strouds so that the knuckles stood out bleached white against the brown skin of his hands. So was I, so was Brannigan. Maybe even Larabee was at that moment because he was strangely quiet after his earlier shout. Then the Old Man whispered, 'I'll give Sheila your love, Bert . . . You bloody-minded, mad old bugger!'

And *Athenian* was climbing up and up, over the black hull below, driving on into the slender conning tower and forcing the whole length of the U-boat ahead of her like a mad dog with a bone in its teeth, unable to stop running to inevitable death.

I saw the cigar hull rolling over and over as it was hurled beam on through the water by *Athenian*'s weight and the two ships, locked together in a Herculean embrace, drove monstrously towards the beach at the far end of the inland sea. That beach, all beautiful and golden, which I'd seen as we first entered.

Someone was screaming a flood of foulness from our after decks but I couldn't take my eyes from the two convulsing ships as *Athenian*, driving under full power, finally pulverised her enemy into the shallows and kept on going up and over and on to the sparkling sand, blazing from end to end . . . driving and tearing with the unholy shriek of tortured metal filling the whole island lake as she tore the bottom right out of herself. Her mast toppled forward into the unrecognisable torment of fire, but even then, she kept on rising unbelievably out of the blood-red water until we saw the flashing, spinning discs of her great phosphor-bronze propellers carving twin canyons deep into the once pretty beach.

Even the cold white cap in the remaining U-boat's conning tower was turned to watch in fascinated horror while the deformity that had been our sister ship came finally to rest. The sounds of her breaking up died away to a muted roar from the white-hot flames eating deeper and deeper into her holds and the black smoke stopped streaming aft and, instead, rose vertically sullen into the clear blue of the evening sky.

And I knew for sure that Bill was dead, like Eric, and Bert Samson and all the rest of *Athenian*'s crowd. All slowly cremating in a twelve thousand ton oven . . .

Then she blew up.

The first explosion, forward of what had been her bridge structure, threw debris and giant pieces of ship high into the air; then the chain reaction followed as, hold by hold, she disintegrated into a million flying, whirling fragments while detonation after detonation fused into one long, ear-smashing roar.

I watched with a curiously cold, almost clinical interest, as the whole of the midships centrecastle rose slowly two hundred feet into the air and fell back into the holocaust, breaking into great slabs of twisted steel. The surface of the lake rose in boiling splurges of foam for a mile towards us as hissing fragments ripped into it like semi-molten meteors.

And then the blast.

Cyclops heeled twenty degrees to port as the first shock waves hit us, fanning out across the anchorage with super-sonic speed. I felt her snub at the anchor cable under the invisible pressure, then we were swinging crazily with some-thing booming against our exposed sides time and time again and the blast catching every unwary man to hurl him backwards, away from the rails, with a contemptuous arrogance. High above the wheelhouse I glimpsed the wooden sides of the monkey island buckle, then whirl away to port, carrying Charlie Shell's little white-painted submarine with them. Then I was lying flat on my back on the deck watching stupidly as the once boisterous, ebullient Fourth Mate took off over the prostrated bodies of the Captain and Larabee and, screaming horribly, crashed head first through the plate-glass windows of the wheel-house in a glittering cascade of razor-edged shards, still attached to the umbilical cord of the Aldis cable.

I lay there whimpering hysterically and trying to dig with broken finger nails into the wooden decking, feeling the ship straining in agony against her cable while the eternal rumblings of the eviscerated *Athenian* kept on beat-ing and beating at us with brain freezing force, until—suddenly—it was over.

The last detonation passed, echoing round the black, overhanging cliffs, and we lay for a moment like dead men. Then Brannigan started screaming dreadfully from his bed of scalpels inside the caved-in wheelhouse and we climbed numbly to our feet, still reeling with the shock of it. I wanted to go straight to Brannigan, to try and stop him screaming like that, but I couldn't—not till I'd looked to see if *both* U-boats had died along with *Athenian*. To see if her suicide had meant something after all.

God, but how I wanted to see that bloody white peaked cap floating in the oil-fouled water.

But no. She was still there, still cruising off our beam, slightly headed away from us now but with the big, black gun already being manned again by her dazed sailors. They must have taken a beating too, though, and I could see a rope being thrown down over the bulge of her tanks to a man struggling in the water. One more minute, however, and she'd be on an attack course again, with us as helpless as before despite all the bloodshed and agony.

Larabee said 'Jesus Christ!' in a shocked voice from inside the wheelhouse, and Evans shouted 'Mister Kent,' above the crackling of ground, broken glass. I turned unthinkingly, sick with despair, and stepped through the shattered door, then froze abruptly at what I saw. I had one brief memory of a gleaming, white skull from which nearly every shred of flesh had been stripped but in which the black hole of a mouth still opened and bubbled, then I was back outside again on the wing, spewing and retching into the now agitated water far below.

And I didn't stop heaving my guts out until the bloody silly gun on our poop slammed deafeningly and a tall column of water rose less than thirty feet from the U-boat's hull.

Which meant we were fighting now whether Evans liked it or not.

CHAPTER NINE

Looking back I suppose it was a chance worth taking. Had the Old Man suspected the things that were going to happen, we would have fought as well and as suicidally as the gallant *Athenian*. It would have been better that way in the long run, as at least every man but one on the ship would have died in the knowledge that he had done so honourably, as so many had done before us.

But, then again . . . does a man in a Board of Trade lifejacket and no top to his head, or maybe with his intestines floating beside him—does he *really* care whether or not he was 'honourably' eviscerated?

Either way, I just stayed doubled over the rail for several stunned moments while I watched the sea tumble back aboard the U-boat and heard the fat little Bombardier's voice from aft screaming, 'Reload! . . . Up fifty! . . . On! . . . On! . . .' then the U-boat's gun was swinging

F

round too, already loaded, as the German sailors moved feverishly in a deadly race against our own gun crew like in some Hollywood Dodge City shoot-out where the first man to draw won the day—except we were competing with four-inch diameter bullets.

Behind me Brannigan had stopped screaming and, above the scrunch of broken glass, I heard Larabee say, 'The poor sod's dead, Captain.'

And Evans's voice, the abysmally sad tone in strange contrast to the text, answered, 'Thank God for that, Mister Larabee.'

Then the German's 4.1 had stopped traversing while Bombardier Allen was still screaming desperately, 'On! . . . On! . . . On, for Chrissake!'

I heard the staccato Teutonic bark slash across the intervening water, '. . . Feuer!' cut short by the whiplash slam of their gun and, in the milli-seconds of eternity that followed I knew already that we'd lost the race. The baddies had drawn first and the Sheriff was already dead.

I had one last view of Charlie Shell on the poop, standing out from the soldiers like a shining knight in his white stockings and shorts, then the hurricane blast of the hit knocked me down for a second time while white-hot splinters of jagged steel whirred and spanged against the after-end of the bridge, wheelhouse and funnel, ripping through ventilators and boats with savage contempt.

I dragged myself to my knees and peered fearfully over the rail, even then praying that I would hear the answering boom from the long-snouted *Phyllis*. But, as my eyes focused through the haze of cordite fumes, I realised I never would—at least, not through the hand of any man on that gun deck.

Oh, the gun was still there all right, with the coat of 1940 paint covering the antiquated 1914 silhouette—but the indescribable shambles of blood and limbs scattered around it symbolised the end of our last hope of leaving Quintanilha de Almeida aboard *Cyclops*.

I wanted to take my eyes from the torn obscenities but I couldn't move a muscle, I just sat there behind the doubtful concealment of the bridge wing, feeling the tears rolling down my cheeks, and watched as the once trim form that had been Charlie Shell dragged itself agonisingly slowly towards the loaded gun, and with infinite care, groped with the one arm it had left for the black, charred, tubby shape incinerated in the gunlayer's seat. Feeling blindly for the firing lever . . . A slow-worm of barely flickering partorgans and limbs, like the little half-man on the sinking U-boat's deck that time so long ago. Would this Kapitan Lieutnant paint a half-Charlie on the side of his conning tower in retaliation? A Second Mate with only one arm and stumps of legs severed at the knee?

The cremated mess of the dead Bombardier slowly keeled over and slopped to the deck as the blind hand trembled and felt towards the trigger. I suddenly hunched in terror as someone started screaming and shouting behind me. Breedie! . . . What the hell was Breedie doing up here on this morgue of a bridge? He should have been sheltering along with the rest of the crowd in the starboard alleyway. 'Charlie? Is that you, Charlie? Oh, for Jesus' sake, Charlie, I'll come for you. Don't move! Charlie . . .'

Then the Spandau mounted on the U-boat's conning tower opened up and the line of white-lashed foam ran across the green water. Up and up our steel sides it climbed, directly under the gun and its zombie part-gunlayer, then Breedie was screaming hysterically as Charlie Shell twitched and rolled over and over with the machine-gun shells sparkling and slamming all around and into him until, mercifully, the thing disintegrated under what was left of the port side taffrail and disappeared over the counter for ever.

And the silence of Quintanilha de Almeida blanketed down again with an almost physical impact.

For a very brief moment.

They'd even got a Tannoy speaker on that submersible killing-machine of theirs.

The metallic, emotionless voice of the man in the white cap cut across to us before the full horror of Charlie Shell's gallant, mutinous death had had time to clear from our frozen brains. 'Achtung, *Cyclops*! Achtung! That was your final warning. Any further resistance will force me to commence firing indiscriminately. I will not stop until every man of your crew is dead . . . Kaput.'

I heard the scrunch of broken glass and glanced round

to see the Old Man watching over my shoulder, ashen-faced. In the background, under the shade of the darkened wheelhouse, Larabee still hovered but I couldn't see the expression on his thin features. Maybe now he wasn't so damned keen to be a hero. The disembodied voice floated across the water again. 'If your master is still alive he will answer, please.'

There was a momentary silence as we looked tensely at one another, then Evans moved forward to pick up the megaphone. I cut in front of him and took it out of his hand, pulling him aside into the cover of the riddled starboard master's ventilator. He glared at me angrily and the white pallor was replaced by a crimson flush. 'What the bloody hell do you think you're doing, Mister? I intend to stop this madness immediately. Or would you rather go aft and take a good, close look at Mister Shell?'

I was already dragging at the rank-bearing epaulettes on my shoulders. 'Get yours off too, Captain,' I said urgently. 'That bastard's liable to take you aboard as a prisoner, same as Henry McKenzie. Remember the *Altmark* last year? Hatches full of M.N. senior officers.'

I threw down my three gold bars and watched as his four followed reluctantly a few moments later, then stepped out to the wing and lifted the megger to my mouth. I had time to notice with a nasty churn in my stomach that the 4.1 was now trained right at me, as well as her four bow-tubes, before I shouted back with all the control I could force into my voice. 'The Captain has already been murdered. This is Kent—Chief Officer. I protest at the massacre of certain members of my crew and warn you I shall report you to the Board of Trade as soon as possible.'

It sounded even sillier when I actually said it but the flat voice from the U-boat betrayed no sign of emotion, amused or otherwise. 'I note your protest, Herr Kent, and have no doubt that your British Board of Trade will take the matter up with my superiors when we have won the war. Until then you will refrain from contacting either them or anyone else by means of your wireless. Do you hear me well, Chief Officer?'

'Bugger you!' I screamed back, in childish frustration.

The German loud-hailer ignored me completely. 'You have ten minutes in which to abandon your ship, Herr

Kent. After those ten minutes have elapsed my First Lieutenant will board you with a search party. Any man found remaining aboard will be shot out of hand.'

A bulky black object was being hauled from a deck hatch on the U-boat's after-casing and I realised that it was an inflatable rubber raft. Grouped round the base of the conning tower we could see several heavily armed sailors, each wearing those peculiarly old-fashioned looking tailed 'Barnacle Bill' sailor hats that the German Navy favoured.

I made one more half-hearted attempt to argue against the inevitable. 'You have shot up my bloody boats. I have several seriously wounded men aboard and I'll be damned if I will . . .'

The white cap moved sharply in the conning tower and the Spandau racketed immediately, cutting a line of foam three feet away from our side and directly under the bridge where I stood. It very efficiently underlined the message that followed. '. . . And you will most certainly be damned if you don't, Herr Kent. You have now got nine and a half minutes left and, if you find it necessary to utilise your port boats, I will expect them to come round to your starboard side where I can see them. I will allow two extra minutes for that operation. Any wounded men you have will be attended to as soon as your ship is abandoned.'

I turned and looked back at Evans inquiringly. I suppose we all did, right then. The Old Man closed his eyes for a moment and I watched the right hand come up and gently, almost tenderly, caress the sanded teak rail, then suddenly the hand clenched into a fist and the grey eyes were staring back at us defiantly. 'Have the boats lowered, Mister Kent . . . any that are still serviceable. Mister Breedie.'

The young kid jumped. 'Sir?'

'I'm sorry, Mister Breedie, but I must ask you to go aft and ascertain that none of the gun's crew are still alive. We have no time to do anything with the bodies at the moment but I will attempt to return to the ship later and perform the necessary functions. Mister Larabee.'

Larabee stepped forward into the sunlight and looked queryingly at Evans. His face was impassive but there was a strangely tense, excited glint at the back of his eyes. 'Aye, Captain?'

'Please be good enough to remove any parts of your W.T. equipment you think fit in order to render it inoperative without actually destroying it. You will conceal them in the hope that we may be able to return and send a signal after the enemy have left.'

The Sparks looked cynical. 'Aye, aye, Sir. But that gear doesn't work so hot under water.'

Evans spoke as he turned back to me, 'They will undoubtedly sink the ship, Mister Larabee, but there is insufficient water under our keel to do more than cover the main deck levels. Please be good enough to do as I ask. And now, John. The boats are well provisioned and watered, I trust?'

I blinked at the change in him. It was like going back three days to before this had all started. He smiled slightly as the suddenly much older Breedie and Larabee clattered away down the ladder, and his red face looked ten years younger. 'Action, no matter how distasteful, John, is infinitely preferable to standing by helplessly and watching men die. I have at least the relief of knowing that the blood has stopped flowing.'

As I turned away to the ladder I heard him arguing placidly with old McKenzie on the engine-room phone, then he hooked it carefully back in its rest and grasped the shiny brass telegraphs for the last time.

The answering clang from deep down below 'Finished with Engines,' seemed very sad. And irredeemably final.

We were still able to use numbers one and three boats, the after lifeboats having taken the brunt of the searching splinters of the Nazi shell. Number one was, of course, already in the water while three port, being already swung out and unbridled, took only about half our remaining minutes of grace to lower away.

I stood as the crew scrambled down the swaying boat ladders after first carefully lowering the wounded, watching them go in their blue jeans or white engineer's boiler suits under the gaudy yellow and blue lifejackets. Two of the deck hands still wore bizarre, bright silk pyjamas though God knows how long it had been since any of us had been in our bunks. Most of them clutched pitiful little bundles of personal belongings and I wanted to cry when I saw the quiet dignity and courage shown by even the toughest, hardest A.B.s. I don't think I've ever felt prouder to be a merchant navy man than I did right then.

Breedie came hurrying along the boat deck and stood beside me, looking sick and dazed. I remembered he'd been aft to the gun and was glad it hadn't been me. Now he was an eighteen-year-old kid with a very old face. I lifted an eyebrow at him and he swallowed. 'All dead, Sir. The whole bloody lot . . .' Then he seemed to get angry and his fists clenched. 'That fuggin' gun. It's still like brand new except, except there's someone's foot in . . .'

His strained voice faded away and his shoulders heaved. I spoke as quickly and as gently as I could, 'You take number three boat away yourself, Dick. Get her forward round the bows to the starboard side as soon as you can before those bastards start getting impatient. I'll collect the Captain from the bridge and join you as soon as possible, he'll probably want to take number one with young Conway and the Chief. Pecker up and chop-chop, son.'

I tried to smile reassuringly but failed and turned away awkwardly to glance round the deserted decks while Breedie swung over the rail on to the ladder. We couldn't have long left now. Everyone gone except the Captain. I started to sweat gently as I imagined what was going to happen to any man fool enough to try and hide aboard after we left. But would they really shoot them? This was the twentieth century, wasn't it? Then I remembered the Spandau shells smashing into the already-dead Charlie Shell and I knew that the man in the white cap meant every word he said.

I hurried forward and climbed the splintered ladder to the bridge.

Evans was standing motionless in the shattered wheel-house when I pulled myself to the top. I stepped through the doors, feeling the glass shards crunching as I moved and trying not to look at the Fourth Mate's body lying contorted in a still glittering pool of blood and jagged crystals. Then a glint of red and white made me look down anyway to see, with a surge of thankful relief, that the Old

Man had covered the shiny bone face with one of the flags from the signal locker on the after bulkhead.

The flag was the red and white cubed 'U'; the International Code signal for 'You are standing into danger.'

Evans half turned as I approached. He didn't smile this time. 'Well, John?'

I saluted awkwardly, it was a thing we didn't normally do but, then again, we didn't abandon ship every day either. 'Numbers one and three lifeboats lowered and manned, Sir. The other two could be patched up but we don't really need them. All hands away in them to the best of my knowledge. We don't have time to search the ship properly.'

He nodded. 'Young Breedie went up on the poop?'

'All dead. The gun seems still to be functioning though. Their shell must've struck around the emergency steering position, the heat, blast and shrapnel did the rest.'

'It's cost a lot of lives, that gun. A lot of lives and not much to show for them.'

I glanced anxiously at my watch. We were due to hear a high-explosive alarm clock in about ten seconds unless White Cap accepted our two packet boats as sufficient assurance that we had surrendered. I turned my wrist to show the Old Man. 'Sir—it's time to go.'

The Teutonic voice cut across to us again, the syllables even harsher and more guttural under the distortion of the amplifier. '*Cyclops* . . . Achtung! You will leave the bridge immediately, Herr Kent, and bring the other man with you also. My boarding party are under the strictest orders to shoot. I can assure you this is not an idle threat. You have thirty seconds to leave, Herr Mate.'

Evans took one last, long look around his bridge. 'They'll sink her, John,' he said, with immeasurable pain in his voice. 'She was such a bloody lovely ship.'

I swallowed nervously. 'Captain, we have to go.'

He turned without another word and walked down the ladder and along the port side of the boat deck, masked temporarily from the U-boat's searching eyes. I suppose if we hadn't met the Chief coming from aft, towards the bridge, things would have been a lot different and I wouldn't have been writing this now.

McKenzie stopped in front of us and glowered ferociously with arms akimbo. I noticed he still had on his red dragon carpet-slippers as he grumbled, 'Bluidy square-heided bastards! Ah've shut down everything but the main generators, Captain. Maybe we'll get back aboard after they U-boat lads leave and in that case we'll be needin' the power on still.'

Evans smiled very slightly. 'Perhaps you're right, Chief. But you should have been in the boats five minutes ago. I trust there is no one else down below?'

'No. Och aye, and another thing, if they buggers think they'll be topping up their bunkers w' my fuel oil I'll be wantin' a formal receipt for it, so ye'll mind and tell them.'

'I'll tell them, Mister McKenzie,' Evans said. 'If they find me that is. Right now you'd better remove those epaulettes of yours or you may have an opportunity to collect that receipt in person.'

I had a nasty feeling we were going to need a formal receipt for the whole bloody ship before they were through but I didn't say anything. The Old Man took a deep breath and, squaring his shoulders, marched towards the forward ladders. I suddenly wondered if anyone had told the amateur bodyguard outside the radio room to shove off. 'I'll nip below round by the radio shack, Sir. Just to check that the after decks are clear.'

The Captain nodded. 'Aye, and we'll have a good look forward as we go, John. The Chief and I will take number one boat away if you would be so good as to look after number three.'

He disappeared down the ladder after McKenzie while I hurried nervously aft along the boat deck. It was very quiet aboard *Cyclops* now. All I could hear was the faint hum of the main generators below trying vainly to dilute the cone of silence over Quintanilha de Almeida. Occasionally I could hear the squeak of oars from over on the starboard side and, once, a guttural shout from the hidden U-boat followed by a distant rattle.

Then, insidiously, I became aware of another sound which seemed to go on and on with irregular persistence.

I stopped just before I turned the corner of the radio room at the after end of the centrecastle. There it was again—a sort of tapping noise, somehow, vaguely familiar.

What in God's name was it? It was almost like a . . . a morse key . . .

A morse key? Oh, please . . . no.

It couldn't be . . . Larabee had been ordered to sabotage the W.T. equipment, then abandon ship with the rest of the crew. Somehow I couldn't convince myself that Sparks was of the hero mould.

But *someone* was transmitting.

And then, suddenly, I knew who it was . . .

Curtis! Of course! With startling clarity it all fitted together. The Third Mate . . . The one man who had left the bridge with ample time to lose himself until the rest of us had abandoned ship. The one man who always seemed to be in the wrong place at the right time, like the after-deck only minutes after that bloody gun had strafed *Athenian*'s W.T. room. I remembered the shocked surprise on his features as we had heeled over under full helm to avoid the U-boat attack, and the strangely silent, thoughtful look when she vomited her crewmen into the slashing shells from *Mallard* and ourselves. I'd thought then that he, like me, had been sickened by the carnage but, if he was a Hun sympathiser, he wouldn't exactly have been waving a joyful Union Jack right then . . .

. . . *If* he was.

And if he wasn't? If he was putting out a genuine call for help, thinking that the rest of the crowd were already safe in the boats? Our transmission must have had the U-boat wireless op, clutching at his earphones in Teutonic agony. Oh Jesus, but I wished that all bloody heroes could be locked up as soon as a war started . . .

Flattening myself against the cold steel plates of the deck housing I sidled aft, towards the rounded corner and the radio room door. It was starting to get dark now, that time of night when colours seem bright and clear-cut with every detail standing out sharply, like when you put on a pair of Polaroids on a blindingly sunny day. I shivered suddenly and felt very exposed up there on the empty deck.

The tap-tapping kept on and I got so scared that I had to stop and close my eyes for a moment. The image of that bloody U-boat's foredeck gun kept on forming in my mind. Maybe it was already swinging on to the W.T. room.

Maybe I was one half second away from a violent, exploding death. They *must* be picking up our signals and monitoring every word we sent. So why, in God's name, hadn't they already fired? I had to get away quickly, into the safety of the boats. Evans and the Chief must have left the ship by now and what was it that White Cap had promised? Any man found remaining aboard *Cyclops* would be shot immediately?

Another thought struck me with stunning force. I'd completely overlooked the fact that the Chief Engineer had stayed behind. Evans and I hadn't met him until we'd left the bridge. The U-boat commander had obviously thought there were only the two of us still aboard the last time he'd hailed us, and now they would have seen two men climbing down the boat ladders. They'd assume that *Cyclops* was already deserted, the boarding party could be on its way across this very minute. Jesus! Perhaps if I ran round to the starboard side and signalled, they'd realise it was all a mistake and let me . . .

But then I took in what the morse key on the other side of the W.T. room door was saying and I forgot all about U-boats, and *Cyclops*, and the automatic rifles under the funny flat hats.

Subconsciously I suppose I'd been reading the key all the time but it was only now that the full import of the transmission penetrated the cloud of fear fogging my mind. My hand reached out for the door handle while I stood for a brief space, staring out over the hideous mortuary of our poop with the shredded Red Ensign still hanging lifelessly from the splintered staff, and listened to the deft professionalism of the operator's keying. I was good at morse, I've already said so, and it wasn't difficult for me to pick up at least the basic text of that remote tapping—the last signal from M.V. *Cyclops*.

S . . . S . . . S . . . S . . . MV CYCLOPS TO ALL SHIPS: URGENT RELAY TO ADMIRALTY: TORPEDOED AND SINKING . . . What the hell? A plain language distress call, and the U-boat wasn't even firing yet, even though she *must* be listening by now. And torpedoed? The controlled rattle continued . . . POSITION P3215-P0330 MASTER AND OFFICERS DEAD NO HOPE OF SAVING SHIP WE ARE ABANDONING . . .

I stood there with my brain reeling. What was all this

about? We weren't torpedoed and sinking. Most of the officers were still alive and safely boating on the unruffled calm of Quintanilha de Almeida along with the supposedly-dead Captain Evans. And there was always a hope of saving the ship—even if we were eventually torpedoed she would only sit level on the bottom with her lower decks awash. An icy cold hand reached up from my bowels and clutched at my stomach. That position the unknown operator had given—it was several hundred miles to the north-west of this blood-stained circle of rocks.

According to what I'd heard just then the Admiralty would now be assuming that we'd sunk in the deep waters of the open Atlantic many miles away from our real location? But they already knew we were heading for Quintanilha. Damn it, they bloody *told* us to come here themselves . . .

The key rattled briefly again as I started to turn the handle cautiously. ALL SHIPS ALL SHIPS URGENT: FORWARD BULKHEADS GIVEN WAY WE ARE GOING NOW GOODBYE TRANSMISSION ENDS . . . And it did, too, as I wrenched the door open and slammed into the equipment-packed cabin fast. Almost fast enough to beat the gun that was snatched from the operator's table by a very steady hand.

It was only a little gun really but, pointed at me the way it was right then, it looked as big as that 4.1 inch on the German's casing.

And I also found that my logical assessment of Curtis as a spy was a bit wrong . . . because Larabee smiled quite nicely and said, 'You shouldn't be here, Mate. This boat's just gone and sunk.'

At first I just stared at Larabee, seeing the cabin starting to spin round me and watching the black hole in the blued gun-barrel gaping wider and wider, while, behind it, the trigger finger slowly whitened as the pressure increased. Almost pleadingly my voice forced its way out from somewhere deep down in my sandpaper throat. 'Wha . . . what was that message you just sent, Larabee? And the gun? Why aren't you down with the rest of the crowd in the boats?'

The smile slipped a bit, but, with sick relief, I saw the finger relax fractionally and rush red again as the blood pumped back into it. But it didn't waver one millimetre. ''Cause I don't think it's a very good idea to go yachting right now, Kent.'

'It's a bloody sight better than sitting here till some Nazi hood blows the back of your head off with a Luger. But that signal you were transmitting? Why, Larabee? This ship isn't sinking, not yet, and certainly not in the position you gave.'

He shrugged but the movement didn't travel as far as the pistol in his hand. '*I* know that, and *you* know that, Mate. But the Admiralty . . . *they* don't know any different. As far as they're concerned *Cyclops* has just gone down in a mile of water a long way from here. They should be sending out the next-of-kin telegrams any time now.'

I leaned back against the door and tried to catch up. The whole thing seemed crazy but I had a horrible awareness that it wasn't—that everything that had happened was part of a sane, calculated operation, and that the planners weren't British either. I moved forward forgetfully and the gun lifted warningly, 'You're a bloody Nazi, you bastard. You're a German agent!'

He nodded and, just for a moment, a wry, almost a nice smile touched the corner of his mouth. 'Do you think it's only the Union Jack that can stir a man to be a patriot, Mister Mate?'

Inconsequentially I noticed that his voice was different, more precise, and I felt the anger surging into my face. He'd fooled me all along the line—all those times I'd seen him as too obnoxious to be anything other than genuine— and now he was still ahead, both he and his Teutonic oppos out there. I started to shake with an almost uncontrollable hatred.

'You're still a bastard, Larabee,' I grated. 'You never had a country. You were spawned in some deep pool of filth . . .'

His trigger finger started to go white again and self-preservation stemmed the flow of abuse I was hurling at him. Suddenly he looked very grim and sure of himself, not at all like the whining, ineffectual little man of a few hours before. I saw that he wasn't even thin and fragile any more—he was lean and tough—because he didn't have to play a part now.

And he intended to kill me.

The gun barrel lowered fractionally until it lined up neatly with my belt buckle and I felt my nails digging deep into the palms of my hands in terror-struck incredulity that this was actually happening to *me*, John Kent, common or garden sailorman . . .

As if from a long way away I heard myself sobbing something—anything—to try and make him let me cling on to life just a little longer. 'This whole mad bloody voyage was a set-up, wasn't it, Larabee? We were meant to come here right from the start. Those goddam U-boats have been waiting for us, not following us.'

The old sardonic expression flickered back momentarily. 'What does it matter to you, Kent? You're dead anyway.'

I ignored the sweat running into my eye sockets. I had to keep his attention. Through the port the setting sun looked wonderfully dear to me. 'Wasn't it, Larabee?' I urged, not daring to move a muscle in case I triggered him, and that bloody automatic, off.

He hesitated, then shrugged. 'You took a lot of convincing. It needed that signal from our mutual friend Rear Admiral Tryst to bring you here, even then.'

I stared at him again. It was getting to be a habit—staring vacantly, I mean. 'How do you know who sent that Admiralty signal, Larabee? It was in code . . .'

My voice trailed off as I finally understood the full story. All the previously disconnected incidents suddenly meshed together—Foley's lonely death, the incinerated *Athenian* operators, Larabee remaining as the only operator in the group. God, we'd even helped them ourselves by disposing of *Mallard*.

He smiled, just a little too impatiently for my screaming nerves. 'I should know what was in that signal, Kent—I wrote it in the first place.'

'And the Captain's original request for instructions from the Admiralty . . . ?' I muttered, already knowing the answer.

He gave it to me anyway. '. . . was never transmitted in the first place. So far as the Royal Navy are concerned this ship is now lying on the bottom a long way from here.'

'But that means you must already have the naval codes, man? You needed them to encode that fake signal from

'Tryst.'

He nodded, a little more absently. I formed the impression that he was waiting for something to happen. But then, so was I. When he spoke again I knew he didn't intend to leave me in anticipation for very much longer. 'We've had the current shipping control codes for a long time, Kent. We're winning this war hands down. A lot of your Allied tonnage has been sunk, it's not always possible for the masters to ditch their confidential bags when they're boarded. No, it's the new ones we want now . . . the ones you've got forr-ad in the strong-room.'

He half turned, almost as if he were listening for something ouside again, then the dispassionate eyes fixed themselves bleakly on me. 'I'm sorry, Kent,' he murmured, 'but you really died before you passed the Formby Light. The *Kent Star* message, those fairy lights that steered you south—all put out by the two U-boats out there . . . but it's really all somewhat academic now . . .'

The gun in his hand started to twist slightly along the axis of the barrel as he increased the trigger pressure . . . and all I could see was the little black hole that got bigger and bigger by the milli-second.

'Christ, man, there's a Geneva Convention,' I screamed, 'I'm a prisoner of war . . .'

His face was as white as his trigger finger. Maybe even a fanatic finds it hard to kill a man in cold blood from a few feet away. But he was having a good try at overcoming his distaste. The last few ounces of trigger pressure were being used up, as a nervous tic dragged the corner of his suddenly bloodless mouth down in a nervous grimace.

'*Mallard* had the same problem, Mate,' he muttered. '*Her* orders said "No survivors" too . . .'

The shot sounded very loud in such a confined space.

I still don't really know what happened during my allocated seconds of killing time, largely because I screwed my eyes up tight and just half-rolled towards him in a sort of airborne foetal position. I felt the smash of a white-hot shell sear my shoulder, then we went down together in a welter of flailing limbs and curses.

The tough, bucko mate inside me grinned savagely as I saw the gun skitter across the compo deck towards the door—then something hard hit me in the face and my eyes stung from the ductile tears that prevented me from seeing anything at all.

Larabee's foot came up into my unprotected groin and I heard myself screaming in agony while the bucko mate image disintegrated into an oblivion of pain. I felt my finger nails split as I scrabbled at the edge of the operator's table, trying to haul myself to my feet. Larabee was mouthing strange, guttural obscenities as he swung the heavy chair at my head.

Frantically I ducked and felt the shards of splintered glass dials lodge in my hair as the front of the gleaming grey transmitter caved in and the blue flashes of abruptly shorted H.T. circuits gave place to the sickly stench of crisping insulation.

Any last ideas I had about actually hitting Larabee disappeared when his deck shoe caught me under the chin. I went down on my knees thinking what a bloody good job the Nazis did in training their agents for every contingency, then I was being sick and watched dully as Larabee snatched up the vagrant gun and backed towards the door.

This time I just closed my eyes and waited to be eviscerated. I couldn't even tense my stomach muscles in anticipation.

On reflection it was probably the funny, choking noise Larabee was making that finally dragged my eyelids open again . . . and froze them wide in an uncomprehending idiot's stare at the sight of the Second Wireless Operator pinned to the wooden door frame by an evilly curved and very rusty cargo billy-hook that someone had driven cleanly through his shoulder blade and muscles.

And a white-faced Third Officer Curtis who was gazing with a look of almost frightened anticipation for my immediate reaction to this strange phenomenon.

'I heard Sparks yelling in German, Sir,' he said apprehensively, 'so I thought I'd better help . . .'

Then Larabee started to scream in a thin, high-pitched key like an animal caught in a trap, while all the time he was fluttering on the hook the way a butterfly does when a kid sticks a pin through it. Curtis slammed him across the face with a piece of four by three and I heard his nose and cheekbones disintegrate along with his consciousness.

I said, 'Thank you, Mate,' with feeling, and watched while the Third Mate was sick in the scuppers, which showed that he was just like me really, and that I'd been as wrong about him as I had about Larabee.

Then the silence of Quintanilha de Almeida was devastated by the sickening smash of the U-boat's Spandau machine-gun opening up, followed immediately by the measured pom . . . pom . . . pom of her one-pounder and the intermittent crackle of small-arms fire.

CHAPTER TEN

For perhaps three million years I stood there, frozen in horror, while I waited for the shells to come pumping and ripping through the wireless room bulkheads, cremating and smearing us to an unrecognisable pulp.

Then, slowly, I realised the shells weren't going to come and, with a different kind of appalled fear, I knew what was happening out there on the sunlit water. I forgot the still suspended Larabee and clawed my way brutally past him, stumbling on the low coaming.

Curtis's eyes were huge with shock. 'Jesus!' he screamed. 'The boats! They're shooting up the bloody boats.'

And suddenly I was outside on the boat deck with the still hot rays of the setting sun blinding me after the darkness of the radio room, and we were crawling on our hands and knees for the cover of the holed wooden hull of number two starboard lifeboat as it hung forlornly outboard under its swung-out davits.

I hardly felt the web of pain gripping my body as the beating Larabee had given me signalled itself. I was too sick and numb with the impact of the scene that opened out before me in the narrow space between the two ships. The killing machine was in gear again, working as smoothly and as efficiently as before, with the U-boat crew silhouetted against the glittering backdrop of the anchorage waters and the whole length of her black casing sparkling with the muzzle flashes of light weapons.

I had time to notice the hungry, predatory shape of her 4.1, abandoned and pointing idly over her bows, then the figure of the one-pounder gunner hanging well back in his straps as he traversed the bell-mouthed barrel across the water, spitting a constant stream of light shells as he swung and—towering above them all—the man in the white peaked cap high in his conning tower, leaning casually, almost disinterestedly, over the rail beside the jolting Spandau mounting.

Then my tear-blurred eyes switched involuntarily to the *Cyclops*'s boats.

All that was left of number three—which should have been my boat—was already down to the gunnels, kept afloat only by the last bubbles of air trapped in the riddled buoyancy tanks under the thwarts while, all the time, bits of shattered oars and canvas and men kept on leaping and up-ending in the foam-whipped pink water as the Spandau bullets lashed the area into a boiling foam. I saw young Breedie's torn corpse still erect at the tiller, then a one-pounder shell exploded just where his chest should have been and the kid vanished in a fine spray of bright red blood and flesh and flying condensed-milk cans from the after stores locker.

Lying beside me Curtis suddenly drew his knees up to his chin and dragged in great gouts of retching, uncontrollable air while I had one more indelible vision of a slowly spreading ring of men face down in kapok-protruding lifejackets, including two in the floating tatters of bright silk pyjamas. Then the line of bullet-lashed foam extended to one side, towards the Captain's boat, reaching and at the same time contracting at its rear like some monstrous, hideous caterpillar creeping over the water until, suddenly, they were all screaming and jerking as the concentrated fire turned on the virgin target . . .

And I was screaming, too.

There must be some kind of horror limit—some level at which one's facility for absorption of the unwatchable is neutralised. I remember only two imprints of the massacre of that second boatload. The first was an angry chief engineer standing up contemptuously, still in his red dragon slippers, bellowing obscene Barrowland oaths at the men who were killing him without a receipt, and the second—most unforgettable of all—the sternsheets of the still immaculate boat, with the words *Cyclops . . . Liverpool* carefully picked out in black paint and, above them at the tiller, the stocky figure of Captain Evans with his arms round frightened little Conway, shielding and at the same time consoling him with a pathetically vulnerable love. Then the Spandau scythed into the two embracing bodies and they merged into one another for ever and ever . . . . . . and I slipped into blessed unconsciousness.

I suppose I was only out for a few seconds but, when I did come round, I remember that I felt absolutely nothing. No horror, or fear, or compassion, or hatred . . . But maybe all I felt *was* hatred, a hatred so deep and intense that it was too great for ordinary recognition. I gazed up at the towering black masts above me, noting disinterestedly that the firing had stopped except for a few sporadic, scattered small-arms shots.

A movement beside me caught my attention and, turning my head, I looked at Curtis, kneeling by now, with the wet smear of tears still glinting on his cheeks. He blinked back through eyes filled with a terrible sadness and I could sense the nearness of hysteria. I tried to forget my own troubles for a moment.

'You remember what Henry McKenzie'd say just now, Three Oh?' I smiled softly, 'He'd say—Keep the heid, laddie . . . Remember?'

Curtis sniffed and tried to muster a weak grin but it vanished as, from the lagoon, a bubbling scream was punctuated by the full stop of a shot. 'Bastards,' he muttered sickly. 'Can't we try to do something, for God's sake, Sir?'

I shrugged, still trying to fight off my own fears. We were as good as dead anyway so it didn't make any difference. 'Sure, Three Oh,' I agreed. 'You fire the Very pistol at them, I'll throw a few rocks.'

He shook his head. 'No, Sir, not really. I've already been aft to the 4.7 . . . She's as good as new, there's even one up the spout all ready for us.'

Of course . . . Phyllis. The fat bombardier's jinxed mistress. I still felt paralysed inside but, by God, how much easier I'd die to see even one shell from *Cyclops* burst among the Nazi butchers on that U-boat casing. But could we? Against a highly trained crew of smoothly oiled automatons? I remembered how Charlie Shell's corpse had jerked and rolled under the hail of shells from the Spandau and started to feel nasty things in my stomach.

I tried not to look too dubious. 'O.K., Mate. But first . . .'

Curtis shuffled anxiously as I inspected the still suspended Larabee, trying not to look too closely at the face, now waxy white where it wasn't bleeding sullenly through the split, jellified flesh. Maybe he was already dead. It didn't really matter, though it would have been nice to have seen him hanged by his neck instead of his shoulder blade. I'd started to search for his gun when Curtis coughed as deferentially as though we were still on the bridge at sea.

'They'll be sending that boarding party away any moment, Mister Kent. Shouldn't we be getting aft?'

I nodded and gave up looking for the automatic—a .38 wasn't exactly going to tip the scales in our favour anyway. A quick, fruitless glance at the shattered remains of the W.T. set and, keeping low, I headed for the after centrecastle ladder. The Third Mate threw one last, bitter stare at the U-boat as it cruised slowly among the sluggishly drifting, humped shapes in the water, then came after me. I saw one sodden lump move slightly as the long black cigar slid past it with a whirr of propellers, then the sea around it whipped into a brief slash of gouting foam as the Spandau rattled, and Quintanilha de Almeida grew quiet again.

There was still one mystery to be cleared up, though. I hesitated briefly at the top of the well deck ladder and turned back to Curtis. 'Incidentally, Three Oh, just why *did* you stay aboard when you should have been away with the rest of the crowd in the boats?'

He smiled a bit and looked embarrassed. 'Silly really, Sir, but when the Captain gave the order to abandon ship I had my best whites on. I figured they'd be ruined in the boats so I nipped below to change into my number twos. I hung my new ones carefully in the wardrobe, then I . . . I . . .'

He mumbled to a stop and looked like a recalcitrant schoolboy but I knew the rest. '. . . then you remembered that the bloody ship was due to be sunk any moment—and with your *best* gear aboard?'

He nodded as I finished for him, '. . . and when you finally came topside, the last boat had gone.'

I turned without another word and slid down the ladder towards the gun on the poop.

I nearly didn't make it as my head rose above the level of the gun deck and I saw the limbs and blood that smeared the scorched wooden planking. For a moment I just hung there, resting my sweat-saturated face against the cool steel of the ladder rail and feeling the dead *Cyclops* heave and roll under my feet. The half orb of the setting sun, now almost concealed by the jet-black landscape, swam crazily and grew larger and larger until it swamped over me in a glaring, blood-red haze.

Then the Third Mate's head bumped into the tight seat of my white shorts and I realised he must have been climbing the vertical ladder with his eyes closed. I didn't blame him either, as I heaved myself over the low coaming and lay full length in the sticky mess.

Curtis flopped cautiously beside me with a grunt of exertion and together we gazed over to where the U-boat still picked its way idly among the flotsam of the silent, floating graveyard. He sniffed with satisfaction. 'Careless sods, aren't they, Sir? Taking too much for granted.'

I saw what he meant. The sporadic shooting had finally ceased as we had crawled on our hands and knees past the steel coamings of numbers five and six hatches, keeping to the port side of the ship, out of sight. Now the crew of the U-boat were standing smoking and talking idly along her casing while they held their automatic weapons under their armpits like some distinguished Highland shooting party after a hard day at the butts. Occasionally a laugh drifted across the darkening water.

I was staring over to where I had a special interest—to where White Cap was leaning placidly on his bridge rail beside the now abandoned Spandau mounting—when Curtis whispered again, 'They must know Larabee's still aboard, Sir. Soon they'll be wondering why he hasn't shown up. Shouldn't we . . .?'

I nodded, thinking with savage satisfaction about the

way the Second Sparks was still hanging on the W.T. office door. Then I remembered we had one more problem. I twisted my head back to Curtis.

'How the hell do we fire this bloody thing?' I muttered.

He stared back in that infuriatingly bland way of his. 'Perhaps, Sir, if I take the gunlayer's seat, you could feed the ammo? Have another round ready to load.'

Even though I knew I owed him at least an extension to my life I still couldn't help glowering like a Chief Officer. 'Do you know what the blazes you're doing, Three Oh? We've maybe sixty seconds of a surprise factor over them and we're running second favourites from then on. We don't have time to read the Admiralty Manual of Gunnery.'

He looked lugubriously solemn. 'Actually I'm R.N.R., Sir. Even been on a gunnery exercise once. I'll have to transfer to R.N. service when we get back.'

I wished he'd inspired a bit more confidence, more like Charlie Shell. But then, Charlie was dead. I took one more hurried glance at our proposed target and noted gratefully that she was still broadside on to us, with the wicked silhouette of her foredeck gun unattended and nosing well over to the other side of the anchorage. A movement abaft the conning tower caught my eye and I could see several men bending over the rubber raft, sliding it down over the pregnant bulge of her buoyancy tanks. I dug Curtis with my elbow, 'They're getting ready to send the boarding party. If we're going, then for Christ's sake, let's go.'

. . . and suddenly, without really realising it, we were both on our feet and running desperately for the gun called Phyllis.

The next few seconds passed in a heart-pounding agony of fumbling with blood-slimed handles and catches and clips, then I had the lid of the ammo locker open and was reaching in for the long, shiny brass cylinders of the shells. Hell! Fuses? Were they fused already? Yes, I remembered Allen had once said they were all set to explode on contact. One brief, shocking sight of an officer's white deck shoe still with a stocking and something else projecting from it—there had only been one man up here

with merchant navy officer's rig when the last futile duel
had taken place—then I was swinging round past other
contorted shapes towards Curtis and the gun.

He was already in the stained gunlayer's seat, spinning
the traversing handle with surprisingly practised hands,
head bent forward and mouth twisted into a half-open
grimace as his right eye glued to the foam rubber cup of
the gunsight while, twelve feet ahead of me, the slightly
belled muzzle cut agonisingly slowly along the submarine's
length. I heard myself whispering to it, whispering because
my throat had gone all dry and constricted with the fear
of what would happen if the gun across the water spoke
first. 'Get round faster, gun . . . Get round faster before . . .'

And then they'd seen us. A startled shout from the U-
boat's deck. 'Achtung!' and suddenly the lounging shapes
were running forward towards their own weapon while a
voice from her conning tower screamed 'Raus! Raus!'
and the white cap was lunging for the butt of the Spandau
still hanging dejectedly downwards in its mounting.

Then Curtis was yelling the same magical incantation
that the fat, incinerated Bombardier at our feet had in-
toned. 'On! . . . On! . . . On! . . .' while I was screaming
at the top of my fear-resurrected voice, 'Oh, get *round*,
you bitch . . . Please get round . . .' and the Third Mate's
hand was blurring on the dull brass traverse wheel. Three
cables away the long black gun had started to swing, too,
while at the same time the Spandau muzzle was sweeping
up towards us . . .

I had my arms round the cold cylinder of cordite-
packed metal, hugging it so tight that I could feel the
raised base rim cutting into my groin, but all I could do
was stare in horrified fascination at Phyllis's snout as it
actually *passed* the high conning tower and still kept on
traversing, turning all too slowly on to the rapidly short-
ening silhouette of the German gun.

'Fire, Curtis!' I bellowed, hating him for being such a
perfectionist, for missing that chance of saving my life.
'Fire for Chrissake, or do you bloody want to die?'

Then the brass wheel had stopped spinning and Curtis's
white arm was stretching out for the firing lever and he was
screaming, 'Bugger you! I'm going to . . . *shoot*!'

And when the muzzle flash had expanded into a hot, cordite-tainted cloud, and the deck had stopped leaping under my feet, the gun on the U-boat's casing had gone and the only member of its crew still to be seen was running round and round in shrieking circles trying to hold his face on with stumps of arms until the demented figure finally stepped blindly into space and rolled, smoking and kicking, down the bulge of her ballast tanks and into the already occupied waters of Quintanilha.

I felt the tears of hysteria streaming down my cheeks as I heard myself laughing and crying at the same time, and shouting, 'Oh you beaut, Three Oh . . . You bloody lovely man!'

Then White Cap appeared over the coaming of the blast-pocked conning tower and felt dedicatedly for the Spandau again while another two figures picked themselves up from the U-boat's after deck and started running for the still unharmed one-pounder. Curtis clawed the breech open and yelled, 'Shut up an' load . . . *Sir*!' as the empty brass case slid out in a cloud of evil-smelling fumes and clanged to the deck between us.

I hardly felt the tips of my second and third fingers slice off when Curtis slammed the breech shut on them, then he was banging the locking bar with the heel of his hand and Phyllis started to veer to the right, back along the length of the U-boat, to where the conning tower gunners were going through their still machinery-precisioned drill.

'Get more shells,' Curtis panted as his brow banged against the rubber cup again. 'More, more, more!'

One brief glimpse of the Spandau finally splitting flickering gouts of flame in the near darkness, the flashes lighting up the water round the black shape of the submarine, and I was lying flat on the deck with my hands clasped over my head while the terrifying drum of heavy calibre bullets climbed the ship's hull below us. Suddenly everything was clattering aind spanging under the hail of supersonic metal. Above me the *Cyclops*'s Red Ensign jerked and flapped grotesquely as crisply edged brown holes appeared in it.

The racketing suddenly stopped as if a sound-proof door had been slammed and I lay for a second blinking stupidly into the strangely indifferent, placid features of one of the dead army gunners. Why had the Spandau stopped? We hadn't fired again? The magazine . . . They must be having to change the magazine over there . . .

Curtis's tight voice filtered through my numbed brain. God but he had guts to have stayed up there on that exposed seat at the gun . . . 'Mister *Kent*! Where the bloody . . .' I raised my head and saw his wide, black eyes against the whiteness of his face.

'Misfire!' he screamed.

Misfire? Oh Jesus! I scrambled to my feet, skidding in the mess below me, ignored it and staggered to the gaping locker. Another round with the pain now shooting up from my torn fingers and I was swivelling towards the gun as the misfire slid backwards out of the open breech and smashed to the deck. Curtis dived for it and grappled for a hold on the slippery, verdigrised cylinder while I frantically pushed the new coned shape from my arms into the spiral rifled mouth. I slammed the breech shut and started shouting at the Third Mate again as he still struggled to lift the rolling misfire. We didn't have time to be tidy. 'Leave it, man. Leave it for Chrissake . . .'

Then he was up on his feet, running for the rail with the shell pulled well into his stomach. 'Get out of my bloody way, Mister!' and the wiry young body was past me and hurling the thing over the taffrail. It exploded as it hit the water and the yellow sea cascaded back over the rail as I stood stunned with the shock of it. And he'd had it buried in his guts two seconds before . . .

The first one-pounder shell from the U-boat burst squarely against the ten-inch port docking bollard five feet behind me just one and a half seconds later.

CHAPTER ELEVEN

I was lying stupidly on my back under the long grey barrel of the gun. Yet I distinctly remembered being behind the breech of it a moment before. Then I stared vacantly down at the empty space where my left foot had been, and started to laugh when I saw the stump of bone and sinew protruding flesh below the brown knee . . . Snap, Charlie Shell! Now I'm getting cut down to your size.

Poor bloody Royal Naval Reserve Officer Curtis. I wonder how many spare parts you're going to need after that hit? But now you're dead and I'll never . . .

I found I'd even been wrong about that when the muzzle flash from *Phyllis* licked down at me and I felt the hair on my floating head singe in the heat. I turned just in time to see the shell land smack at the base of the U-boat's conning tower and watched interestedly as White Cap came up out of his perch like a human cannon-ball on the end of a jet of smoke. Just at the top of his arc the cap fell off as he hung, momentarily suspended, above his beautifully trained crew, then fell, a perfectly ordinary little corpse, back to join Evans and McKenzie and Conway and the rest of *Cyclops*'s crowd as they bobbed obscenely in the Quintanilha Polka.

And the Third Mate's smoke-blackened face, with a deep cut above the eye pouring blood all down his right cheek, hovered above me for a moment, looking at the embarrassingly untidy stump of my severed shin bone, then his voice said tightly, 'Hang on, for God's sake, Sir! I'll be with you in a sec . . .'

Then I started to scream with the pain from a foot that wasn't even there, while the gaping muzzle above me flashed and smashed thunderously God knows how many times, with the high-explosive fumes belching down on me and charring my skin. All around the tanks of the now burning, listing U-boat, men were jumping into the water as the shells from *Phyllis* searched out the vital spot in her forward torpedo room.

Until one found the first sleek warhead in her tubes and she started to blow up as ton after ton of amatol fused into one long, brain-bursting roar, and *Cyclops* was snubbing at her cable in terror for the second time while Curtis clawed at the slime on the deck beside me and said over and over again, 'Jesus, but the trigger position's different to the one in the manual . . .'

And I finally passed out thinking, what a funny thing to say when you've just killed a hundred men.

I remember coming round again and seeing Curtis through

a haze of pain, framed against the gun barrel that still slashed across the scope of my vision. It was pretty dark now and, above and behind him, the clear blue sky sparkled with a myriad of tiny, twinkling stars. The white teeth showed reassuringly in the shadow of his face as he smiled softly, holding up a strip from his torn shirt.

'Tourniquet, Sir,' he said. 'I'll try and rake up some morphine once I've got you fixed up. Anything else you want?'

There was, but I didn't think even the admirable Curtis could manage that.

I wanted my leg back.

I remember the way the bile choked me as Curtis applied the torniquet. Then more floating in a morass of delirium. It seemed an expensive way to go about shearing a bloke's limb from his body. Two million pounds' worth of ships on the bottom . . . My damned leg was worth more than Betty Grable's. I started to laugh, then cry, then laugh and cry all at the same time, until Curtis gave the stricture one last, gentle twist which wasn't quite gentle enough, and I toppled into the blackness of a billion slimy horrors . . .

When I next opened my eyes it was to find myself propped against the pedestal of the gunlayer's chair with the warm gleam of the brass firing lever just above me. I tried to move my leg and couldn't. In fact I could hardly move anything at all, not from the waist down, yet at the same time I didn't feel much pain—more a sort of numbness, an impression of drifting just beyond the fringe of a terrible, threatening agony.

A clang behind me made me twist slightly to see the Third Mate slamming shut the cordite-stained breech mechanism. He glanced down and smiled nervously, 'Thought I'd leave one up the spout. Just in case . . .'

In case of what? There were only corpses out there now, Curtis . . . sundered, life-jacketed shells of men and, maybe, a few ghosts out of all the dead sailormen. He knelt down on one knee beside me and shivered. 'Cold,' he said. 'It gets pretty cold out here at night, doesn't it?'

I tried to grin painfully back at him because I knew he was looking for comfort too, and he held up a cautionary finger. 'Don't try to talk, Sir,' he said. 'I've given you a

shot of morphine from the emergency pack. Your leg . . .
I've tied it off as best I can. Maybe if we can get you
forr'ad to the . . .'

He stopped talking then—rather abruptly—and his eyes
looked wide and surprised for a few seconds. Almost hurt,
if you know what I mean. There was something else
slightly different about his face, too, but it took me nearly
the same time to realise what it was.

He'd now got *three* eyes.

As he keeled forward into the space where my leg
used to be I noticed something else that struck me as odd
—he didn't have any back to his skull. And then I found
out why . . .

 . . . because the little hole in his forehead was the same
diameter as the one in the end of Larabee's gun.

Larabee—it must have been Larabee, though you couldn't
have told from the grotesquely deformed mask of a face
above the radio operator's epaulettes on the smashed shoulder—Larabee heaved himself laboriously over the break
of the ladder and sort of half-rolled towards me with a
muffled sob of agony. He was still pretty well in control
of the little automatic, though . . .

I sat there, staring stupidly into the back door in Curtis's
head, as he climbed painfully to his feet, stood swaying
against the backdrop of the stars, and said, 'Heroic bastards!'

I felt the closing agony very near. Suddenly I didn't
care any more, so I put my arms around poor, misunder-
stood Curtis and whispered, 'For Christ's sake, get it over
with, Larabee . . .'

In the darkness I could still see the flecks of spittle at
the side of the slashed mouth as he shook his head deliberately. 'Get up, Kent. I want to see you take it on your
feet.'

Which was ironic, really.

I felt the tears wash into my sandpaper eyes as I lay
there under the gun feeling very lonely. Larabee started
to shake uncontrollably and I knew he, too, was near the
end of his tether. He dragged in a great gout of agony-
laden breath and stumbled forward a couple of paces. I
thought he was going to pass out right then but he re-

covered and, clinging on to the depressed muzzle of Phyllis, jerked the automatic savagely in line with my belly again.

'Get *up*, Kent,' he muttered, ''cause if you don't I'll see it's only the last shot that kills you . . . an' I've still got five left.'

I took one, last, long look at him, thinking how much he still looked like a butterfly on a pin as the barrel of the 4.7 merged into the silhouetted blackness of his chest—then I started to get up.

I raised my arm numbly, feeling for a hand-hold above me while the sickness rose higher and higher in my throat.

When my groping hand found the firing lever it was cold to touch—just like the brass handles of the bridge telegraphs that time when the Frenchman went . . .

. . . and suddenly Larabee just ceased to exist. Or most of him did, anyway.

The rest of him remained for perhaps a milli-second longer—until the furnace-hot gases from Phyllis's muzzle flash had crisped the white deck shoes and stockings and shorts, to a crinkly brown—then Larabee's legs, and pelvis, and quite a lot of his torso, folded into one another as they collapsed.

And the tears streamed down my face as I screamed with the first lick of the unbearable agony which was overcoming the morphine as it drained out of my system . . .

LAST WATCH

TO WHOEVER MAY FIND THIS MANUSCRIPT:
The events I have described seem to have taken place an eternity ago yet, in fact, I know that only a few weeks have passed since the last but one crewman from Group H 24 S died so violently. I can't be more specific about times and dates because so many days were spent in a twilight half-world of shock-filled pain and semi-delirium immediately after that bloody gun on the poop fired her final salute.

The radio equipment is smashed beyond repair. Larabee has got his revenge on me because, unintentionally, he's condemned me to the life of a Twentieth Century Ben Gunn—except that, instead of cheese, I've had a desperate craving for morphine.

I thought, for a time, that I was going to get better. I've eaten well, and rested for weeks while scribbling this log, and I'd even started to hope again. When I found I had the strength to patch up number four starboard boat and lower her I really imagined I had a chance of escaping. I buried Curtis—and what parts of Larabee I could find. And young Brannigan from the shattered wheelhouse. The little bible did come in handy after all, Captain. And not just as a story book.

And then, two days ago, I started to notice a curious, clinging, sickening odour that seemed to follow me wherever I went—a stench of living putrefaction—and I knew that the malevolent gangrene was going to kill me before I'd even got half way to the Cape.

Why did I write this fragment of history . . .? Well, I had to, didn't I? As a duty to those shipmates of mine who were already dead, so that there would be a record of their passing.

I'm leaving *Cyclops* now—if I can make it to the bottom of that damned accommodation ladder. It's funny how you still cling to hope, even when you've used it all up a long time ago. There's another silly thing I find myself hoping for. That—when this catalogue of agony *is* finally found—there's going to be a small space left for quite a lot of names at the bottom of that war memorial of the Old Man's . . .

EPILOGUE

The Commander sat for a long time after he had finished reading the last page of the yellowed, painfully scrawled manuscript. It wasn't until he heard a gentle knock at his cabin door that he swivelled stiffly in his chair. He noticed with surprise that the early morning sunlight was streaming through the forward ports, lighting up the shrivelled, curled sandwiches and the cold, untouched coffee pot of the evening before.

'Good God,' he thought, 'I've been sitting here all night.'

The First Lieutenant pushed the green curtain aside and stuck through his tousled head, looking at the unshaven Commander with respectfully concealed interest. 'Morning, Sir. The working party's ready to leave for *Cyclops* now. Do you have any instructions for them before they go?'

The Commander levered himself wincingly to his feet and looked out of the port, blinking in the warm sunlight. Three hundred yards away the old ship lay unprotestingly at the end of her rusty cable, as she had done for over twenty-five years. He turned to the young First Lieutenant.

'You and I are going over too, Number One.' He suddenly wondered about the little bible—had Kent replaced it in the drawer of that deserted chartroom, under the shelf with the bearded Jack Tar tin? He hoped so—it would be fitting for what he intended to do.

He rubbed a hand over the stubble on his chin and glanced out of the port again. There were a lot of dead men under those silent green waters. He knew they had a Red Ensign aboard, but did they have a German flag too? Either way, perhaps those long gone sailors from *Cyclops* and *Athenian* would like to see the Red Duster flying over their ships for the last time. He closed the manuscript and smiled sadly at his First Lieutenant.

'Have the hands muster at eleven hundred, Number One. We have a duty to perform . . . before we disturb anything at all.'

A short time later—while the survey ship's ratings assembled gravely on her after-deck, standing to attention in their gold-badged number one dress and with all eyes fixed on the simple ceremony being conducted on the aged ship's poop—the Commander allowed his fingers to brush briefly against the breech of the very old gun called Phyllis.

And even while he was reading from the battered little bible he still couldn't stop snatches of long-forgotten sentences from drifting through his head. Like—'Now you remember, Charlie Shell . . . Only a *little* submarine, mind?'

. . . and names like Breedie and Brannigan, and Evans, and Samson and McKenzie and Curtis . . .

. . . and Conway, and Eric Clint and Bill Henderson . . . Please God that a certain John Kent also entered that place where Chief Officers voyage eternally together . . .

And the Commander saluted the Red Ensign as it climbed slowly up the scarred staff and fluttered proudly once again over the rusty ship resting forever in that distant inland sea.